The Prodigal's Return

The Prodigal's Return

Cast of Misfits

Woodrow Dawson, aka WD – an alcoholic who gets a second chance in life.

Madeline Dawson – WD's ex-wife and natural born busybody who still holds out hope for her husband.

Joyce Dawson – WD and Madeline's daughter who is trying to fill the void in her life with work.

Chloe Dawson – WD's granddaughter, a Millennial who is looking for answers in all the wrong places.

Stephen Dawson – WD and Madeline's first born who isn't satisfied with what he has.

Ben Dawson – WD and Madeline's second born who is always looking for an angle.

Blaine Dawson – WD's father, who lives for one thing; to see his family united.

Truman Dawson – WD's younger brother, who had it all but didn't realize it until it was too late.

Ron and Edith Pauley – Boomer's parents learn.

Luke Pauley – aka Boomer – a seventeen-year-old spoiled brat.

Tony and Emma Estes – Tramp's parents

Travis Estes – aka Tramp – a teen with much to learn.

Bob Grayson – Senior partner with Grayson, Grayson, Estes and Pauley law firm.

Ellis Grayson – Junior partner with Grayson, Grayson, Estes and Pauley law firm.

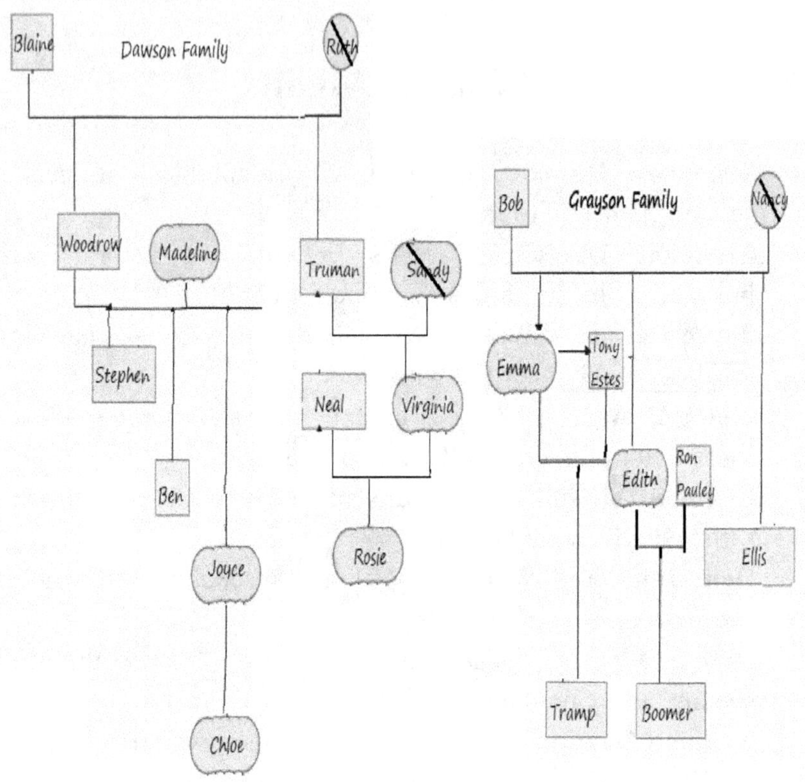
Blaine
Dawson Family
Ruth
Bob
Grayson Family
Nancy
Woodrow
Madeline
Truman
Sandy
Emma
Tony Estes
Stephen
Neal
Virginia
Ron Pauley
Edith
Ben
Ellis
Joyce
Rosie
Tramp
Boomer
Chloe

Chapter One

My Name is …

A set of yellowed headlights from an aging pickup truck appeared in the distance.

The driver slowed, rounded the corner and approached a stately old church building in the center of town. A soft amber glow emanated from the basement windows of the sanctuary, while above it spread a canopy of velvet salted with tiny specks of light.

As the pickup entered the parking lot, a dozen leathery wings stirred. Sharp talons scraped the roof of the old building and scores of red eyes watched with evil intent at the figure exiting his truck. Unheard, a low growl percolated from the throat of the leader of a hoard of demons.

"Shall I kill him, master?" a shriveled, emaciated demon asked, his mouth dripping with froth.

The spirit of hatred, a hulking beast with horns protruding from either side of its head, glanced sideways at his underling. He had no love for the man walking across the parking lot, neither had he any love for those who served under his command. He sought power and more of it. If killing this mortal would advance his cause, then so be it, but if letting him live would do more harm to God's kingdom, then he would let him live.

Knowing there was a strong possibility that this man might change his ways, he gave a nod to the weak-willed, sniveling imp cowering next to him. "Yes," he said in a low, breathy tone. "Kill him."

The smaller creature's craven eyes danced with wicked glee. With bony fingers he gripped his spear and spread his leathery wings. "With pleasure, my lord."

The creature flapped his shriveled wings wildly, barely able to give him lift from his perch on one of the gables. Once he'd reached forty feet above the earth, he lowered his head and plunged downward; his spear ready to pierce through the man's heart.

Suddenly, lightning split the inky night. Prince Uriel, one of God's powerful angels stepped from his hiding place. In one swift move, his gleaming sword sliced off the wormy demon's head. It plopped to the ground with a soft thud and rolled down the hill. A millisecond later, a host of bright, shining angels appeared. Their presence illuminated the night sky and sent the black forces of evil screaming.

With his sword dripping with the creature's black blood, Prince Uriel guarded his charge until he reached the basement door of the church.

Once the man was safely inside, Uriel released a cautious breath and looked to his leader. "That was close," he said, wiping the stain from his mighty sword.

Prince Camael, the commander of a legion of angels, gave assent to his friend. "Yes, Prince Uriel. Were it not for the Lord God warning us, this man would be dead by now."

Prince Uriel, clothed in white array with a golden breastplate, took his place next to his commander. "Has the Almighty told you why it is so vital that this man live?"

His commander shook his head allowing a few braids of silky white hair to fall from under his silver helmet. He widened his stance and stared at the receding forces of evil. "No. I only know God has a purpose in everything He does. It is always good, and it always amazes me. I look forward to seeing how this will play out. Now take your place. I see movement."

***

Oblivious to the unseen battle which had just taken place, the man entered the lower section of the church.

Inhaling a nervous breath, he waited indecisively. *How many of these meetings have I attended over the years only to find myself back where I started?*

After a beat, he stepped inside the brightly lit room and looked around. No one seemed to have noticed him. For that, he was glad. Wearing khaki slacks, a plaid cotton shirt with the sleeves rolled up and loafers, he wondered if he was over-dressed. Seeing a dozen folding chairs, some empty, some taken, he joined the group and took a seat.

At precisely seven o'clock, Emit Ferguson, the group's facilitator, stood. "Welcome everyone to our weekly AA meeting." Glancing around, he paused and smiled. "I see a couple new faces. Before we go over the twelve steps to recovery, would you please introduce yourselves?"

The newcomers exchanged nervous looks.

Finally the man stood. "My name is WD and I'm a drunk!"

A chuckle bubbled up in the throat of the group's facilitator. "Uh sir, we don't call ourselves drunks. We call ourselves alcoholics. Like the sign on the door says, Alcoholics Anonymous," Emit said in an even tone.

Jamming his hands into his pockets, WD said, "But I'm not anonymous," his frustration growing. "My name is WD, that's short for Woodrow Dawson! And I'm not an alcoholic. I'm a drunk!"

That brought a round of laughter from the normally somber group.

"Shh, everyone be quiet," Emit said, trying to quell their mirth. "Sir,"

"And stop calling me sir. That sounds like you're talking to my father. I'm WD or nothing," his voice shook with emotion.

"Why?" asked one of the ladies, a middle-aged housewife with sagging shoulders. "Don't you like your father?"

WD leapt to his feet, his pulse pounding in his ears. "Don't you ever mention my father. He's the reason I'm a drunk in the first place," he said vehemently. Hands shaking, he rubbed the stubble on his chin. "I need a—"

"—We all do mister," another man blurted. "That's why we're here. We drink too much, especially when we're agitated, and you sir, are agitated."

"Yeah, 'the more I drunk, the drinker I get,' someone sang out.

As if on cue, another round of laughter erupted.

WD plopped heavily in the metal chair making it groan under his weight. "I wasn't agitated until you people began badgering me about my past."

The man to WD's left leaned forward and placed his elbows on his knees. "Now we're getting somewhere. What is it about your past that's gotten you so agitated? We're just trying to get to know you."

"Yeah," the first woman said. "You come in here dressed all preppy like you think you're somebody. Why don't you tell us what's really bugging you?"

For a moment, WD sat stunned by the bluntness of her statement. He had his reasons, his secrets, his pain. They all did—even the facilitator. But why single him out? After a beat, he took a deep breath and let it out slowly.

"All right, I confess—"

"—Now we're getting somewhere," Mr. Ferguson, exulted. "First confession, then admission, then recovery. Right group? That's our motto."

The group let out a collective groan. "Yes, first confession, then admission, then recovery," they said in monotonous unison.

"So let's have it," said the large Black-American man to his right.

It wasn't a request.

Chapter Two

The Confession …

"My father was—"

"Don't go blaming your old-man," the first woman interjected.

WD extended his hands. "But it's true. My dad was a real pain in the butt: demanding, over-bearing. Even my mother, God rest her soul, admitted it. He lived hard and drank harder."

"Nothin' wrong with hard work," said one of the members.

"Or hard liquor," someone else muttered under their breath. That brought a ripple of laughter which Emit quickly quashed. A beat passed without WD's answer.

"What kind of work did he do?" Ferguson probed, trying to keep the conversation going..

WD let out a heavy sigh. "We lived on a large ranch out west…in Oklahoma. We raised cattle mostly, but we also herded sheep. I hated those things."

"At least it was an honest living. My dad was a drug dealer," a man across the circle added in a gruff voice.

WD pierced him with a pair of gray eyes. "But did he beat you? Did he make you do the worst job on the ranch?" It wasn't true, but it amplified the pain he bore from his father's verbal abuse.

A woman shot up her hand. "Yeah, my dad beat me and worse."

"That's enough. Let the man speak," Emit said.

"What was the worse job on the ranch?" The woman who started it all off asked in a curious tone.

WD bristled. "Cleaning up horse sh—"

"I think we got the idea," Emit interrupted. "That's not so bad, was it?"

WD shook his head dully. "Nah, not really. I usually only shoveled about half of it anyway. I kinda had a rebellious streak running through me. Never like taking orders." He chuckled gruffly. "As punishment for one of my misdeeds, my dad ordered me to put a fence around the garden plot behind the house all by myself. If you know anything about Oklahoma, you know it can be brutally hot in the summer. That week it was particularly miserable. And my lazy good-for-nothing younger brother, Truman, just stood in the shade and laughed."

The man to his right shifted and looked him in the eyes. "What'd ya do? Your dad that is."

WD stared back at him, his hands forming hard fists. "We argued; said some harsh things. In the end, he won, but I intentionally didn't finish it. I put down all but one fence post just to spite him." His voice grew cold as ice.

By now, every member of the group sat on the edge of their seats.

"Tell us, what did your old man do?" they nearly said in unison.

WD forced a half smile. "Nothing, I didn't give him a chance to beat me again. That night, I packed my belongings and high-tailed it out of town; haven't been back since."

"But what about your mom?" The woman across the circle asked. "Didn't she defend you and stand up to your old man?"

WD's head hung low. "Mom was too afraid of him so she kept her mouth shut. A year later, she died," he croaked out.

"And your dad, is he still alive?" someone else demanded.

Feeling the pressure to make a clean break from his past, WD bolted from his chair and headed for the door. "I think I've done enough confessing for one night," he said over his shoulder.

Just before he hit the door, it burst open and the local sheriff filled the entrance. "Sorry to break up your AA meeting Mr. Ferguson, but I'm looking for a man named Woodrow Dawson. I understand he may be here."

WD skidded to a stop.

All eyes pointed accusingly to him.

"That's him," the wiry man sitting next to WD's empty chair blurted.

All at once, two burly police officers appeared with wrist restraints.

"Woodrow Dawson, I have been ordered by the court to transport you to an emergency receiving facility for a mental evaluation. If the clinician determines you are a threat to yourself or others, you will be admitted to a mental health facility for further evaluation. Also, you have the right to an attorney. If you can't afford legal representation, the court will appoint one to your case. Do you understand your rights?"

WD struggled against the restraints, but was in no condition to put up much of a fight. "Yeah, yeah, I guess so," he finally admitted.

"Take him outta here," the sheriff said with disdain. "And put him in the backseat of the police cruiser." Turning to the shocked group, he said, "Sorry for the interruption, but we've been looking for this guy ever since that big warehouse fire. Now go back to what you were doing." Then he disappeared through the door.

"That's too bad," Emit said to the group. "I thought we were making some real progress."

"On who? WD? Not on your life. That man's a lost cause," the first woman said with finality.

***

Prince Camael, having heard the woman's comment, grimaced.

Leaning closer to his lieutenant, he said, "Prince Uriel, I want you to stay close to Mr. WD. Take Prince Leo and a quadrillion of my most powerful forces and guard this man. Let's show these mortals that no one is a lost cause when God wills it to be."

Uriel fisted his chest. "It is as you wish, my lord."

Chapter Three

Evaluation and Consultation …

Nearly three days had passed since WD had been taken into custody; three grueling days of tests, questions and more tests.

Finally, just before the time limit for the 72-hour hold rule expired, the doctor examining him entered the room where he'd been kept. It was a small, sparsely furnished room with a row of dingy florescent light bulbs, its only source of illumination; that and a narrow slatted window high on the wall. If WD could have moved the bed, which he couldn't because it was bolted to the floor, but if he could have, he would have seen the old church from where he'd been taken.

The doctor, an aging man nearing retirement, took a seat on the only other piece of furniture in the room; a metal chair. It too was held in place with heavy bolts. The file folder, which he held close to his chest, bore the name, Woodrow Dawson.

He laid it on the table and said, "Take a seat Mr. Dawson. I've got the results of your analysis."

WD forced a hard swallow and obeyed without comment.

"As you were informed when they brought you in," he began, "Form 1013 authorizes the state to hold you involuntarily against your will. This gives us time to assess your condition."

"My condition," he spat. "Who authorized the state to take me into custody?"

The doctor shifted nervously in his chair. "I'm not at liberty—"

"—Was it my kids?"

The doctor scanned the floor with his eyes. "I-I—"

"It was!" An oath escaped his lips. "Those dirty devils. I knew they were out to get me."

Palms held in a calming position, the doctor tried to reign in his patient's growing agitation. "Look Mr. Dawson, we've gone over this before. No one is out to *get you*," he fingered air-quotes.

"Then who?" he demanded. "No one else—"

"—No one else cares that much for you WD. Your adult children were only thinking of your well-being." He let that sink in before pressing on. "You are aware that the authorities are investigating the fire which burned your warehouse down, aren't you? They are considering you their prime suspect. If convicted, you could be fined $50,000 and or sent to prison for up to twenty years. Couple that with insurance fraud and you're looking at thirty years in prison."

Hands extended, WD said, "But I didn't do it. Yes it's true I owed the bank a lot of money, but I was working out a deal to sell off some of my parts stores. And I certainly wouldn't have burnt the place down with me inside it. That's crazy."

The doctor leveled his gaze as if to say, *yeah, you are crazy.* "When the fire and rescue squad arrived, they found you face down, stone-cold drunk. Your BAC was around 35%. You had drugs in your system—"

"Pain-killers."

"And they found a gun near you."

"I can explain."

The doctor waved off his excuses. "I'm not your judge WD. Neither am I your attorney, but you might consider getting one. In the meantime, I am authorized to confine you to a mental health facility for a term of six months. If your attorney is smart, he can use the report I'm filing on your behalf as your defense."

"But I'm not suicidal, and I'm not insane."

The doctor stood and stepped toward the door. "Like I said, I'm not your judge. Look, just do your time; keep your nose clean and in six months this will all be over."

WD started to protest, but the doctor stepped out of the way and let two large orderlies holding a restraining vest enter the room.

"Please sur, don't give us no trouble," the one orderly said with compassion. "It will only make it harder on us and you."

WD saw the tenderness in the man's eyes and sheepishly complied. "I may be complying on the outside, but I'm fighting you on the inside," he said through gritted teeth.

"It's all right by me, suh. Just so's you obey. I'll be pulling fer ya," he said as he cinched the last strap in place.

Chapter Four

Stoneybrook Mental Health Facility …

WD stared at the calendar in his room, "Four more months," he muttered.

"Four more lousy months in this stinking place," referring to Stoneybrook Mental Health Facility. He had undergone nearly every kind of test, procedure, and protocol the medical professionals could conceive. Despite his claims that he was as sane at the next guy, and as innocent as the pope, he was declared mentally unfit to participate in society, and sentenced to an additional four months of incarceration.

His only visitor was Chloe, his sixteen-year-old granddaughter. She had become his rock, his source of strength. She was also his only source of information from the outside, and what he'd heard disturbed him. Thankfully, she was the only person who not only believed him, but who believed in him.

His ex-wife, Madeline, the woman who'd given him their three children, Stephen, Ben, and Joyce, had visited him twice. Both times ended badly.

It left him depressed and agitated.

He knew in his heart Madeline still loved him. He also knew he still loved her. But as far as he was concerned, reconciliation was out of the question, especially since they had divorced twenty-five years ago. Truth is, they were mutually incompatible. With her being a good Christian lady and him being a drunk, he had no illusions of ever getting back together.

His short career in the Navy ended with him being wounded in action. For his sacrifice, he had received a Purple

Heart, and an honorable discharge. While in rehab, he met Madeline Turner, his physical therapist. Six months later, in 1973, they married. Their marriage lasted fifteen years and produced three children.

Three children who hated him.

The pain from the wounds he'd received on the battlefield drove him to seek help from the Veteran's Administration. But the doctors weren't interested in curing the source of his pain. They were only interested in giving him more drugs. When the drugs became ineffective, he turned to alcohol. At least, that's what he told himself every night before he collapsed on the couch or on the floor. It didn't help that he had trouble keeping a job. His employment record looked like Swiss cheese.

Finally, after years of going in and out of rehabs and bars, he decided to take control of his life. For the next three years he stayed dry and clean. By 1995, he was 46 and had built up enough good credit to apply for a small business loan. With it, he opened WD's Parts Supply. For the next four years, he provided Richmond Hill, a community about 20 minutes from Savannah, Georgia, with auto parts, and tools.

Then disaster struck.

In 1999 hurricane Floyd, a category two hurricane hit land bringing 110 mile an hour winds and displacing two million people across six states. It took him years to rebuild the business. But with hard work, he expanded the company by opening several more stores. It seemed like he had finally beaten back the demon of alcohol.

With his 38-year-old son Stephen, running the day-to-day operations of the business, and Ben his 36-year-old brother keeping the books, he was left to focus on getting new clients and overseeing the company. But then, something happened which changed everything. In 2013, sales began to fall off, bills went unpaid, inventory disappeared. He suspected one of his store managers was stealing from the company, but he couldn't figure out who. With pressure mounting, the drinking returned. And with it came the guilt, the depression, and all the old demons.

His relationship with his two sons went from bad to worse. It didn't help to have them constantly nagging about his drinking. What little communication he had with Joyce, his daughter, ended in harsh words. He'd never forgiven her for getting pregnant out of wedlock at the young age of 16.

Now at 64, his life, his marriage, his relationships with his children, his business was in shambles. And then there was the fire which burned the company's warehouse to the ground.

Now he found himself facing the real possibility of jail-time.

He needed a way out.
He needed a friend.

***

"How is your charge getting along?" Prince Camael, asked his longtime ally.

Prince Uriel straightened. He had been overseeing WD's affairs since his incarceration. So far, no demonic activity had been seen. "There has been some suspicious activity, some of the older residents playing with a Ouija board and one widow lady pretending to tell everyone's future." He smirked. "We all know how their futures will turn out."

Prince Camael nodded grimly. "It is appointed unto men once to die and after that, the judgment."

A shudder ran the course of Uriel's muscular frame. "One never gets used to seeing these poor souls pass through the valley of the shadow of death."

Placing a strong hand on the princes' powerful shoulder, Camael lowered his tone as a senior resident shuffled past their hidden position. "Though unseen by human eyes, it was uncanny how perceptive some of the more Godly saints could be. Some, on their death-beds would even exclaim, 'There they are—the angels have come to usher me home!'"

Uriel smiled, his face gleamed with the brightness of the morning sun. "Yes, that is a sweet thing. As to your original question—WD is getting increasingly more disquieted."

"Is his heart softening toward the Gospel?"

A beat passed before Uriel gave a reply. Time for the mortals was so short. "I'm afraid not. He is so bitter, I'm not sure anything can get through his hard heart."

A deep sigh sounded from his commander's throat. "Well, we will see about that. I must report to the Almighty, as if He doesn't already know. Nevertheless, it is my privilege to stand before His Holiness and report any progress in bringing this soul into the fold."

Smiling broadly, Uriel hooked his thumbs in his golden utility belt from which a massive sword hung. "What an honor. To see the King of kings and Lord of lords singing and rejoicing over the rescue of one of His image bearers. That must be a sight."

Commander Camael returned his smile. "Tell you what, depending on WD's decision to place his trust in the finished work of the Lord Christ, I will personally invite you to the celebration."

Prince Uriel's grin broadened, then faded. "And if not?"

His commander's piercing blue eyes took on a distant expression as if seeing through the tunnel of time; seeing

WD's missed opportunities, his wrong decisions, his heart growing hard. "Then it grieves me to say, we will have to stand by and allow the evil one to take one more lost soul to Hell."

Though only slightly shorter than his commander, Uriel lifted himself to his full height. "Not on my watch, my lord. Not on my watch!"

Chapter Five

A Friend in need is a friend indeed ...

Arnie Winowski, a fellow resident at Stoneybrook, stared across the checkerboard table at his friend.

"Are you going to move or sit there staring into nothingness." His heavily rimmed glasses sat precariously on his rounded nose.

The two older men played checkers nearly every day. Some of the time Arnie would win, some of the time WD would. The rest of the time the game would end on a draw. Today was no different. They had gathered in their usual spot in front of a large picture window. Outside, spread an emerald lawn dotted with live oaks festooned with Spanish moss.

WD jolted back to reality. "What?" he asked testily.

"I said, it's your move. Are you going to play or do I need to get another checkers partner?"

WD rubbed the stubble on his chin. "I'm sorry Arnie. It's my wife…my ex-wife. She paid me a visit earlier today and it's got me all upset."

Arnie's owl eyes rounded. "Oy vey. Well she's gone now, so put her and your visit behind you. You can't let little things come between you and your serenity."

"My serenity," he harrumphed. "I've got no serenity, no peace, no nothing." He returned his gaze out the large pane glass window.

Spring had arrived and with it, came all the colors of green, yellows and pinks. The groundskeepers maintained the property with the utmost care. Even as he stared out the window, someone wearing goggles and ear protection strolled by blowing grass clippings off the sidewalk.

Amidst the roar of the leaf blower, WD heard Arnie saying, "I win, you lose—again." He picked up his checker and hopscotched across the playing board. Then he added, "Know Jesus, know peace. No Jesus, no peace."

WD straightened and looked his friend in the eyes. "What's that supposed to mean?"

The older man, in his late seventies, let his shoulders rise and fall. "It means what I said it means. If you know Yeshua Adonai…Jesus as your Lord and Savior, you will know real, lasting peace. If you don't Him, you will constantly be fighting yourself and others. Thus, no peace."

"There you go, preaching again."

"Not preaching, just one thirsty man telling another thirsty man where to find the Water of Life."

WD shook his head ruefully. "I need a drink, and not water."

Arnie leveled his gaze. "That's what got you landed here in the first place, ya schmuck."

"That's not exactly true."

"You're a drunk, aren't you?"

"The professionals say I have a disease."

Arnie leveled his gaze. "What? Do you want to spend the rest of your life being poked and prodded by those professionals? That's meshuga...crazy. Or are you going to take responsibility for yourself?"

WD slouched back in his chair. He knew Arnie was right. He'd been running from his past, from God, from his responsibility nearly all his life. *Where would it end?*

"Arnie, I know you mean well, but, I've done too much."

"Not so much that God can't fix it. If He could make a man from the dust of the earth, He certainly can reshape him into His image. All you need to do is turn over the reins of your life to Him. Confess the sin of rebellion and unbelief. Trust Him as your Savior and He will make His abode in your heart. By His grace He will begin the process of cleaning out the sin in your life. He will make you a new man."

Shaking his head, WD stood. "I'm not ready, Arnie. Maybe someday, just not today." With that, he strode off in the direction of his room.

***

The next morning, WD awoke to find an ambulance sitting outside the facility and a body draped with a white sheet being hurriedly wheeled down the corridor.

It was Arnie Winowski. He had died in the small hours of the night. An orderly found his body on the floor where he apparently had been kneeling in prayer. An open Bible and a prayer list lay next to him. At the top of the prayer list was two letters…WD.

***

"I can't believe I missed it," Prince Uriel said regretfully.

He stood just outside Arnie's former residence with hospital staff rushing past him as if he wasn't there. "I was so absorbed with watching over WD that I totally missed the death angel until it was too late."

Prince Camael materialized and held his friend's sad gaze. "Do not grieve my friend. I have it on good authority that all things work together for good to those who love the Lord God, to those who are called according to His divine purposes. Right now, Mr. Winowski is rejoicing in the presence of his Lord and Savior."

Prince Uriel took in a shaky breath. "But what about his friend WD? There is no one left to witness to him. How will he ever come to repentance?"

His senior commander smiled. "He being dead, yet speaketh, my friend. Trust me, Almighty God is not finished. Now go, set a guard around WD. Do not let the demon of despair or discouragement anywhere near him. Meanwhile, I have something I must do."

Prince Uriel squared his broad shoulders. After calling for reinforcements, he doubled the number of angelic hosts encircling WD. Then, with his eyes piercing the murky plains between light and darkness, he placed his hand on the hilt of his sword and said, "Not this time, you old serpent. Not this time."

***

"What happened to old Arnie?" WD asked a fellow resident.

He had not left the hall, rather, he stared into Arnie's now empty apartment.

The man stood bleary-eyed; not quite grasping the gravity of the situation. "I-I don't know," he said with uncertainty. "I know Arnie had some medical issues, but hey, we all do. He never complained, at least not to me."

A woman wearing a pink robe and fuzzy bunny slippers stepped next to the two men. "He was such a nice man. I'm going to miss him."

WD pulled his gaze from the unoccupied room. "Did you know him well?"

She nodded, "Yeah, he was my husband," an impish twinkle danced in her eyes.

Taken aback, WD gaped at her. "He never mentioned he had a wife, let alone that you were living in the same facility."

The woman lowered her voice to a near whisper. "It's a secret. Don't tell." She glanced around mischievously. "We got married in the chapel a year ago."

The man next to WD nudged him in the ribs and shook his head as if to say, "Don't press the issue."

Wisely, WD followed the man's lead and let the subject drop. "I wonder where they'll have his funeral," he said as the crowd of onlookers broke up.

Hearing his musings, the director of the facility turned and faced him. His face was haggard and tired. "He and his family made all the arrangements months ago. He wanted to have a memorial service at the Baptist church where he attended. It's not too far from here. The pastor will probably officiate the service. If you want, I can arrange for transportation to the service. Of course, you will be under constant surveillance, so don't get any ideas."

WD nodded. The thought about leaving the facility never occurred to him.

Now it had.

Chapter Six

Breakfast at Stoneybrook ...

Breakfast in the dining hall was as somber as a morgue.

The usual laughter and bantering between the residents was replaced with grim faces and whispered words.

WD entered the room and got in line. Taking a tray, he waited for the servers to fill his plate with scrambled eggs, grits, toast, bacon, and mixed fruit. He stopped at the coffee urn and poured himself a mug of the black brew before finding his seat at his assigned table. The chair next to him was empty, reminding him of Arnie's passing.

As the other two residents took their places, WD nodded. "Are you going to the memorial service?" He asked as the man reached for the salt and pepper shakers.

Ed Noble, a man suffering from depression and suicidal tendencies, blinked absently a few times. "Yes, at least I hope it will be open to us—"

"Crazies?" WD interjected.

"Not crazies," the woman sitting across the table from him chided. "We are here because," she lowered her voice, "because each of us have our own way of dealing with problems."

Ed chuckled. "Yeah, like getting plastered," his near hysterical laughter broke the somber mood.

Residents glanced scornfully at him.

"Shh, lower your voice," WD said. "Arnie was a good friend and we should respect his passing."

Silence settled around the table until finally Ed spoke up. "Arnie was always talking to us about Jesus. Did he do the same to you?"

WD set his fork on the table and nodded glumly. "Yeah, just yesterday he told me that we are not guaranteed of tomorrow, that we need to be ready to meet Jesus at any time."

The woman harrumphed, and spoke out of the side of her mouth. "I guess he put that theory to the test."

Her sarcastic tone irritated WD. Rather than respond harshly, he stood and sauntered over to an old upright piano. Its tired keys boasted of a life well-lived. Some keys lacked their ivory coverings, others lacked their ebony. It reminded him that, like the old piano, he too would someday be rendered unusable and be discarded, and forgotten.

But not today.

Today he would honor his friend's passing. As a boy, his father insisted he take piano lessons. Between his ranch chores, and schooling, he studied the piano and eventually developed a modicum of success. It was one of the only tasks his father had given to him, which he actually completed. Sitting on the rickety stool, he began to play one of the few hymns he knew by heart. *Amazing Grace.*

Within minutes, the room was filled with singing as elderly voices joined into one. Even those individuals whose cognitive skills had long departed them, suddenly, as if waking from a long winter's nap, awoke and began to sing. Albeit, their articulation was a bit slurred and their voices a bit shaky; they sang with delight. When the music ceased, they returned to their blank stares. It was a moment WD determined never to forget. Not for a long time.

***

Once breakfast was cleared, the residents were free to go their respective ways.

Some had appointments with their psychologists. Others went to physical or occupational therapy. WD glanced at the calendar on the wall. He was scheduled to see his attorney, and as usual, the man was running late. Usually, when he had some free time, he filled it with a good book. He hated watching the news on the big screen television. It, like the newspapers, was built around doom and gloom. *If it bleeds, it leads*, he remembered someone once saying.

For a moment, he considered returning to his apartment and retrieving his book when a familiar face appeared on the other side of the main lobby. It was Chloe, his granddaughter. His heart quickened just a little. Despite the fact that she had only recently turned sixteen, she appeared much older. And underneath all that black eye shadow, purple lipstick and white powdered face, was a very attractive girl. He had to admit she was a carbon copy of Madeline, his wife…ex-wife, Chloe's grandmother.

As she skipped between tables, the male resident's eyes followed her every move. The elderly sainted women, however, cast contemptuous glances both at the girl with the orange stripes in her hair and the men who, by all intents and purposes, were junior-high boys again.

"Hey, G-Diddy. What-suh?" she said as she leaned over and pecked him on the cheek with a light kiss.

"Ouch!" He winched, playfully as if it hurt.

She giggled. "G-Diddy, why do you always act like it hurts when I kiss you?"

He smiled sheepishly. "I'll tell you if you tell me what 'Suh,' means."

She shrugged off his question. "It means, what's up, you know, like, what's happening?"

He stood and led her to a quiet corner where a couple of unoccupied wing-backed chairs awaited them. He took a seat in one of them and patted the other indicating he wanted her to sit. He'd never gotten used to her hip lingo, but he enjoyed trying to.

"I see. Well, as to why I winch whenever you kiss my cheek; it's because it makes you laugh and that makes me happy."

Chloe, wearing tattered blue jeans with holes in the knees, flip-flops, and a tight top which revealed her midsection, crossed her legs. Chin in hand, she nodded. "I'm glad it makes you happy. You're the only one I can talk to who really understands me," she said, looking down at her black painted fingernails.

Chloe had been his only visitor ever since his incarceration began. Her weekly visits were a highlight in his ordinarily mundane days; that, and the course in millennial speak.

After a few minutes of small talk, he pushed himself up with a slight groan. Then, taking her by the hand, he said, "Let's go outside. It's such a lovely day."

She smacked her gum and continued to chatter; her flip-flops flipping and flopping with each short, choppy step.

He led her through the lobby and out onto the veranda which ran the length of the building. The broad, tongue and groove porch had been recently painted forest green and smelled new. Down the steps they went and found an unoccupied concrete bench. He sat and motioned for her to do the same.

"You look, ragged G-Diddy. Have they been ghosting you?"

WD knew what she was getting at. Or at least he thought he knew. "No, they haven't been ghosting me. They've actually been treating me okay. It's just that," he paused as an orderly pushing another resident in a wheelchair passed them. "It's just that a fellow resident, a man named Arnie, passed away last night."

Her darkened eyes rounded. "Fur rel? That's cray," she exclaimed.

"Yeah, I know. No one expected him to die; especially not me."

Another bubble of gum popped. "Well, what are they going to do? Did someone off him or what?"

"No, no one 'offed' him. He just died of natural causes. But it's got me thinking."

Another bubble, another pop. Two more residents hobbled along the uneven brick walkway before WD spoke.

"Plus, my attorney is dragging his feet and the doctors don't seem to be in any hurry to release me. If I don't get out soon, I'll end up like ol' Arnie—dead."

"You mean dead, dead? Not dead like something was really funny, dead," she said, her hands flailing wildly. "That's a drag man. I'll help you bounce any time you're ready."

He guessed her meaning and nodded slowly. "I appreciate the sentiment, but a person doesn't just walk out of this facility. It would take planning and preparation. And even then, the authorities would come looking for me. It would be bad publicity." Lifting his hands like a banner he continued, "CRAZY MAN ESCAPES FUNNY FARM." He paused and lowered his voice. "If I attempt to go home, they'll be there waiting for me. And if I went to a homeless shelter, well—" he let his unfinished sentence hang like a slow pitch curveball.

Chloe shook her head letting the sunlight dance on the red and orange streaks in her naturally raven colored hair.

Reaching up, she fingered one of the three studs jutting from her left ear as if she was planning his escape.

At four foot ten, she was a bundle of energy. A sophomore in high school with a 4.0 GPA, she was the co-captain of her volleyball team, a team that placed second in the State. Plus, she had a voice that would make the angels weep. Her role as the lead singer in a number of school musicals brought offers from a number of talent agencies.

"I can't even," she muttered. "So what are you going to do?"

WD stood, jammed his hands in his pockets and began to pace. "I'm working on it."

Chloe joined him as they strolled along the well-maintained sidewalk. "Me and my Fam are planning to take a road-trip during the Spring break. We've stashed food, clothes, money, whatever. It'll be a blast from the past," her blackened eyes wild with excitement.

"So you're thinking about running away from home…again?"

Chloe's face darkened. "Nah, it's just for a week. Mom will be gone to a conference or something and won't even miss me. Anyways, I need a break from her just as much as she needs a break from me."

WD raised his eyebrows. "For real?"

She eyed him impishly. "It's fur rel. Not for real." She formed air quotes. "Anyways, recently, mom's been ridin' my case about keeping up with the house cleaning, my grades, my dance classes—"

"—Your dance classes?! I hadn't heard about that."

"Yaas, but it's really basic, I mean—"

"Boring? I remember you told me the meaning of basic the last time you visited me. Well look, do as she says. She means well. And don't do as I did and run off to the circus."

Her mouth gaped, her eyes rounded like moons. "You were in the circus? That's rad, man!"

WD smiled ruefully. "Nah, I didn't actually join the circus, but I did hook up with the rodeo the summer after I graduated. I was young and buff. I bucked broncos, road bulls; the works. Ah, those were the days. Later, around September or October, I joined the Navy." A dreamy smile crept over his face.

"G-Diddy, you never told me you were in the rodeo."

He sighed heavily. "Girl, there's a lot I haven't told you. So how's your mom?"

Chloe scuffed the ground nervously. "She's really busy at the hospital. They've got her pulling three twelves in a row. When she comes home, she crashes on the couch. I gotta drag her to the bedroom and get her tucked in. It's a real bummer."

WD listened without commenting. He could only imagine how hard it was being a single mom; trying to put food on the table and keep a roof over their heads.

"And your G-Ma? Is she still mad at me?" He just wished things were different—maybe someday. He pushed aside those thoughts.

Chloe shook her head. "Nah, she's over it. Whatever *it* was."

More secrets.

"So when is your Spring break?"

Chloe held up seven fingers each painted black.

"Seven days or seven weeks?"

"Days, G-Diddy. And then we are gonna blow."

"Seven days, hmm? Where are you and your *Fam* heading?"

Her face brightened. "Florida baby. To the beaches, the sun and the surf. Me and my squad are going to biv on the beach, cook hot dogs over a campfire and chill," her eyes danced with anticipation.

WD watched her animated gyrations. "Sounds like a plan. What'd ya think your mom will do when she finds out you ran off with your *Fam*? And she will find out."

She shrugged. "She'll probably ground me for life, but I'll just sneak out. Like I said, she's so out of it when she comes home all's she does is crash. She won't even miss me."

The wheels in WD's mind began to churn, but he kept his thoughts to himself.

Chapter Seven

Arnie Winowski's Memorial Service …

Soft music played in the background as a small group of mourners gathered near the front of the church auditorium.

On the communion table sat a picture of Arnold Winowski surrounded with a few bouquets of flowers. An open Bible in front of the photograph completed the ensemble. At exactly eleven o'clock, the pastor stood, approached the wooden pulpit and cleared his throat. This was not his first memorial service and by the look of his congregation, it would not be his last.

"Friends, fellow believers, we are here to pay our last respects to our friend and fellow believer, Brother Winowski," he paused and scanned the sparse crowd.

"To most of us, he was known as Arnie. He was a faithful witness for Christ despite his…problems. The demon of opioids was the bane of his life, but Arnie was an overcomer. If Arnie could stand here today, he would want you to know these four things; life is short, death is certain, eternity awaits and God loves you."

WD rubbed his sweaty palms on his pant legs. He and a few others from the mental hospital had been given permission to attend the memorial service, albeit, with a heavy presence from the local police department. Sitting on the padded pew three rows from the front, he listened with renewed interest.

"Folks, there are two inescapable appointments on all of our calendars. The first is April 15th." His chuckle was met with empty stares since most of the attendees hadn't paid income taxes in years. "And the other appointment we all have is with the coroner." He paused to let the uncomfortable moment pass. Scanning the faces of the people, he said, "As you can tell, none of us are getting any younger and there are no guarantees of tomorrow. Our friend Arnie would tell you this, however, trust Jesus as your Lord and Savior today."

It didn't take much convincing for WD to realize he was a dirty, rotten sinner. That was apparent to all. How to solve his sin-problem was the question.

The pastor's gentle voice called him back from his musings.

"Jesus is a friend of sinners. The Apostle Paul said in I Timothy 1:15, *This is a faithful saying and worthy of all acceptation, that Christ Jesus came into the world to save sinners, of whom I am chief.* You see friend, no matter how bad you think you are, Paul was worse, and yet Jesus died for him and redeemed him."

As the pastor droned on, WD felt the Holy Spirit tugging drawing him toward the light. Eyes pinched shut, he yielded to the wooing of the Spirit. "Lord, you know I'm a dirty, rotten drunk. I've cursed your name and wasted my life running from You. And I am tired—tired of sinning—I'm tired of running. Come into my heart. Wash it clean with Your blood and save me. In Jesus' name I pray."

From the corner of the platform, the organ began to play, *Lord, I'm Coming Home* and WD's wet eyes popped open. Everyone stood and began to file out. As he joined the others, one of the policemen who'd been assigned guard duty sidled up next to him. WD swiped the tears from his eyes.

"Sorry for your loss, WD. You two must have been close."

WD took a halting breath. "Thanks, we were," his words came out hoarse, ragged. "But I wasn't crying—I think I got some lint in my—." Suddenly, he felt the Holy Spirit's conviction. He'd been such a liar that telling a lie came as naturally as breathing. "Uh, yes, we were close, but that's not why I was crying. You see, what that preacher said made a lot of sense to me, and I just asked Jesus into my heart. I'm a changed man, officer."

The policeman, not one to be impressed by a jail house conversion, nodded unconvincingly. "Well, we'll see if it's real, WD. You don't have a very good track record of getting yourself cleaned up you know."

Hands raised in surrender, WD continued. "I'm not saying I'll be perfect, Lord knows I've got some bad habits. But I've been dry and sober for the last two months and by God's grace, I'll stay that way for the rest of my life."

Again, the officer nodded. "Okay, that may be so, but you still have four more months to go and even then—" he didn't need to finish his statement.

WD knew what awaited him if the insurance fraud and arson charges were pursued.

He joined the others who were standing on the sidewalk waiting for the bus to arrive. Hands in his pockets, he glanced heavenward. *Is it my imagination, or do I hear singing?* He listened more closely. *Yes, definitely. Someone is singing.*

***

Prince Leo felt his commander's presence even before he appeared.

Cocking an eyebrow, he said, "I take it you just left the King's throne room?" His Scottish accent echoed softly in the ethereal air.

Prince Camael's humming continued. "As a matter of fact, I did. Have you ever heard God sing?"

His lieutenant shook his head; his fiery red hair shimmered in the sunlight. "No, not yet, I hope to one day."

Camael hiked up his silver girdle. "It is something you will never forget. Tell you what. I am personally assigning you to WD's granddaughter. Guard her well."

"But, but—"

"No buts. I know she is wild and unruly. But she needs God's grace as much as anyone—more perhaps. So here's the deal. It will be your responsibility to be her guardian angel. Take as many hosts as you need and set a hedge of protection around her. Do not let the demon of lust and addiction take control of her. Understand?"

Leo's grin broadened revealing a choir of pearly-white teeth. Giving his leader a crisp salute, he said, "Aye aye, sir." Then, pointing to four other angels, he said, "You there, come with me." In a flash of blinding light, the five heavenly hosts disappeared leaving only a slight swirl of air.

Chapter Eight

Escape from Stoneybrook ...

The short ride from the church to the mental hospital gave WD time to consider his new situation.

The case against him was pretty convincing. Even though he had four months left under the watchful eyes of the mental health facility, there was the strong possibility that he might be interned there indefinitely. The prospect of spending the rest of his life in that place made his skin crawl.

He had to get out.

He had to make things right.

All at once a plan began to form.

It was Wednesday and over the next two days he began to take closer notice of the staff and vendor's movements. He knew already that the oxygen supply truck came every Tuesday and Thursday with regularity. They entered the service gate which was lightly guarded. And the men delivering the oxygen cylinders didn't have to pass through any security checkpoints. Wearing common overalls, they moved through the loading area with little or no supervision. If he could acquire one of those overalls, he just might be able to blend in with the delivery crew and leave with them.

What could go wrong?

❈ ❈ ❈

Prince Sariel, his name meaning Prince of God, joined the delivery crew as they loaded dozens of oxygen cylinders into the rear of the delivery truck and strapped them in place.

Unaware of his presence, the men bantered and joked about what they planned to do this coming weekend.

Most of their talk involved sensuality and lewdness which made Sariel want to intervene, but that wasn't for him to decide. It was his responsibility to see to it that everything was in place for what was to transpire.

***

Having familiarized himself with the break room, the locker room and the cleaning supply room, WD knew where he could commandeer a set of overalls.

He just needed time to make his move when no one was looking. Plus, it had to be when he was not scheduled for anything else. Just before he bolted, it suddenly dawned on him; *I have no identification, no driver's license, no credit cards, and no money. All my personal belongings were confiscated when they took me into custody. And the only person with the key to the locker where my belongings are is my psychiatrist.*

Thinking quickly, he made his way down a long corridor to the doctor's office.

"I'm here for my appointment," he said through the Plexiglas window.

The nurse glanced up from a stack of papers. "Oh, I'm sorry, didn't they tell you? The doctor was called away. Something about a—well it doesn't concern you anyway. You'll just have to come back next week," she didn't sound too apologetic.

Suddenly, a buzzer sounded and she glanced at her computer screen. "If you'll excuse me, I'm needed elsewhere." She pushed herself back from her desk, stood and exited the enclosed office.

As she rushed by him, WD stuck out his foot and caught the door before it clicked shut. Once the squeaking of the woman's rubber soles on the polished floor faded, he made his move. Quick as his legs could carry him, he entered the nurse's office, slipped around her desk and entered the doctor's office. Fortunately, the man, in his rush to leave, had forgotten the wad of keys to the locker room.

He snatched them up. With his pulse pounding in his ears, he set off in search of the locker room. He just hoped his movements would go unnoticed by the ever-present security cameras. With care, he methodically picked his way along the corridor until he reached the door marked, Staff Only.

Fingers trembling, he fumbled with the keys until he found the one to the door. Slipping inside, he discovered the room was empty except for a wall of lockers. Not knowing which one was his, he made an educated guess. Since his uniform, his room, even his personal ID bore the number 3636, he guessed the locker holding his personal belongings would be the same.

He quickly slipped the key in its slot and turned it.

Bingo! Inside the locker was his wallet with all his credit cards, his driver's license and all the currency he had when they picked him up. Even his slacks, shirt and shoes were neatly stacked on a shelf. In no time, he had dressed in his street clothes and was retracing his steps. Then he made his way to the storage room where an unclaimed set of overalls hung.

Hastily, he tugged them over his street clothes and headed for the loading dock. A lean supervisor wearing a stubby-brimmed ball cap stood with a clipboard in his hand. He nodded as WD moved past him. The delivery crew was busily moving oxygen cylinders and other gasses from the truck into the storage area. Thinking quickly, he grabbed a hand cart, loaded a cylinder onto it and wheeled it into place.

A few minutes later, the rear of the delivery truck was empty. He locked the hand cart in place and joined the crew in the back seat of the delivery truck.

Within minutes, they left the loading dock, passed through the security gate and were rumbling along the highway. Thankfully, the men were too tired from a long day to do much talking.

When the delivery truck arrived back at the company's warehouse, it was late in the day. After parking the truck in its assigned slot, the driver and crew got out and headed for the break room to clock out.

This was it.

It was now or never. WD counted to one-hundred waiting for the men to enter the building. Once the last of them had disappeared, he slipped out of his overalls, stashed them in a trashcan, and casually walked to the street. Then he disappeared into the gathering gloom.

***

Standing in the shadows, Prince Uriel and a few other hosts of light watched WD disappear into the night. "Good work, my brothers.

Lord Camael will be pleased. Now stay close, I don't want the evil one to tempt him to turn aside and enter one of the dens of darkness."

In an instant, the angelic hosts encircled the lone figure walking along the sidewalk.

Chapter Nine

The Mysterious Ride Home ...

As WD made his way along the uneven sidewalk, a driving rain began to descend, soaking him to the bone.

It was April 1st, and WD thought, *What a fool. I wish I'd grabbed an umbrella from the locker room before I took off. Oh well. No point in second guessing myself now. I just need to keep my head down and stay focused.*

His house was situated several miles away, and on a good day, he could have made the hike in about an hour. But with the rain and wind blowing in his face, he guessed it would take much longer. If he didn't get there soon, the authorities might get there first. He was sure his home would probably be one of the first places they would look the moment they discovered he was missing. Picking up his pace, he pushed through the darkening night.

Out of nowhere, a car appeared and slowed to a stop. The passenger door popped open and someone yelled, "Get in."

Unsure what awaited him; WD lowered his head and peered inside. It was the delivery truck driver.

"Get in man!" he demanded. "You're going to catch pneumonia."

WD swiped the rain from his face and climbed in. "Thanks, I was beginning to think I'd have to swim all the way home."

The man chuckled and gave him a sideways glance. "And where's that? Your home, that is."

WD did some quick calculating. Lying was not an option; not anymore. But telling this man the truth could get him in a lot of trouble. "It's on the other side of town. You can drop me off at the 7-Eleven near my house. I need to pick up a few things anyway."

Not missing a beat, the man said, "You're one of them…one of the residents of the, the—"

"Mental hospital?"

"Yeah, the psyche ward, funny farm."

"Was a resident. I'm now a free man."

The driver smirked, "Yes, but for how long? Say, you're not a serial murderer, are you?"

WD smirked. "If I was, I wouldn't tell you. Actually, they had me there to help me get over my drinking problem."

"Did they? I mean, are you going to the 7-Eleven to buy booze? 'Cause I don't want to be responsible for—"

WD waved off his concern. "Look man, I'm not going to buy booze. I'm a changed man, no thanks to the psyche ward. Thankfully, I heard the gospel and it…Christ Jesus changed my life. I now have a better reason to live."

The driver's face brightened. "That's real good to hear my friend. I'm a believer and a former alcoholic. Were it not for God's grace, I don't know where I'd be. Is there anything I can do besides giving you a ride home?" he asked, reaching for his wallet.

The sincerity of the man's question took WD back a moment. He'd always admired people who'd demonstrated true kindness to a total stranger. But this was different. This time he was the recipient of such kindness.

"Well, for starters, you don't have to drop me off at the 7-Eleven after all. You can take me all the way to my house."

The man refocused his attention on the road ahead. With the windshield wipers working overtime, the driver pushed through the storm in silence until they reached the road which led to WD's house.

"It's just up ahead on the right," he said, pointing with his index finger.

The car rolled to a gentle stop along the curb and the driver twisted around. "Look man, you don't have to worry about me going to the authorities. As far as I'm concerned, we never met. But be assured you'll be in my thoughts."

WD extended his hand and gripped the driver's. His firm grip reassured him that indeed, the man was as good as his word. "You are a God-send my friend. Thanks."

The man squeezed his hand firmly, then released it. "Well, I must be going. Stay safe."

WD nodded and climbed out. After shutting the door, he stepped from the curb and began a steady pace in the direction of his house. He didn't take notice of the direction the car went, but looking back he didn't remember seeing the car turn around. Neither did he hear it accelerate away. As he stood wondering, he glanced down at his clothes.

They were completely dry.

***

Prince Uriel guided the car around the corner, stopped and got out.

"That was interesting," he said to himself. "Cars are much slower than I thought. Speaking of that, I'd better find WD before he enters the garage. I wouldn't want him to do something he'd regret."

In a blink of an eye, he disappeared and took up a position in the upper rafters of the aging garage. Seeing the other members of his team, he gave them a thumbs up.

***

The rain which pelted him earlier had ceased leaving deep puddles of muddy water.

He dodged the worst of them, but unfortunately, missed a few and got his shoe wet in the process as he made his way up the walk to the front door of his house.

A rumble of thunder echoed in the distance making him wish he'd chosen a better night for his escape. If his old pickup truck refused to start, his chances of escaping were very thin.

He arrived on his front porch just as another roll of thunder sounded overhead. With his heart pounding in his ears, he fished the house key from his pocket, unlocked the door and entered.

"Ah, it's good to be home," he said in a low tone.

Inhaling, the dank, stale air assaulted his nose. After all those months, the faint stench of alcohol still lingered in the air. All at once the demon of liquor pounced on him, trying to bury its talons into his mind.

It's okay to take just one drink. No one will know. After all, you deserve it," it whispered

WD's hands slicked, and the moisture in his mouth turned to dust. Heart racing, he cried out, "Oh Lord, help me to resist the devil," even as he reached for the handle of the refrigerator.

***

"No!"

Prince Uriel clapped his hand over his mouth with one hand and with the other, sliced the air between himself and the lizard-like creature which threatened to crush WD's skull.

The demon snarled and hissed. "He's mine, all mine!"

Another broad stroke of Uriel's sword and the demon leaped back. "Not so fast demon. My God has redeemed this man's eternal soul. He belongs to Him now, so back off!"

The demon, one of the mightier princes of the power of the air, lashed out at Uriel with his barbed tail. Uriel knew better than to tangle with this beast. Giving a whistle, he signaled for reinforcement. A bolt of lightning flashed and Prince Camael appeared, his sword swirling like a buzz-saw.

For a moment, the demon hesitated. "I will not yield," he bellowed and threw himself at the two angels of light.

Standing back-to-back, the angelic hosts swung their swords. Unknown to WD, the battle continued until the leathery creature made one mistake. He overextended his reach and miscalculated the length of Camael' sword. It sliced through his thick hide. In an instant, black, oily goo spurted from its throat. The beast gasped knowing what was next.

Prince Uriel, though only slightly smaller, was fleet of foot and quickly danced around the beast's tail and rammed his spear into the demon's heart.

"Nooo!" his anguished cry echoed as he descended into the abyss.

***

Shocked by the sound of rustling wings and the clash of swords, WD glanced around, looking for its source.

In the unseen mayhem, dishes vibrated, chairs danced across the floor and the lights flickered.

All at once, everything fell silent.

Breathing hard, he waited for his heart to slow and his mind to clear.

Gone was the urge for a drink. His hand dropped to his side and he turned and ascended the stairs. Knowing he had only a few minutes to make his escape, he quickly pulled an old suitcase out from under the bed, flung it open and began to throw what few belongings he had into it. Then he grabbed his shaving kit, filled it and shoved it into the suitcase. After latching the buckles, he dragged it down the stairs.

Then he flung open the back door and made his way to the garage. It wasn't much, but the old building had served as his getaway from the world's pressure. It was also where he used to tinker on his vintage pickup truck. He hoped one day to fully restore it and go to antique car shows. Now all he cared about was whether or not it ran.

Chapter Ten

Surprise, Surprise …

Hiding in the rafters of the old garage, Prince Leo had heard about all the vulgarity he could stand.

The spirit of lust had embedded is talons in at least two of the figures below him. The spirit of blasphemy and indulgence hung thick as smoke in the air. It was clear the prince of darkness was closing in for the kill. Leo was about to release a burst of light and drive the demons into the depths of the bottomless pit when he heard footsteps.

"Soon," he told himself.

Relaxing his grip on his bow and arrow, he waited and watched. Seconds ticked as a man approached the door.

***

As WD neared the garage door, he noticed it hung partially open.

"Hmm, I certainly hope no one broke in and stole all my tools," he muttered.

Reaching for the handle, his hand was arrested. *Is that voices I hear? And is that laughter?*

"Kids,' he complained. "I hope none of them have a gun. I'd hate to get shot in my own garage."

After taking a reassuring breath, he grasped the handle, yanked the door open and stepped inside. Through the glow from a single light bulb, he saw three figures; two guys and one girl. They were smoking, laughing and swaying to the asymmetric rhythm of rap music. One of the figures bolted upright and sucked in a sharp breath.

"G-Diddy!?" her words came out slurred.

"Chloe?!"

Her head lolled to one side as she tried to push herself up. With effort, she wobbled to her feet and climbed from the bed of the pickup truck.

"What are you kids doing in here?" WD demanded.

The two young men quickly snuffed out their smokes. "What are *you* doing here, old man?" they asked in unison.

The blue haze crackled with tension.

Chloe stepped away from the truck and approached her grandfather. Her glassy eyes burned with defiance. "G-Diddy, I thought you were—"

"—You thought wrong young lady!" he snapped. "And who are these, these guys?" he asked, trying not to sound accusatory.

The one leaning on the hood of his truck pushed himself up on unsteady legs. His glazed eyes stared unfocused back at him. "And who are you?"

Chloe cocked her head and spoke over her shoulder. A joint of marijuana hung between her fingers. "This is my granddaddy. I told you about him. He's cool." She took a long pull from her joint, savored the moment before releasing a column of blue smoke.

A lanky boy in sagging britches clamored from the back of the truck and stood next to Chloe.

She wormed her arm around him, and said, "This is Tramp, his real name is Travis." Eyeing the other boy, she said, "that's Luke, but everyone calls him Boomer. These are the Fam I was telling you about. We were just getting ready to bounce," she sneered.

Bile rose in WD's throat knowing what would happen if and when these two scumbags ever got their hands on his granddaughter. He rejected the thought that they might already have.

Keeping his voice level, he said. "Uh, guys. This is my pickup truck and I need to be going, so would you kindly remove yourselves? I'm in a bit of a hurry."

Chloe eyed him coldly. Under the light of the 60-watt bulb, she looked like death warmed over. *Gothic,* WD thought, *it's more like ghastly.*

The butterfly tattoo on her neck appeared to be a new addition to the others, but he refused to acknowledge it. He had a tattoo on his forearm. It was an anchor with a chain wrapped around it, so he was in no position to judge. Albeit, he'd received it while in the Navy long before she was born.

"G-Diddy, how'd you get out of—of," she glanced around not wanting to say Mental Hospital. "How'd you get here anyways? Now you screwed up everything."

WD backed away from her, not wanting to inhale her marijuana laden breath. "Maybe it's better you don't know. Now which one of you has the keys to my truck?"

Boomer squared his shoulders defensively. Lifting his hand, he waggled them between his fingers. "What's the hurry, old man? Like Chloe said, we are going on a road trip and it doesn't include you. So beat it!" His voice took on an edge.

This isn't going to end well, WD thought. *Two against one aren't good odds. Well, one is high as a kite, so the odds are better. But what about Chloe?*

After a moment of reflection, he offered the young man a weak smile. "I'm guessing neither of you are old enough to drive. You're what, sixteen?" looking at the glassy-eyed boy who'd slumped to the concrete next to the truck.

"Seventeen, but I just have a learner's permit," slurred Tramp.

"And you?" WD demanded, glancing at Boomer.

"Same."

In a move which surprised them both, WD grabbed the keys from Boomer, and yanked the door to the pickup truck open.

"Then it's settled. I'll drive you to Florida. Then we go our separate ways. Deal?" He glanced at Chloe, then at the boy leaning on his truck.

She stared defiantly back at him.

If looks could kill. WD thought.

Finally, Chloe cocked her head and caught one of the young man's eyes. He nodded his approval.

WD released a tight breath. "Then it's settled. Grab your stuff. Like I said, I'm in a bit of a hurry."

Tramp moved with surprisingly more energy than WD expected. Within two minutes, he, Chloe and Boomer had tossed their sleeping bags, backpacks and a few sacks of groceries in the back of the pickup truck.

"Get the door," WD barked over the rumble of the truck's engine.

Chloe jumped from the back of the truck and swung the door further open. WD eased the pickup from its resting place. After closing the garage door, she climbed in next to her grandfather. Boomer and Tramp squeezed in between her and the truck door.

"Hold on," he said and popped the clutch causing the truck to lurch forward.

***

Prince Leo released a pent-up breath.

"And you want me to stay with that girl all the way to where?" he asked his leader. "It was all I could do to keep from chopping off the heads of those two ruffians," he said with a slight Scottish accent.

Prince Camael watched a trio of demons following the truck. "Not just you, I am going along with you. Those demons can only be dispatched by prayer and fasting, and I know of no believer strong enough to do such a thing. It is our job to protect Chloe and WD from falling into the wiles of the evil one. So let us be going. We have many miles to go before this is over."

With a swirl of air, the angelic band rose skyward and gave chase to the fleeing pickup truck.

Five minutes later, a black and white police cruiser drove passed WD's residence.

Chapter Eleven

The Drive to Florida …

"I smell sulfur," Prince Selaphiel, one of Prince Camael's forward guards, said.

His sensitivity to subtle changes in the ethereal space between the natural and the supernatural was acute. His keen eyes and sharp senses had kept Camael and his hosts from stepping into many ambushes over the millennia.

Prince Camael's hand immediately grabbed the hilt of his sword. "I sense the presence of a great evil. Be on guard. We are entering the domain of Satan's most powerful spirits," he whispered as he and his company angels sped along the highway.

By the time WD and his traveling companions neared the Florida state line, it was nearly nine o'clock. What remained of the sun was obscured by the presence of the evil one. Although there wasn't a cloud in the sky, the air cooled and the wind picked up. In the growing darkness, Prince Camael knew the forces of darkness were gathering. He saw the spirit of lust with its talons buried deep in the minds of the two boys sitting next to Chloe. But she was no lily-white flower. Her mind was in the grips of anger and bitterness, not to mention the wicked thoughts of indulgence.

"Lord Jehovah," Prince Camael cried out, "Send reinforcements. The cause is too great, and the need is greater."

In an instant, the sky lit up with a thousand shafts of light as Prince Raphael, one of God's mightiest cherubs led a myriad of the heavenly warriors to their rescue. Above the speeding pickup truck, angels and demons clashed. To WD and Chloe, it was just another early summer storm. In reality, it was the continuation of the conflict of the ages.

Miles later, the storm subsided, the sky cleared, and the face of a smiling moon appeared. With the forces of evil reduced to a handful of cowardly spirits, Prince Camael saluted his companion. "Thank you my brother. Were it not for you, our purpose might have been thwarted."

Prince Raphael sheathed his golden sword. Glancing down at the young men in the front of the pickup truck, he said, "The problem is those young men. Their minds are so filled with lust that they invited the enemy's attack. May I suggest you send one of your angels to cause them to fall into a deep sleep? At least then, they won't be thinking about the young lady sitting next to them."

Prince Camael removed his silver helmet and rubbed the place on his head where a demon's club had struck. He winced. "I won't let that happen again. Your suggestion is duly noted. It is as you wish."

Within minutes, the boys drifted off to sleep. With their heads lolling on each other's shoulders, their snoring nearly drowned out the roar of the engine.

***

Hands gripping the steering wheel, WD's mind swirled with a thousand questions.

Was Chloe just using me to get away from her mother?

Had she made the same mistake Joyce made sixteen years ago?

Who were these boys and what interest had they in my granddaughter?

What would happen to me if I get caught carrying minors across a state line?

These and many more questions plagued his thoughts.

He was so angry with Chloe's behavior that he wanted to bend her over his knee and give her a good old fashioned whoopin', but that would probably only drive her further away. Of course she was angry. Why wouldn't she be? He'd caught her smoking dope with a couple of knuckleheads. Who knows what was on their minds.

Finally, with the moon illuminating the rolling landscape, he summoned the courage to break the tense atmosphere.

"What were you thinking, running off with those two hoodlums?"

Chloe uncoiled her arms, her hands still in tight little fists and released an angry breath. She turned her eyes in his direction. They were painted black and had grown hard.

"You callin' my tribe hoodlums?" She followed up her question with a few choice expletives. "Look at you. You're a drunk, and an escapee from a mental hospital. You've got no room to judge me." Her words assaulted him like angry bees.

Taken aback, WD had not expected such vitriol, not from his granddaughter. For as long as he'd known her, she'd never spoken to him like that. Biting his lip, he blamed it on the company she'd been keeping.

He nodded. "You're right. I am a drunk and I did just escape from a mental hospital, but that doesn't mean I can't see what's going on. You're about to screw up your life with those two—" he resisted the temptation to say what he really thought of the young men.

Chloe let out an angry huff, crossed her arms over her chest and peered straight ahead. "They're my friends. All yours are dead. I wish you were, too," she said through clinched teeth.

WD wished the same thing. *What have I gotten myself into? Now even my granddaughter hates me.*

An uncomfortable silence grew between them giving him time to consider his situation. He was taking three under-aged teens across a state line without parental permission. That's three counts of kidnapping. If they possessed marijuana, there's drug trafficking added to a long list of other crimes he'd already committed. He needed to dump these losers and fast.

Suddenly a thought occurred to him.

Over the years, he had developed a friendship with some commercial fishermen. From time to time, they needed parts for their fishing boats, and they came to his parts store in search of them. As a result, they had invited him to go deep sea fishing, drink beer, and occasionally catch a marlin or a shark.

Currently, however, they were holed up in a fishing camp located deep in the Okefenokee Swamp. Hoping his friends had not relocated to their summer port, he increased his speed.

By 9:45 in the evening, the scenery along I-95 had changed from tall pine trees to live oak trees covered in Spanish moss. Seeing their looming figures draped in the fog reminded him of a scene from Jurassic Park. All he needed now was to see a Tyrannosaurus Rex emerge and charge after them.

Chloe roused. "Where we headed?"

WD kept his eyes on the road, hoping they had gotten far enough from any dragnet the police may have set up.

So far, none appeared.

"Like I said, I'll take you to Florida and drop you off."

"Then where are you going?"

He shifted slightly, but kept his eyes straight ahead. "I've got some things to do before I turn myself in."

"You're what?" her face turned slightly ashen. "You'll go to jail for sure."

"What do you care? You were just using me to get away from your mother. All those times you visited me…you were planning on stealing my pickup truck and shack up with—" he clapped his hand over his mouth. "I mean, go on a road trip. You never really cared about me, did you?"

"That's not true," she said defensively. "When your stinking warehouse caught fire and when they hauled you off, I believed in you. I still believe in you." She finished her statement with a few choice words.

WD bristled. "You sure didn't act like it back in the garage. And by the way, I don't appreciate you using my Lord's name so cavalierly. You may not believe in Jesus, but I do and I'll not stand for you using His name in vain."

She slumped deeper in the seat. "Sorry!" She didn't sound sorry, but he accepted her apology with grace.

"All right, with that settled, let me say, my plan doesn't involve three minors. I've got a lot of miles to cover in a short time and I can't have you three—" he glanced to the side and pointed with his forehead. "I can't have you dragging me down. Anyway, your mother, not to mention the police, the mental hospital, and who knows who else, will be on my tail like white on rice. So as soon as I can be rid of you, the better."

She took a hard swallow and glanced at the changing landscape. "This doesn't look like Florida. Where ya taking us?"

He avoided eye contact and kept driving.

They had left the interstate and were entering the small town of Folkston. *With any luck, we'll get to the fish camp in another thirty minutes.*

All at once, a black and white police cruiser appeared out of nowhere and pulled up behind them. WD eased his foot off the gas pedal. Heart racing, he prepared to stop and face the consequences. A moment later, the policeman turned on his lights and siren, and accelerated around him. In a heart-racing instant, he was gone, leaving WD and Chloe panting.

"That was close," she said, clearly shaken.

Tramp stirred. "What happened dude?"

"Nothing," WD said, glancing in the rear-view mirror.

Chloe shifted slightly away from him. "Go back to sleep, bruh," she added curtly.

The boy shrugged his shoulders and slumped back down like a whipped pup.

"Do you always talk to your peeps like that?" WD asked.

Chloe's shoulders slumped. "Yeah, what of it?"

Knowing it wasn't a real question, he let silence fill the cab.

Chapter Twelve

The Fish Camp …

After leaving the paved highway, WD drove his pickup truck along a narrow sandy road for another twenty minutes.

It was nearly 10 o'clock at night by the time they reached the main road leading to the heart of the Okefenokee Swamp.

Outside, a chorus of crickets sang the night away. A giant bullfrog made his presence known and something black dashed across the road as the truck's yellowed headlights cut two thin shafts ahead of them.

All at once, the courtyard of the fish camp appeared in the distance, and WD brought the truck to a halt. He cut the engine and let the night settle in. The fish camp as he called it was nothing more than a few block buildings separated by tuffs of saw grass, discarded boats and rusting cars.

In the light of a single streetlamp, pot-bellied men in grungy overalls moved about the sandy campground at a measured pace. No one seemed to be in a hurry. No one seemed to have taken notice of the visitors either.

Out of nowhere, a man sporting a long red beard appeared next to the cab.

"What's your business here?" his voice boomed in the darkness.

Chloe sucked in a sharp breath and pulled back.

Tramp and Boomer shot upright like they'd been jabbed with a hot iron.

WD, his window rolled down, his elbow over the door frame, flicked on the dome light. "It's me—WD," he said in a casual tone.

Taking a greasy handkerchief from around his cannonball sized head, the man mopped his brow and let out a low whistle.

"If it ain't ol' WD. I thought you were stuck in the funny farm."

WD grinned sheepishly. "Oh hey, Jimmy. I was, but I got out for good behavior. I ain't kilt anyone so's they thought I was rehabitchuated."

The man let out a belly laugh and called out to a few of his friends. "Hey guys, look who just showed up."

Three rather large men paused from loading their gear on to a fishing trawler long enough to acknowledge WD's presence, then returned to their labor.

"Ah, don't mind them. Their just sore 'cause you refused to supply us with that 1997 Mercury Villager drive shaft."

WD pushed the bill of his baseball cap back and rubbed his forehead. "If anything, I should be sore at them for not paying me for the last one."

"Not paying?! We paid that bill in full. Is that why you drove all the way out here in the middle of the night to accuse us of cheatin' you?" he colored the air with vulgarity. But he wasn't through. "Didn't your bookkeeper tell you?"

WD's mouth gaped open. "Nah. I heard nothing about getting paid. I thought—"

"You thought wrong, ol' buddy," the man spat.

Hands extended, WD said, "Hey, I'm sorry. I never got the paid invoice. I let Stephen handle all that."

"Then you'd better get with him. 'Cause you've got a rat in your barn."

WD reached and pulled the handle of the truck so he could climb out. Once he'd extracted himself, he scanned the area. Not much had changed. "I'm sorry. I'll do that when I get back." He waited for the man's response.

Nothing.

"I guess you haven't heard."

"Heard what?" the man said, then spat a wad of tobacco juice on the sandy ground.

"That I'm being investigated for arson and insurance fraud. They think I set my own warehouse on fire and then tried to kill myself."

A groan sounded from the cab of the pickup truck and WD glanced over his shoulder. Chloe slumped deeper in her seat.

"No, I haven't heard that. Did you do it?" he asked as he stuffed a fresh wad of tobacco in between his cheek and gum.

"If I did, would I admit it to you? Of course I didn't do it."

"Then that proves you've got a rat in the barn. Perhaps you should check on the whereabouts of your sons when that fire started."

Another groan sounded from the truck's cab.

"'Nuff about your insurance troubles. What brings you way out here in the middle of the night?" He swatted a mosquito with his fat hand.

WD cast an accusatory glance at the two boys in the pickup. "I brought you some live bait," he said with a chuckle.

Tramp, who had been watching the conversation in silence, suddenly spoke up. "Hey wait a minute. You said you were going to take us to Florida."

WD turned on the youth. "This is Florida ya dumb bunny," emphasizing every letter. "We are about three miles inside the Florida state line. I kept my side of the bargain. Now shut your trap and get out of my pickup!"

He left the boy no room for negotiation. Grabbing Tramp by the shirt, he yanked him out of the cab. "You too Chloe. Get your stuff and get out."

"But—but—"

"No buts. You wanted a road trip to Florida. and you got it. These men will show you a real good time. Won't you, Jimmy?"

Jimmy eyed the scrawny youths with disdain. "Looks like we've got us a couple of snowflakes and a mouthy white bit—"

"—Hey watch it. That's my granddaughter you're talking about. It was her idea to take a road trip with these two scumbags. I'll let you guys sort it all out. In the meantime, I've got some housecleaning to do. If you can keep an eye on them for a week or so, I'll get them on my way back."

"Hey gramps, that's not fair. You lied to us." Boomer said and pulled his fist back.

Instinctively, WD blocked the swing and sent him sprawling.

Chloe shrieked then turned the air various colors of blue.

WD turned on her. "Chloe, if you say another word, I'm going to personally throw you to the fish."

She clamped her hand over her mouth, then stomped away into the darkness.

While the two young men collected their camping gear, WD and Jimmy sauntered off to discuss how they were going to handle three unruly youths. Once WD handed Jimmy a wad of hundred-dollar bills, the two men shook hands. With their business concluded, WD retook his place behind the wheel of the pickup truck.

"By the way, WD. That's a nice set of wheels. You ever think about sellin' it?" Jimmy asked in a lighter tone.

WD patted the outer side of the door. "Yes, yes I have. Let's talk about it when I get back. How 'bout that?"

Jimmy nodded. "Sounds like a plan. Now get outta here," he said and slapped the side of the truck.

WD saluted the other men, cranked the engine and pulled away.

He had a long drive ahead of him and much to think about.

***

Prince Camael waited until the roar of the engine faded before assembling his lieutenants.

"Prince Leo, I want you to follow Miss Chloe and see to it that no harm comes to her."

He narrowed his eyes. "That won't be easy, my lord. She's as much a danger to herself as she is vulnerable to attack by the wicked one."

Camael acknowledged his statement with a slow nod. "I'm inclined to agree with you. Take Prince Cassiel and Prince Haniel with you and set around the clock guard over her."

Turning to Prince Raguel, a giant angel bearing a trident and a round shield etched with markings in a heavenly language, Camael said, "I'm assigning you and Prince Zadkiel to keep watch over those two young men. I believe the Almighty has big plans for them, but be aware: their minds are corrupted with the filth of this world. It was their evil imaginations which nearly cost us this leg of the journey."

The two powerful angels took their positions in front of their commander and saluted him sharply. "We go in the name and strength of Almighty God," they said in unison.

Then they descended through the night sky and sat on the camping gear next to Tramp and Boomer.

Chapter Thirteen

Welcome to Reality …

Prince Zadkiel had just taken his position on the north side of the fish camp when he noticed a dark shadow creeping across the sandy courtyard.

In human terms, it was 10:30 p.m. In the spiritual realm, time meant nothing. "Do you see that?" he asked Prince Raguel in a low tone.

His ally nodded. "Yes, it is the spirit of wickedness. I have been tracking its movements as the moon slides further to the west."

Their eyes followed it until it slithered into one of the sheds. As embedded as the spirit of lust was in the two boys' minds, it wouldn't be long before the devil himself showed up.

Prince Raguel shifted his weight from one foot to the other, his sight peering between the two dimensions—the physical and the supernatural. "You want that I could materialize as one of the men and dispatch that lizard before he has a chance to sink its talons any deeper in those boy's minds?" He loved posing as an old Jewish goldsmith or carpenter.

Nodding, Prince Zadkiel gave his friend a pat on his broad shoulder. "Good thinking, but be on guard."

Raguel tapped the hilt of his sword. "Always." In the blink of an eye, he was gone.

***

"Now let's get one thing straight," Jimmy said, as he eyed the two boys. "I've got one rule around here. Do as I say and I won't feed you to the alligators." He nodded in the direction of a pen housing several very large alligators.

"But you can't keep us here against our will. Isn't there a law against that?" Boomer protested loudly. "My dad's a lawyer and he's going to—"

Jimmy widened his stance. "As I understand it, you boys asked Mr. Dawson to take you to Florida. He didn't force you. You came willingly. Right?"

"Yeah," they muttered weakly.

"I can't hear you. Right!"

"Yeah, but not here. Not to this God-forsaken place," Travis said belligerently.

Jimmy shook his head. "Now you've gone and done it. You've insulted my home. Show me your cell phones," the palm of his hand extended.

"What?" they protested in unison.

"You heard me. Give me your cell phones."

Reluctantly, the two boys fished the phones from their pockets and placed them in Jimmy's fat hand.

He eyed them with interest. "Pretty new. How long have you had them?"

Tramp puffed his chest. "My dad gets me a new one every year."

"Yeah, me too," added Boomer. "If you don't let us call home, my dad will take you to court for all you have."

"Is that so! I guess you'll be getting new phones next year." Before they could stop him, Jimmy tossed the phones over the fence into the alligator pen.

"Hey, you can't do that!" protested Boomer.

"Rule number two. Keep your mouths shut until I say so."

"But—"

Jimmy stepped so close to Boomer that his rotund gut knocked him back a step. "Look here, sunny boy, until WD returns, you're all mine. I'm going to teach you snowflakes not only how to work, but how to work hard. And the more you gripe and complain, the harder it's going to get. Now grab your gear and follow me." He took a step, then stopped. "Hey wait, where's that girl who looks like death warmed over?"

Travis and Boomer exchanged confused expressions.

"Got me," Travis said.

Jimmy called to one of his crew. "Hey Bubba, you seen a dead girl walking around here?"

The man cocked his head. "Say what?"

"WD dropped off these two snowflakes and a girl dressed in Gothic, but she disappeared. Could you see if you can find her?"

Prince Raguel, dressed in grungy overalls offered him a toothy grin. "She couldn't have gotten far. There's no place to go."

"Just try and find her before the alligators do."

With a nod, he set off in the direction of the dirt road leading to the fish camp.

"Let that be a lesson to you. Ain't no gettin' outta here. We are circled by a swamp filled with cotton-mouth snakes, man-sized mosquitoes and man-eating alligators. This fish camp is the only safe haven for miles."

Tears formed in the boy's eyes, but they kept their mouths shut and followed Jimmy to the bunkhouse.

Chapter Fourteen

On the Road …

After leaving the fish camp, WD drove a few more miles until he came to a fork in the road.

Cutting his wheels, he sped up causing the tires to rumble on the washboard surface of the sandy road. "You can come out now Chloe," WD called over his shoulder.

Rustling sounded from the bed of the truck and Chloe's head popped out from under a tarp.

Slowing, he said. "You might as well ride in the front. Climb on up here."

Being careful not to lose her grip, Chloe clambered over the gunwale, opened the door and climbed in. Her multi-colored hair stood on end. The black eyeliner had bled down her cheeks from crying, and she looked like a zombie.

Arms crossed, she pooched her lip, and asked, "How'd ya know I was back here?"

WD glanced over at his granddaughter. "I'm no dummy."

She huffed.

He chuckled.

"You might as well face it. We are traveling companions for the next week or two."

She gawked. "I gotta be back by next Monday."

"This might take a bit longer."

"But my grades."

"You should have thought about that."

"I didn't know you were going to abduct me."

"Consider this a field trip—you'll learn a lot."

She cut her eyes in his direction. "Where are you taking me?"

WD changed gears and sped up. "Correction, where am I going? That I can't tell ya; at least not yet."

"Why not?" her voice was raspy from the dust swirling inside the cab.

"Because, I haven't decided what I'm going to do myself."

"Fur rel, bruh!? You kidnapped me and my tribe. You drop them off with a couple of losers, and you abduct me and you don't have a plan?!"

WD rubbed the back of his neck. "Wait one cotton-pickin' minute. You climbed into the bed of my truck. Nobody forced you to do that. Now hand me your phone."

She eyed him for a second. "You're kidding me." Her voice turned flat.

Shaking his head, WD extended his hand. "Nope. Give me your cell phone. I'm not kidding."

She huffed and began to root through her bag. "There," she said, slapping it in the palm of his hand.

He eyed it for a few seconds, then tossed it into the brackish water which collected along the dirt road.

"Hey, you can't do that!" She protested, but it was too late.

"I just did. Now let's get a few things straight. First, you chose to take this road trip, and you planned on stealing my truck. Then, when I get you to Florida, rather than sticking with your tribe," he formed air quotes with his fingers, "you climbed into the flat bed of this pickup truck and left with me. Does that about sum things up?"

She pressed herself deeper into the seat. "I want to go home."

WD lowered the gear, rounded a curve and accelerated.

"Not going to happen."

"Why G-Diddy? You don't want me. Nobody wants me. I hate you."

"So now we're getting somewhere. All of those visits to the hospital; they were just to gain my confidence so you could learn where I kept the keys to the truck."

She let out a four-letter word.

"And another thing," WD continued. "For the duration of this road trip, you will speak in common English, no 'F' words, no foul language, no blasphemy. You got that?"

She gaped at him, her eyes round, her jaw hanging.

"Don't look at me like that young lady."

She harrumphed, "You're so basic."

"English."

"Boring," she muttered in a sing-song voice.

"I can handle boring," he said with a half-grin. "But before it's over, you'll thank me."

"Whatever." Closing her eyes, she leaned her head against the door and grew quiet.

Good, thought WD, *Now perhaps I can figure out where I'm going.*

***

Sitting atop the pickup truck, as it rumbled along the sandy road, Prince Leo grinned at his commander.

"This is going to be interesting."

Prince Camael adjusted his silver helmet. "How so?"

Prince Leo released a low chuckle. "Aye, laddie, that girl has a lot of spunk. I'd hate to be on the receiving end of her vitriol."

Giving his companion a wan smile, he said. "It's all bravado. Beneath that crusty surface is a struggling, hurting soul for whom Adonai died. It is our privilege to guide her to the light."

"I certainly hope the saints are praying. Without those prayers, our efforts will be in vain," Leo added, the wind whipping his red hair.

"I don't know if they are praying or not, but I do know there is one saint praying," said Camael, glancing at the man driving the pickup.

Chapter Fifteen

Stoneybrook Mental Health Facility ...

Angry voices rose from behind the closed doors of the Stoneybrook Mental Health Facility.

But they were not human…

"I told you, I have no idea where WD went," said the spirit of arrogance, a short, stubby, frog-like spirit with a potbelly and bulging eyes. He prided himself on his superiority.

"Then find them you fool," ordered his commander. The tall lanky, lizard-like spirit of intolerance, towered over the smaller spirit. His eyelids narrowed into slits; his chest heaved with pent-up hatred.

Arrogance sputtered. "My eyes have been blinded by the light. How can I?"

Intolerance swatted the smaller spirit aside with his leathery tail. "Enough of your whimpering. I gave you one simple task, watch WD, but no, you got distracted. You thought you knew better." His tone grew sarcastic. "And now we've lost track of not only one human, but we've lost track of three; a young, easily manipulated girl, and two lug-headed boys. We had them right where we wanted them, then poof, they were gone."

While the demons argued and accused each other, their counterparts; the leadership and staff of Stoneybrook had their own problems.

***

"The police are the last people I want to talk to," Sam Lott, the head of Stoneybrook Mental Health Facility, said as he scanned the room filled with sleepy people.

He had called an emergency meeting with his staff, and expected everyone to be at the top of their game.

Will Thornton, his chief psychiatrist and WD's primary clinician, ran his hands down his elongated face. He had aged years in the last eight hours. "Look Sam, we can't risk WD being out on the lam for more than a day. If he tries to hurt himself, it will be on us for not reporting his escape."

"Perhaps he didn't escape. Perhaps he's somewhere on the compound," Ed Huntley, the head of physical and occupational therapy, suggested.

Don Sutherland, the head of security, leaned his chair back on two legs. Arms over his broad chest, he said, "He's not here. I had my men do a thorough room-to-room search. They checked under every bed, in every closet, in every locker, and every nook and cranny of this facility and nothing—nada."

Sam shifted uncomfortably as his secretary relayed a message to him in a low tone. "Gentlemen, ladies, my secretary just got off the phone with Joyce Dawson, WD's daughter. I wanted to check with her to see if perhaps WD had gotten a one-day pass to visit her."

"I never issued him a one-day pass," Sutherland said in his own defense.

"It's not the first time someone faked a one-day pass Don," Sam said, his tone level. "That aside, she confirmed my worst fears that indeed WD has escaped. Then she went on to say that Chloe, her daughter has gone missing."

A ripple of anxiety spread through the room like a fog causing the mortal and immortal spirits to stop and listen.

"Who reported this and have they gone to the police?" The question came from Britney Brice, his chief legal counsel.

Sam clinched his fists and pounded the table. "Joyce Dawson, WD's daughter; the girl's mother and no, she hasn't contacted the police yet. But she is threatening to call the newspaper if we don't get ahead of this, and fast."

"How do we do that if we don't involve the police?" Thornton said. "He's not only a danger to himself, now he's endangering his granddaughter."

Sam nodded. Releasing a sigh, he said, "You make a compelling case, make the call. We'll just have to deal with the public reaction as it comes. In the meantime, Ms. Brice, would you and your team prepare a statement condemning Mr. Dawson's actions? Something like, 'we are working closely with federal and local authorities in order to resolve this unfortunate situation, Blah, blah, blah.'"

She nodded, stood and quickly exited the room.

***

The clock on the wall read 7 a.m. and already the police department was a bevy of activity.

"Look ma'am," Sheriff Wooten said. He had already been over this with Boomer's mother. Repeating himself was not something he was accustomed to doing. "It's Spring break. Boomer and his friends are probably just letting off steam. You remember how it was when we were—" He pulled the phone from his ear so the others could hear.

"Yes, but you don't know my son. He's a good boy, never gave us a lick of trouble. He's a straight 'A' student. Just ask the principal of the high school."

The boy is not all his mother thinks he is, the sheriff mused.

He knew for a fact that the boy had been caught smoking under the bleachers a number of times. On another occasion he was caught cheating on an exam and would have been suspended had his father not intervened. Ron Pauley, the boy's father, and one of the attorneys in the Grayson, Grayson, Estes, and Pauley law firm, was well known for throwing his weight around and often did.

"Look Mrs. Pauley," the sheriff interrupted, "we will look into this, but really, it's too early to put out an Amber Alert on a couple of teen boys the day after school let out. Give it another day before you panic."

"Another day—panic!" her voice spiraled up an octave. "That's my boy out there. Some ax murderer could be carving him up as we speak."

The sheriff released a tired huff. He had no patience for hysterical mothers. Handing the phone to his deputy, he refocused his attention on more pressing matters.

"Sir, there's a call on line one for you," his secretary said. "It's Sam Lott, head of—"

"I know who Sam is. We golf every Friday." Cursing under his breath, he punched the button on the phone. "Hey Sam, what's going on?"

He waited, not moving as Sam filled him in on the details.

"How long has he been missing?"

The room fell silent. All eyes turned in the sheriff's direction.

"Twelve hours, you say?"

He waited.

So did every deputy, every beat cop, and every secretary.

"And you have done a thorough search of the—"

Another pregnant pause. His underlings exchanged quizzeled expressions.

"Yes, but I had to ask. And you say his granddaughter is missing too. She wouldn't happen to be friends with Travis Estes and a boy named," he scanned his notepad. "Boomer Pauley, would she?"

Another uncomfortable pause filled the connection.

"All right, that confirms what I suspected. It sounds like we have reasonable cause to put out an Amber Alert and an APB for Mr. Dawson. We could very well be looking at kidnapping charges on top of an already growing list of crimes Mr. Dawson is being investigated for.

After hanging up, he scanned the room. "Don't just stand there. Put out an Amber Alert and get a warrant for Mr. Dawson's arrest. We've got to get ahead of this, or the press will eat me alive. Now get moving."

No one needed more motivation than Richard Waterman, the District Attorney. He was already leading the fight to bring WD up on charges of arson and insurance fraud. Now he had this to add to his list and he was thirsty for blood—Woodrow Dawson's blood. At this point, he wasn't sure how the law firm of Grayson, Grayson, Estes, and Pauley was involved, but going up against them would be a real game changer.

***

The spirit of destruction smiled wickedly.

Humans are so easily manipulated. He rubbed his clawed hands together. *They are so full of pride. All I had to do was hint that they might be publicly humiliated, and they go into self-preservation mode.* A wicked chuckle bubbled in his throat.

Chapter Sixteen

Grayson, Grayson, Estes and Pauley Attorneys at Law…

Truman, Blaine's youngest son, cursed his bad luck.

The fact that he had the full run of ranch meant little to him. After high school, he enrolled in the University of Oklahoma and carried a duel load, Ranch Management and Geology. Upon graduation, he returned long enough to inform his father that he was taking a job with the Bureau of Ocean and Energy Management (BOEM). However, with his mother's passing, and his father's declining health, the day-to-day operations of the ranch fell on his shoulders. Reluctantly, he set aside his lucrative career and stayed home to run the ranch. But he never forgave prodigal brother for what he did.

Having done his homework, he had discovered a vast oil deposit beneath the ranch, but when he presented the idea of setting up a drilling operation on the ranch, his father balked.

Soon afterward, their relationship went from bad to worse. At the present time, they were not speaking.

He blamed his father's failing health on his brother.

He blamed his bad luck on his brother.

Unaware of WD's troubles, Truman and his attorney, Ms. Beth Taylor, flew to Savannah seeking the advice of his old friend and college buddy, Bob Grayson.

Bob Grayson, the senior partner of the Grayson, Grayson, Estes and Pauley law firm was known for being an aggressive and formidable presence in the courtroom. However, due to a series of poor decisions, the law firm had fallen onto hard times. Cash-strapped, Bob listened to his friend's complaint.

"Truman, my advice to you, is get in your father's good graces."

Truman stood and began to pace the plush carpet; his hands jammed deep in his pockets. "I've tried, but as long as my older brother is alive, Dad is holding out hope that he will return. If that happens, he'll cut me out of his will."

Bob placed his elbows on his massive desk and templed his fingers. "And how do you know?"

Retaking his seat, he said, "You should know, you provided the documents making me the executor of father's Last Will and Testament."

The savvy attorney nodded. "So why are you coming to me?"

Truman glanced at his personal attorney who withdrew a few sheets of paper from her attaché case. He took a look at them and handed the proposal to his friend.

"If WD shows up I stand to lose millions of dollars from the drilling rights not to mention my position as chief executive of the ranch. What I'm proposing is that we form a shell corporation with interests in the drilling rights to the Circle D Ranch. If Dad signs the lease, we stand to make billions of dollars."

The cagy attorney stroked his chin. He wasn't a stranger to shady deals and this idea tickled his interest. "I'll need some time to think and consult with the other attorneys, at least with Tony and Ron. I don't think Ellis will go along with it."

"Suits me, but time is of the essence."

"Time is money," Bob quipped.

"How much are we talking about?"

Bob scanned the documents, then laid them aside. "One million dollars."

Truman felt the blood drain from his face. "Where am I going to get that kind of cash?"

Bob stood and came around the desk. Folding his arms across his chest, he leveled his gaze. "You might try talking to Stephen and Ben, WD's two sons. From what I've heard, they seem to have plenty of cash on hand."

***

Bright splashes of sunlight dotted the hardwood floor in Stephen Dawson's apartment.

He and Ben had interrupted their morning routine to assess their situation and plan their next move. His apartment, though not extravagant, was well-furnished. Plush carpet occupied the foyer, a recently acquired couch and armchair with matching end tables completed the ensemble. His only indulgence besides gambling, was buying paintings by local artists.

"This is not how things were supposed to happen," Stephen complained. "The plan was to get Dad permanently committed to the mental health facility. Then have his name removed from the company's insurance policy making us the sole beneficiaries of the insurance claim."

Ben, having already embezzled nearly several million dollars from the company, needed a plausible cover up, and the fire provided the perfect one. It not only consumed all of the contents within the warehouse, but it also burned all the financial records. Having their father named as the primary suspect in the fire was just icing on the cake.

"And we also can't afford to have Dad's name remain on Granddad Dawson's Last Will and Testament. According to Uncle Truman, when the old man dies, he'll leave most of the estate to our drunken father. If that happens, he'll squander every dime he gets his hands on." Stephen cursed.

"Yes, and then there's the matter of the oil and gas lease," Ben added.

Stephen nodded and walked over to the counter where a bottle of Jack Daniels sat. He grabbed a tumbler from the shelf and poured an inch of the brown liquid into it. After taking a swig, he wiped his lips with the back of his hand and poured a second shot.

*****

The front door slammed and Joyce marched in.

"Isn't a bit early to get drunk?" she said condescendingly.

She hated seeing her two brothers complain about their father's behavior and then act just like him. Frustrated at being called to her brother's apartment after pulling another long shift, she plopped onto the couch and kicked off her shoes. She had just gotten off work and was foot-tired and irritable. Being called to her brother's apartment was the last thing she wanted.

Stephen gulped down his booze and retook his seat. "That's only my second drink, I can handle it, so be quiet."

Joyce stood and padded into the kitchen. "What's this all about?" she asked. "With Dad and Chloe missing, I've got enough to worry about."

While Stephen and Ben debated their own troubles, Joyce fixed herself a mug of coffee. After pouring some vanilla-bean flavored creamer into the black brew, she took a sip and savored the moment. Closing her eyes, she did something she'd not done in a long time…pray. "Dear Lord, I know it's been a while, but I really need you. Chloe is missing, Dad is, is…" her prayer morphed into tears as she sobbed her way back to the cross.

While she prayed, her brothers plotted.

***

"I wonder why Dad never took us to meet the old man?" Stephen said, referring to their grandfather.

The only connection they had with their extended family was with Truman, their uncle. Earlier that month, he and his lawyer, Ms. Taylor, had stopped by the office unannounced. Obviously, WD wasn't there. According to Truman, had their paths crossed, it wouldn't have been pretty. It was then he informed them of their grandfather's failing health, the proposed oil and gas deal, and the need for them to kick in a million dollars to get the ball rolling.

"How convenient, having Dad arrested for kidnapping could work to our advantage," Stephen said in a low tone.

Stirring her coffee, Joyce returned to the living room.

"Why did you let Chloe spend so much time with him?" Ben asked accusingly.

Joyce blinked. "Say what?"

"You heard me. Why did you let your daughter get so close to Dad? He never gave us the time of day, growing up." Ben complained.

Joyce bristled at the accusation. "Look, Benji, I didn't *let* her spend time with him. Someone around here has to work for a living. You know she's as independent as a hog on ice."

Ben stood and stretched his legs, a smug expression on his face. "She gets it good and natural. I remember you were pretty wild when you were sixteen. Getting pregnant with—"

"Shut up, Benjie. How many girls did you—"

"All right, all right, you two." Stephen cut her off before she said too much. "There's no point in us fighting among ourselves."

"So why the urgent call?" Joyce asked, unaware of her brother's troubles.

Ben stepped in front of the large pane window and watched a bird eating from a feeder. "We just wanted to know if you've heard from Chloe. Is she all right?"

She shook her head. "No, but earlier I spoke with the sheriff, and he said they were going to put out an APB. Hopefully they will find them soon."

Chapter Seventeen

A Visit from the Sheriff ...

Joyce had just returned home when someone knocked on her front door.

Her heart quickened. *Maybe it's Chloe. I'm going to kill that child for staying out so late without telling me.*

The knocking continued.

Expecting to see Chloe's ashen face, she reached for the handle.

"Mrs. Dawson, it's Sheriff Wooten. Could you open the door? I have a few questions."

She felt her heart stop.

Fighting to keep from collapsing, she yanked the door open.

"Sheriff Wooten, any news?" she asked, her hands clutched under her chin.

"Morning, Ma'am, may we come in? It will only take a few minutes," he said as he and his deputy pushed their way into the foyer.

The deputy, a young man with the name Franks embossed on a shiny new brass badge nodded as he entered the apartment.

"Of course, Sheriff, anything to help get my daughter back." Her voice broke and she fought back a tear. "Take a seat gentleman." She motioned to the couch.

"That's why we're here, Mrs. Dawson." Rather than following her instructions, they took two seats with the sun at their backs.

"You may or may not know this, but both Travis and Boomer's mothers called us as soon as they realized their sons were missing. I was wondering why you called Stoneybrook before you called us."

A slight wave of irritation swept over her and she shifted uncomfortably. "Sir, I didn't call them. They called me around 6:30 this morning asking me if WD showed up on my doorstep."

"Had he?"

She shook her head, a strand of raven hair fell across her eyes and she tucked it behind her ear. "No, why would he visit me?"

The sheriff shrugged. "I don't know, Mrs. Dawson. Do you know exactly when Chloe went missing?"

Joyce did some quick calculating. "I was scheduled to go out of town for a week of in-service training. So when I got up around six in the morning, I wanted to talk with Chloe and set the ground-rules for the week. But when I checked her room, she was gone."

"Didn't that bother you, Mrs. Dawson?" the deputy asked.

Joyce fingered the hem of her blouse nervously. Her parenting skills were sorely lacking, but she wasn't about to admit it to these officers.

"At first, I thought she just hadn't returned from a party with friends. It was the last day of school you know and kids do things like that, but when I called her cell phone and got no answer, I got worried."

The sheriff jotted a few notes on a small notepad. "And that was…?"

She pinched her chin between her thumb and forefinger. "Oh, around nine."

"Did you notice anything missing—clothes, money?"

Joyce nodded slowly. "Why yes. All the above."

"And do you know the other two teens who'd gone missing? Their mothers reported them missing earlier this morning."

Joyce felt heat creep up her neck.

"Do you think they might have gone somewhere together?" she heard the sheriff asking.

Joyce sat upright. *This was news to her.* "What were the names of the boys?" she asked tentatively.

Sheriff Wooten flipped back a few pages of his notes. "Ah, here it is. Their names are Travis Estes and Boomer Pauley. Do either of their names mean anything to you?"

At the mention of the names Estes and Pauley, Mrs. Dawson took a sharp breath.

The deputy pulled out his notepad and scribbled something.

"No, sheriff. You know how teens are. They have their own tribe—no adults allowed." She gave them a faint smile which didn't reach her eyes.

"Would you be able to give us Chloe's cell phone number? If she uses it, we may be able to track it. Also, her credit or debit card numbers. If she tries to use them, the bank will alert us, and we will be able to zero in on her location."

She acknowledged his request with a slight move of her head. "I'll see what I can do." then she proceeded to dig through her purse looking for the requested information. "Ah, here it is," lifting a small business card with the numbers neatly written on its reverse side. Handing it to the sheriff, she released a nervous sigh. "Will that be all?" hoping it was.

The sheriff took the proffered card and shoved it into his shirt pocket. As he pushed himself up, he paused and retook his seat. "There's just one other thing that's been bugging me. Well, maybe two. As you know, the authorities at

Stoneybrook reported earlier that WD had gone missing the same time your daughter did; don't you think that's a little odd? I understand they were close."

Joyce bit her lip to keep from coloring the air blue. "No, I don't. They got along quite well, which is more than I can say about my relationship with either of them. Especially since he's been—" she let her voice fade.

"Incarcerated?" the deputy asked.

She shook her head. "Yes, that would describe it."

"Doesn't that worry you, him being suicidal and all?"

Joyce narrowed her eyes. She despised her father, but the thought of him doing something nefarious to her daughter was outrageous. "No, he loves her. He wouldn't let anything happen to her. The fact that both of them have gone missing is a mere coincidence."

The deputy shifted in his chair. "Were you aware that your father's vintage Chevy pickup truck is also missing?"

The room fell deathly silent.

"No! I hadn't heard that. Can you trace it?"

The sheriff and his deputy stood. "We've put out an Amber Alert and an APB. The Georgia State Police and local jurisdictions are on the lookout for it. Can you give us a better description of the vehicle?"

After jotting down its license plate number and color of the pickup truck, the sheriff took a step toward the door. Thank you, Ms. Dawson, I think we've taken up enough of your time."

***

Outside, Deputy Franks leaned close to the sheriff as they descended the steps.

"Did you notice the reaction when you mentioned the names Estes and Pauley?"

The sheriff nodded. "I did."

"Aren't their fathers' partners with the Grayson and Grayson attorney group?" the deputy asked.

"Yep! The one and the same."

The deputy let out a low whistle. "No wonder Mrs. Dawson didn't want to admit that her daughter had anything to do with those two boys. There could be a huge lawsuit in the making, and this could get real messy before it's over."

"You got that right," the sheriff said as they climbed into the police cruiser. "Those guys live for things like this."

Chapter Eighteen

Joyce calls Ellis Grayson ...

The moment Sheriff Wooten and his deputy left, Joyce grabbed her cell phone from the counter and dialed a number.

A young receptionist's voice came on the line. "Hello, Grayson, Grayson, Estes, and Pauley, attorneys at law. How may I direct your call?"

Joyce gulped some oxygen. She had not called this number in over sixteen years. *Why now?* She wondered.

"Could you put me through to Ellis Grayson?" dreading the ensuing conversation.

"One minute. Let me check to see if he's available."

The minute long wait made her heart pound in her ears. When the receptionist returned, she said, "I'm sorry, Mr. Grayson is in route to a meeting with a client. Is there anyone else you would like to speak with?"

I don't even want to speak with Ellis, but I have to. "No, this is Joyce Dawson, the mother of the missing girl. Could you give me his cell number? Maybe I could speak with him as he's driving."

"Oh, yes, of course. I think that is possible. Here it is."

Joyce jotted it down and punched in the number. It rang twice before being answered.

"Hello? This is Ellis Grayson who is this?" He sounded irritated.

Joyce hadn't spoken with her former boyfriend in years; sixteen to be exact. But this was an emergency. Taking in a calming breath, she began, "Ellis, it's me, Joyce." She heard the screech of wheels and guessed he'd nearly run off the road.

Heavy breathing preceded, "Why on earth are you calling me? Especially now!"

"Then I guess you already know the answer," she said, her words clipped.

"Well dah. Of course I know. But why?"

She heard the car come to an abrupt halt and assumed his business meeting had just been put on hold.

"Because this involves our daughter and your two law partners' sons running off together. Now tell me, what you know and when did you know it." It startled her how forceful she could be when it involved her daughter.

Ellis huffed into the phone. It was obvious he didn't like being on the business end of an inquiry. "I probably learned it about the same time you did, Joyce. What's this about your father allegedly kidnapping them?"

Joyce tried to relax but speaking with Chloe's father brought back a world of emotions; some good, some bad.

"I'm not certain. It could just be a coincidence, or they could have planned this together. I know Dad wasn't happy being held in a mental hospital on charges that he was suicidal. And his lawyer is a total loser. Not to mention the fact that Chloe visited him nearly every week."

The lawyer to which she referred was commonly known for his weak performance, but Ellis refused to engage in talking trash about a fellow attorney. Changing the subject, he said. "Look Joyce, I'm really sorry that I've been an absentee dad. You know how my father is; overbearing, controlling et al. I can see that now. But back then, I was young and stupid. It was his idea to pull me out of public school and put me in an exclusive, private school. And then when it came to college, it was his choice to send me up north. Even now, as junior partner, I feel like I am constantly under his thumb."

Joyce listened as long as she could. "Ellis, I hear what you're saying, and I don't doubt it's all true. But you have no idea how hard it is raising a child, going to nursing school and working twelve-hour shifts. You could have at least called, sent Chloe a birthday card with a few dollars in it or a small gift."

"Okay, okay. Guilty as charged. I feel bad enough without you laying a guilt trip on me. Tell you what. I'd like to somehow make it up to you. I'm going to set up a $10,000 reward fund for information leading to Chloe's safe return."

"Throwing money around. Is that your way of soothing your conscience? Make it matching funds, and you might get some responses."

He sighed into the phone. "No Joyce. That's not what I'm trying to do." He paused when she didn't speak, he said, "All right, matching funds."

"Good. Look, I've gotta go. Let's keep in touch. Okay?" She shocked herself by being so bold.

A long pause sent ice chills through her blood. *What were you thinking? You idiot,* she chided herself.

"Yeah, sure, I think I'd like that. Maybe, say…coffee?" He sounded sincere, but then, he was a lawyer after all. He made a living at sounding sincere.

She smiled at the phone anyway. "Coffee it is."

Chapter Nineteen

Of Crickets, Mosquitos and Alligators ...

Rather than taking the paved highway leading back to civilization, WD cut his wheels and accelerated along a narrow sandy road.

He had been driving in circles for hours trying to decide what to do. Finally, with the moon peeking through the mossy trees, and a thick fog creeping up from the swamp, he'd made up his mind. But he couldn't do what he needed to do with Chloe tagging along. Neither could he take her back to the fish camp. There was only one thing left for him to do. As his mind cleared, he realized he'd gotten turned around. *In the fog, all the roads look the same*, he told himself.

"Lord, guide me, and give me wisdom as I deal with Chloe." he whispered.

Chloe roused. "You say something?"

WD kept his eyes on the two narrow beams of light. "Nah, go back to sleep."

She didn't.

Sitting upright, she peered around. They were surrounded by tall grass, deep shadows and pervasive fog. "Where are we anyways?"

WD chuckled. "If I told you, you wouldn't believe it."

She gaped at him. "Try me."

He shrugged. "Okay, we're somewhere in the middle of the Okefenokee Swamp."

Her mouth fell open. "The Okefen-what?"

"See, I told you. The Okefenokee Swamp, the largest black water swamp in America."

"Blackwater, that sounds scary," she said, scanning the night.

"It is, especially if you get lost out here. This swamp covers about 1000 square miles and has over 120 miles of trails. You could wander for months without seeing a living soul. If you're lucky, and not get eaten by a monster alligator, you might run into 'Swampies.'"

"Swampies?!" her eyes rounding. "What are they?"

WD couldn't help his mirth. "They're people who live out here. This is their home."

She took a hard swallow. "Like those men you left Tramp and Boomer with?"

He whistled the short version of '*Dueling Banjos,*' the theme song from the movie, *Deliverance.*

"Not very funny, G-Diddy. Fur rel, are those guys—"

"Sorta. But that wasn't their permanent home. They are deep sea fishermen. They just bivouac here during the winter months."

"English G-Diddy. What's bivouac mean?"

He chuckled. "You know…biv. It means they stay out here temporarily."

Eyes stabbing in every direction, her lips rounded. "Oh."

"Speaking about 'Swampies, you're going to meet one."

"Fur rel?" a slight tremble in her voice.

WD gave her a sideways glance. "Yup, for real."

"When? Like now?"

He grinned. "Like in about two minutes." He rounded the last curve and brought the pickup truck to an abrupt halt in the sandy clearing. Ahead, in the shaft of his headlights, stood an aging cabin surrounded by tall Live Oak trees and saw palmetto bushes. On its porch stood a dark-skinned woman about four foot three. Her grizzled hair had been tugged back into a bun. Her eyes seemed to burn with an inner glow. In her hands was a double-barrel shotgun.

"Is she a witch? This is so dank." Chloe muttered.

"Dank means musty. Is that what you mean?"

She waved her hand animatedly. "No, it means 'cool.'"

WD grabbed the handle of the door and yanked it open. "You may not think so after you meet her."

"Oh?!"

"Get out and let me introduce you." Without waiting, WD climbed out of the cab and strode into the beam of light from the pickup. "Don't shoot. It's just me, WD. I brought someone I'd like you to meet."

"What? No good morning Miss Winnie?" Her craggy voice sliced through the sultry air while all around them myriads of crickets serenaded the night away. The only other disturbance was the occasional guttural burp of a frog.

"It ain't morning yet, Miss Winnie." Cocking his head, he called out, "Chloe, step outta the truck and meet my friend."

Chloe, her arms wrapped around her waist, came up behind her grandfather. He pulled her from behind him and shoved her forward. "Miss Winnie, this is Chloe. She's my granddaughter. Chloe, this is Miss Winnie. We go back more years than we'll both admit."

The older woman lowered the barrel of her shotgun and stepped off the porch. Bony hand extended, she said, "Nice to meet you, Chloe. Your grandfather speaks very highly of you. Won't you two come inside? No sense in all of us gettin' eaten by those pesky mosquitoes."

As she spoke, she slapped a large bloodsucker which had attached itself to her slender forearm. "There, that'll teach you to attack me."

Turning, she trudged up the steps and guided her guests into the cabin. Once inside, she shut the screen door and made her way to the kitchen. Overhead, a kerosene lantern suspended by a rope provided the only illumination. Its yellow glow cast eerie shadows throughout the house.

The cabin was a fifteen by thirty foot structure. The front room contained a cook stove and a sink on one side, and a thread-bare couch and an avocado-colored armchair on the other side. A short hall connected two small bedrooms and privy. In the center stood an aging table with a couple of equally aging chairs.

No television, no radio, no computer, Chloe noted.

"Take a seat," Miss Winnie said in a gravelly voice. "Let me get you some victuals."

Chloe glanced at her grandfather as if to say, "English, please," but said nothing.

"Thanks, Miss Winnie, but really—"

She cut him off with a wave of her bony hand. "I'll hear nothing of it. You've probably been ridin' around in that old beat-up pickup truck for hours wonderin' if you should stop here. And now that you did, well it's the least I can do. Now tell me why you came out here while I fix you two somethin' to eat. You do eat ham don't you, young lady? I hear kids these days are going vegan," she huffed. "Such foolishness."

Chloe shrank an inch; eyes big as saucers, she gulped. "Y—yes ma'am."

Miss Winnie sliced off a large piece of ham and placed it between two pieces of homemade bread. "Yes what? Yes, you eat ham or yes, you're a vegan?"

Chloe looked to her grandfather for help.

"How 'bout I eat the ham. Chloe is a bit of a health nut. I think she'd go for a healthy piece of toast with some of your homemade Muscadine jam."

Miss Winnie's toothless grin said it all. "One piece of toast smothered in goat butter and Muscadine jam comin' right up," she cooed.

Chloe's eyes watered.

WD chuckled.

Patting her hand, he whispered, "It'll be okay, girl. Just try it, you just might like it."

She nodded sullenly.

Soon the house was filled with the aroma of fresh brewed coffee, ham and goat cheese and toast. While they ate, WD sipped coffee from a chipped mug and filled her in on the most recent news; his drinking problem, with which she was well acquainted since it was her white lightning that contributed to his former condition. When he spoke about the warehouse fire, Chloe squirmed in her chair and looked sick.

Miss Winnie busied herself cleaning up the kitchen. "Anything else?"

WD's face brightened. "As a matter of fact, there is one other thing. A few days ago, I had a come to Jesus moment," he said, then waited for her reaction.

Hand to her chest, Miss Winnie's eyes filled with tears. "I knew it! I knew there was somethin' different 'bout you. Why didn't you say so in the first place?"

Extending her scrawny arms, she pulled him into a tight embrace. "That's the best news I've heard in a coon's age."

Chloe looked at her grandfather. "English?"

They both ignored her question.

"My friend, Arnie Winowski, God rest his soul, passed away a week ago and the authorities were good enough to let me go to his funeral. It was there I heard a clear presentation of the gospel again, and I prayed to receive Christ into my heart. Since then, I feel like a new man."

"That's 'cause you are," Winnie added with a twinkle in her eyes. "God is in the process of makin' you new every day. But you need to do yo part. You got to study the Word and do what the Good Book says," she said with a confident nod.

WD rubbed the back of his neck. "I'm tryin,' Miss Winnie, but drink had such a hold on me. No thanks to your brew."

She lowered her eyes. "And for that, I am truly sorry. I've stopped makin' that poison ever since the day I came to know the Lord. Now it's Georgia sweet-tea or nothin'."

WD raised his coffee mug as if saluting her. "That and black coffee."

As they talked through the night, Chloe wobbled over to the couch and curled up in a ball like a kitten. Soon her soft, rhythmic breathing took over as she slept the hours away.

Chapter Twenty

Breakfast at Winnies ...

Shafts of golden sunlight jabbed holes in the lace curtains making bright spots on the heart pine floor.

Tiny particles of dust floating in the air glowed like fairies in the quiet morning. A slight breeze entered through the screens causing the curtains to sway, and a shadow moved.

Miss Winnie emerged from her small bedroom dressed in tattered overalls, barefoot, with strands of grizzled hair poking out from under a threadbare straw hat. This was her home, her kitchen, her domain, and she ruled it with kind benevolence.

She glanced at the girl sleeping beneath a stack of hand-sewn quilts. Her gaze moved across the room to WD. He was like a son to her. She'd known him nearly all his adult life; ever since the day he stumbled across her home in the middle of the swamp.

He had delivered some parts to a couple of men at a nearby fish camp and had gotten lost. After driving the back roads of the swamp for hours, he arrived on her doorstep bone weary and dehydrated. Back in those days, she'd made a good living providing the community with the best homemade brew this side of the Mason-Dixon. Her fortuitous encounter with WD had blossomed into a long-term friendship.

But then a tent revival came to town, and she went out of curiosity. One evening the evangelist preached loud and long, and she felt the tug of the Holy Spirit on her heart. At the altar call, she yielded to His sweet invitation and walked down the sawdust trail. At the front, she met a woman who took her aside and showed her the way. That night, she gave her heart to Christ. Then, as a new believer, she was baptized in the black waters where she had grown up.

Knowing that WD was on his way to Heaven, made her heart leap for joy. Eyes watering, she set about making cat-head biscuits and sawmill gravy. She hoped the girl could stomach her brand of cookin'. If not, her only other option was starvation.

***

As the small space filled with the aroma of coffee, bacon frying in a pool of grease and fresh baked biscuits, Chloe roused.

"Mornin' girl. Sorry, I'm not so good with names," Winnie said apologetically.

Chloe rubbed the sleep from her eyes and gave an ample yawn. "That's okay, neither am I. It's Chloe."

Winnie turned to face her, a spatula in hand. "Well, Miss Chloe, the privy is just around the co'ner. You can freshen up there before breakfast. I hope ya like biscuits and gravy."

Chloe wrinkled up her nose but said nothing as she dashed around the corner clutching a quilt close to her body.

As the door shut, WD roused. "Is she gone?" he asked amidst a yawn.

Winnie eyed the closed bathroom door. "Yep. It's safe."

WD grabbed his shirt and skipped barefoot out the front door in the direction of an old outhouse. After a few minutes, he returned. "I thought she'd never get up. What time is it?" glancing around for his watch.

"It's somewhere between dawn and noon. I don't pay much attention to the clock these days."

WD smiled, "Ya don't say. I think we talked all night."

She chuckled. "Yeah, I think we did."

Their conversation paused when Chloe emerged from the bathroom. Her multi-colored hair had been combed back and the white powder and black eyeliner had been scrubbed from her face.

"That's a big improvement," Winnie noted. "Girl, you one beautiful child."

Chloe glanced at her grandfather, uncertain what to say.

"Yup, she's a spittin' image of her momma," WD said, giving his granddaughter a gentle hug. "Sleep well?"

She pierced him with a pair of black orbs. "Mostly, except when you two started laughing. But I ignored it. I love the smell of those quilts," she said eyeing the stack still lying on the couch.

Winnie smiled. "They came from that old cedar chest. Would ya kindly fold them and put'em away while I finish fixin' breakfast?"

Chloe smiled, "That's cool." She stood and went to work. When she finished, she clutched the last one to her chest and inhaled. "It's so, so peaceful out here," she sighed deeply with a dreamy expression on her face.

WD stepped beside her as she stared out the window. "So, you want to stay here with Miss Winnie another night?"

She sucked in a sharp breath. Eyes wide she said, "I didn't say that. It's just that—"

WD couldn't help but smile. "I was just kidding. You stay here, you work, that's the rule. Right Miss Winnie?"

The older woman waved her spatula like a scepter. "That's right. You work, you eat. No work—no eat."

Chloe quickly stepped to the cedar chest and shoved the last of the quilts inside. "There, now do I get to eat?"

WD and Miss Winnie nodded, "Yep!"

Chapter Twenty-One

School of Fish Camp ...

Dawn came early in the Okefenokee Swamp.

With a rooster crowing the day into existence, Tramp and Boomer released a unified groan. "Someone shut that stupid bird up," Boomer growled.

Tramp jammed his head under the thin pillow in a futile attempt at keeping out the repeated cacophony. The bunkhouse where they'd spent their first night was nothing more than an uninsulated plywood structure with screens covering windows and a screen door. The only comforts provided were two thin mattresses and a couple of well-worn sheets.

All at once, Jimmy's rotund form filled the door frame. "Wake up ladies, time to earn your keep." Then he blew an air horn bringing both boys to upright positions.

"Breakfast is in ten minutes. Be there or go hungry." He turned and strode off in the direction of the mess hall.

After much complaining the boys crawled out of their bunks and dragged themselves to the block building which served as the outhouse. After washing the sleep from their faces with sulfury smelling well-water, they towel dried their hair. Then, dressed in the same clothes as they slept in, dashed to the dining room. Inside, they found a number of men gathered around a wooden picnic table eating and talking sports. They ignored the two youths as they lined up to receive their food.

"What is this?" Tramp asked.

The cook, a balding man with a growing waistline and a soiled apron didn't miss a beat. "It's cheese grits, scrambled eggs and bacon all rolled up in one. Now sit down and eat it or you'll be wearing it."

The boys looked at each other, their eyes rounding. No one had ever spoken to them like that before. It was a new experience; the first of many.

After breakfast, Jimmy ushered them out to the courtyard.

"Today, we're going to learn how to stack crab traps. Then, we'll load up and go over to a port near Fernandina Beach where we'll put out to sea. I'll take you to my favorite fishing spot. I hope you boys ain't some kind of environmentalists, 'cause we are about to put a dent on the crab population." He chuckled at his own joke.

Tramp clutched his stomach. "I think I'm going to be sick."

Boomer's face had already turned a deep color of green. "Me too."

Jimmy tossed the two a pair of tattered gloves. "Here, put those on. They'll protect your pearly white hands. At least for a few hours. Now follow me."

He led them to a shed. Stepping inside, they were immediately assaulted with the stench of rotting fish. Eyes watering, the two boys fought to keep their breakfast down. Stacked to the ceiling were wooden baskets with chicken-wire tacked to the frames.

"Okay boys, I want all those crab traps loaded on the back of that truck," he pointed with his domed head.

"This is going to take all day," Boomer griped.

"It had better not," the man growled. "And if I catch you snowflakes slacking off. I'm going to place my size eleven boot up your—"

The two boys began loading the traps before he finished his statement.

***

Prince Raguel couldn't hide his amusement.

He and Prince Zadkiel had watched throughout the long night for any sign of the enemy.

None had shown themselves. Nevertheless, their wariness had not lessened. Going out to sea had its own dangers and they were concerned that they might venture into the principality of one of Satan's mightiest demon…the spirit of fear.

"Perhaps we should send for additional support," Prince Zadkiel suggested.

Glancing at the size of the commercial fishing trawler, Prince Raguel gave an appreciative nod. "I agree. If they run into a storm, we will have our hands full. I will dispatch a message before we leave."

He stepped from Zadkiel's presence, caught a small bird in his hands and whispered in its ear. Then he released it. "Now go, fly with the winds and bring word to our Lord."

With the flutter of wings, the bird ascended heavenward.

***

The commercial fishing trawler cut through the heavy surf like a bull in a China-shop.

Its powerful bow slammed into the oncoming waves parting them asunder, sending salty sea-spray in all directions and soaking the boys to the bone. They sat huddled in the cockpit, their faces as green as a spring apple.

"You boys better get a grip on your breakfast, or it will be all over the deck. If that happens, your first lesson will be how to swab up your own puke" Jimmy barked over the roar of the turbine engines.

The two young people looked at each other and forced down a hard swallow.

Once they had reached their destination, about three miles off the Florida coast, Jimmy throttled back on the engines. They purred like two well-fed lions.

Speaking to his crew, Jimmy said, "All right guys, it's show time. Get to work."

Immediately, the experienced crew members began lowering the crab traps into the sea while Tramp and Boomer stood out of their way. Their time would come soon enough. Once the traps were all gone, Jimmy made sure the orange floating marker was in place and let it fall overboard.

"Good work men. Tomorrow, we'll do it all over. Hopefully, with any luck, we'll catch us a mess of crabs. Then we'll rewind and do it all over again." He took his place at the helm, revved the turbines, and pointed the trawler toward an orange ball sitting on the edge of the earth.

***

"I'm glad that's over," Prince Raguel said, his aquiline complexion slightly gray.

Prince Zadkiel released a low chuckle. "If you think that was bad, you should have been with me and the Apostle Paul the time when a violent hurricane struck. That storm lasted two weeks. It was all I could do to keep from being thrown overboard." He gazed into the distant past.

"What did you do?" asked Raguel, clearly interested.

Prince Zadkiel shifted his stance. The two angels had taken their position on the rear deck of the fishing trawler and were keeping an eye on a large, black cloud which seemed to have been following them.

"As commanded by the Lord God, I appeared to the Apostle and said, 'Paul, do not be afraid, for you must be brought before Caesar; and indeed, God has granted you all those who sail with you.'"

Like a child hearing a bedtime story, Prince Raquel's eyes widened. "What happened? Did he survive?"

Zadkiel's smile broadened. "Yes, yes, he did; he along with the other one-hundred and seventy-six souls. But it was not without the loss of the ship along with all its cargo; dashed upon the rocks.

The captain and ship owner should have listened to Paul when he warned them not to venture out to sea at that time of the year. But that was not the end of the story."

"It's not? What happened next?" Raquel pressed.

"They were shipwrecked on a small island and were rescued by a local tribe of people. They invited them into their village and provided them with food and shelter. While the Apostle gathered wood, a large serpent attacked him and sank its fang into his arm. Thinking this was God's way of punishing him for some evil deed, the villagers watched and waited. But when they saw that the poison had no effect on him, they changed their minds and thought he was a god."

Prince Raquel shook his head. "How foolish those mortals can be."

Suddenly, the storm clouds to the east lit up with bolts of lightning. A few seconds later, the low rumble of thunder reached them. Fearing the oncoming storm would catch them before they reached port, Captain Jimmy increased his speed in an attempt at outrunning it.

"C'mon, Prince Raguel, put your back into it," encouraged Zadkiel.

Together, they nudged the trawler along until they reached the safety of the port.

As the ship entered the 'No Wake' zone, the two angels ascended heavenward. Their task was done for now. Now it was time to take up guarding positions.

With drinking and carousing on the minds of the ship's crew, they knew danger and evil would be lurking nearby.

Chapter Twenty-Two

Making Plans, and Making Deals ...

No sooner had Miss Winnie and Chloe taken their seats at the breakfast table than WD began—

"I've been thinking," he said between bites.

"That's dangerous," Miss Winnie quipped.

WD ignored her comment. "I could turn myself in and face the consequences, or I could hide out here in the swamp and start a new life."

Winnie shook her head vehemently. "Nope, not a good plan."

"Which one?"

"Neither," both women said in unison.

Winnie continued. "As I see it, if the authorities get their hands on you, they'll put you away in that funny farm for the rest of your life. And stayin' out here ain't a good idea either. You'd have to go to town for supplies sometime and someone would see you and turn you in. Then what would I do with Miss Chloe? I'm not her momma."

"Hey, wait a minute," Chloe protested. "I can't stay out here indefinitely. I've got school, volleyball practice, dance—"

"Hold your horses, young lady," WD said, his hands held up. "I was planning to send you home on the next bus."

"A bus?!" her mouth gaped. "That's so, so basic."

Miss Winnie waved her hands animatedly. "Would ya stop arguing for a minute?" Looking at WD, she said, "My advice is, make things right with ya family; starting with ya father."

The news struck WD like a bolt of lightning. "My father?"

She nodded. "Yep. From what you told me, that's where ya problems began."

"What? Wait a minute!" Chloe interjected. "I didn't even know your father was still alive."

WD chased a chunk of egg around his plate. "Well, that's a touchy subject. My dad and I haven't been on speaking terms for years."

"Forty-five to be exact," Miss Winnie added. "Don't you think it's time?"

WD swallowed the last of his coffee. "I don't relish the thought."

"He might be on his death bed."

"He might shoot me the moment I get within range."

"He'll probably miss."

"Knowing my dad, probably not."

Chloe glanced between the two adults. "Why? What'd ya do?" clearly incredulous.

WD rose from the table and placed his dirty plate in the sink. "It's a long story."

She mopped up the last of her gravy with a bite of her biscuit and shoved it into her mouth. "I've got time. By the way—I'm convinced that was the best breakfast I've ever eaten."

"Better than pop tarts?" WD kidded.

Her forehead wrinkled. "Way."

After they washed and dried the dishes, Winnie excused herself and headed to the chicken coop muttering something like, "She's your granddaughter."

As her small frame disappeared out the back door, WD touched Chloe's elbow.

"Walk with me," he said.

She wiped her hands on a towel, folded it and placed it on the counter. "What suh?"

WD took a step in the direction of the front door. "There's something I want to show you."

Interest sparked in her eyes. "What is it? I hope it isn't one of those man-eating alligators."

"Don't worry, it's not. Now follow me."

He led her to the back of the cabin to an aging block building covered with vegetation. Grabbing a handful of vines, he pulled them back revealing a rotting wooden door. After he had cleared enough of the foliage, he tried opening it.

It resisted.

He shoved harder.

Nothing.

A few more attempts and getting nowhere, he said, "All right, I guess we'll just have to play rough."

Putting his shoulder against the door, he shoved with all his might. It scraped the concrete floor angrily as he pushed it open. Once inside, he tried the light switch—nothing.

"I should have known, he muttered and began to yank the yellowed newspaper from the windows. Within minutes, shafts of muted light streamed in revealing a 1968 Ford Mustang.

"No way!" Chloe exclaimed.

"Way, and it's all mine."

"Say what?"

"Yup, I made the deal last night; my old pickup truck for this baby. You love it?"

Chloe eyed the convertible with growing interest. "Does it run? I mean—"

"Nope, at least, so Miss Winnie says. I'm about to give it a complete overhaul. I can see already that it needs tires, probably brakes, a tune up, oil change, belts and who knows what else."

Chloe jammed her hands into her back pockets. "That'll take, like forever," her voice swirled upward like smoke from a chimney.

He lifted the hood. "Watch out!" He yelled leaping back as a flock of birds took flight.

Chloe screamed and dove for cover. Then she stood, chuckling. "That was way cray."

Wiping his brow, WD retook his place and peered inside the engine compartment.

"I think Miss Winnie ripped you off, G-Diddy."

"Nah, I knew from the start what I was doing. I'm guessing it might take a week. But heck, we've got the time."

"Maybe you do, but remember, I've got school and mom will be home at the end of the week. She's gonna freak out."

He let her statement pass without comment and began to check the belts.

Leaning against the hood of the vintage car, Chloe scuffed the ground. "Well if you expect me to help you, forget it. I don't know anything about cars. Especially old ones and I don't what to learn."

WD lifted his head. "That's fine, I'm sure Miss Winnie can find plenty to do around here."

Straightening, he found a scrap of cardboard and began making a list of items he would need to get the car running again. After a few minutes, he folded the cardboard in half and jammed it into his back pocket. "I'm going to town and get some supplies. I want you to stay here with Miss Winnie."

"What?! Wait. You can't leave me here," she protested. "I might get eaten by one of those people-eating alligators."

"Man-eating alligators, Chloe. I don't think they'd like the taste of you, anyway."

Still pouting, she harrumphed. "Not funny."

He fished the truck keys from his pocket. "Well, you for sure can't go with me to town."

"Why not? You think I might run away?"

He hiked over to the pickup truck, got in and cranked the engine. "Just stay here and do what Miss Winnie says. Is that too much to ask?"

As he pulled away, she stuck her tongue out at him.

"I hope a mosquito lands right on your tongue," he called over his shoulder," as he drove away.

Chapter Twenty-Three

God Loves to Talk to Girls While They're Fishing ...

As silence reclaimed the swamp, Chloe heard her name.

Turning, she saw Miss Winnie standing on the back porch, two fishing poles in her bony hands. "Girl, come along. We've got supper to catch."

"Say what?"

Miss Winnie lowered her eyelids. "Just follow me."

"But I don't know how to fish."

The older woman cocked her head. "That's okay. I'll teach ya. Actually, ya don't have to do much. Ya just have to know what the fish are hungry for and bait the hook so's it doesn't see it, and wham, ya got a fish."

Chloe shoved her hands in her shorts and trudged reluctantly along behind the woman. The narrow dirt path, lined with ten-foot-high stalks of bamboo, led deeper into the swamp. At times, the path would disappear under black water, then reappear as a few rocks or a rotting plank of wood. "Watch ya step, girl," Miss Winnie called out.

It was too late; Chloe had missed her step and landed knee deep in mud. "Shoo, this place stinks," she said, pulling herself up from the goo.

A low chuckle bubbled up in Winnie's throat. "It should, it's been here since the dawn of time. Now come along before something worse befalls you."

The path weaved another half mile through the swamp and ended at a small clearing. Ahead, a sagging wooden dock jutted into the brackish waters.

"This is my favorite fishing hole," Miss Winnie said in a hushed tone. "If you listen, you can almost hear the voice of God." She said God the way preachers used to, with awe.

Chloe's forehead wrinkled. "How do you know it's God's voice and not some—" she whispered, "demon?"

Miss Winnie's face brightened. "Oh, that's easy, girl. If it agrees with God's Word, it's the Lord. If it contradicts His Word, then it's not."

And that settled it. For the next several minutes while Miss Winnie prepared the fishing gear, Chloe contemplated what she had said.

"Take a seat, and we'll get started directly," Miss Winnie's craggy voice brought her from her musings.

On the dock sat two rusting lawn chairs. Half of their webbing hung loosely from their metal frames. The other half looked like they might break the moment she sat down.

Miss Winnie nudged her forward. "Go ahead, girl, take a seat. I'll bait the first hook and get you started."

Chloe bit her lower lip and gingerly inched her way along the dock. Then she eased into one of the lawn chairs. After a moment, she relaxed and began to breathe again.

"Here, take this," Miss Winnie said, offering her a cane pole.

"There now. Pay close attention, 'cause I'm not gonna show ya twice."

Then she proceeded to bait the hook with a minnow she had taken from a small bucket. "Toss it as far as ya can, then watch that bobber," she said, pointing with her bony finger at the red and white ball. "When it goes under the water, give the pole a sharp yank," she said instructively.

After she baited her own hook and cast it on the opposite side of the dock. Then she took a seat in the other lawn chair and waited. As the minutes stretched, Chloe began to wonder if they were ever going to catch something. She sighed heavily and placed her chin in the palm of her hand.

"Patience girl. If ya want to be a good fisherman, ya gotta learn patience. Actually, fishin' ain't all that hard. It's the bait that does all the work."

Chloe shifted to get a better look at the elderly woman.

"Yep. That's the same way Satan does his dirty work. He knows just how to tempt us. He knows what we want and hides his wicked old hook inside it. The book of James chapter 1 verse 15 says, Every man is tempted when he is drawn away by his own lusts. Then, when lust hath conceived, it bringeth forth sin: and when sin is finished, bringeth forth death. Take you for instance."

"Me? Why me?"

Winnie eyed her for a second. "Yes, you. There you are in your short-shorts, your tank-top showing all that silky white flesh. What boy wouldn't want to get his hands on you? And take that football jock; all buff and handsome. Ya think I don't know the way young people think? So does the devil and he gets ya into a compromising situation where the temptation is too great, and ya got sin."

Chloe felt her face heating and took a hard swallow. It was the closest thing to the famous Birds and the Bees lesson she'd ever had. Suddenly her pole bent, and she yanked it up. "I got one!" she exclaimed.

"Yes, ya do. Now carefully drag 'em in."

Uncertain what to do next; she lifted the tip of her rod. At the end of the fishing wire, a large, fat catfish struggled to get free.

"Here girl, let me hep you." Taking a fishing net, she scooped the struggling fish up and placed it on the dock. With care, she removed the hook and strung the fish on a stringer.

"Now it's your turn to bait the hook, and don't forget what I told ya. The devil is smart, but by God's grace, you can resist the tempter."

She followed Miss Winnie's instructions and soon had her baited hook in the water. "I guess that's how I came to be. My mom and some guy surrendered to temptation. Does that mean I am tainted?" Her voice broke and a tear leaked down her cheek.

Miss Winnie touched her arm. "No, girl. You ain't tainted. You were wonderfully and marvelously made in the image of Almighty God. That's not to say you're not a sinner. We all are, but no dearie, ya ain't tainted. God loves ya just as if you were conceived within the bounds of marriage. My advice to you is this: stay under your momma's authority and keep ya sef pure. Don't ya let some guy go pawing all over ya."

Chloe nodded sullenly. "I wish I knew my dad. Maybe things would be different."

As Miss Winnie dragged in her first catch of the day, she said, "Maybe so, maybe not. Bu'cha got a momma who loves ya very much."

Chloe huffed. "I doubt it. All she does is work and sleep. She has me doing all the cleaning and laundry and still expects me to keep up with my grades."

Winnie leveled her gaze. "Girl, ya momma is doin' the best she can to put food on the table and a roof over ya head. So don't cha go badmouthing her. I'll not hear a word of it."

Eyes watering, Chloe returned her attention to the bobber floating in the brackish water. Out of the corner of her eye, she caught movement. The bony skull of a large alligator took shape as it swam past the dock. Fearing the monster might climb up and snatch her, she jumped, nearly knocking Miss Winnie over.

"Girl, whaddaya doing?"

Eyes round as saucers, she pointed at the swirling water.

"Oh him, that's Tick-Tock. Ya know, from Peter Pan? Like the crocodile that swallowed the alarm clock and follows Captain Hook around."

The information did nothing to allay Chloe's fear. Keeping one eye on the bobber and the other on Tick-Tock, she retook her seat and continued to fish.

***

As the sun began to lose its hold on the day, both Chloe and Miss Winnie proudly displayed six fat fish on their stringers.

With a groan, Miss Winnie pushed herself up on uncertain legs and waited for the blood to reach her toes.

"These old bones," she said with a wry smile. "'C'mon girl. Let's call it a day. We've still gots to clean these fish. Then I'll teach ya how to fix them so's they literally swim down ya throat." An impish twinkle danced in her eyes.

Two hours later, they had the catfish skinned, breaded and frying in a cast-iron skillet. Stirring the cheese grits, Miss Winnie wiped her brow with the back of her hand. "Miss Chloe, why don't cha fetch your granddaddy. It's gettin' close to suppa time."

Chloe finished setting the table and said, "Yes ma'am," then disappeared out the front door. "

"And tell him to hurry. I'm hangry," she said.

Chapter Twenty-Four

Car Repairs and Long talks …

As the sun lost its battle with the approach of night, crickets and bullfrogs began their nightly celebration having survived yet another day.

For that, they had reason to rejoice, as did WD. He had been working on the vintage Mustang for the last two weeks and had just finished tightening the last nut on the oil pan when two muddy feet appeared.

"Miss Winnie says its dinner time. You need to quit and wash up before it gets cold."

He rolled out from under the Ford Mustang, stood and pushed out the kink in his back with a groan.

"Is that so?"

Using the cash he had saved up to repair his pickup truck, he made multiple trips to the parts store, and the junk yard to buy tools, and parts for the Mustang. Standing back, he admired his work. Not only had he given the car a complete tune-up, oil change, replaced the brake pads and drums, replaced the belts and battery, but he'd cleaned the interior and washed and waxed the outside. In the light of a single bulb, the antique glistened like a new car.

"Ain't she a beauty," he said admiringly.

Jack, Miss Winnie's pit-bull, growled in response. For the last fourteen days, Jack had been his only companion. Not being a dog person, however, he and the dog hadn't gotten along that well. Mostly, the dog laid in the shade and watched with passive interest.

Chloe, wearing an apron over her tattered jeans, cotton shirt with her sleeves rolled up, nodded. "Yaas, it's bussin."

WD cocked his head. "Isn't it a bit warm to be wearing a long-sleeved shirt?"

She glanced down at the blue plaid shirt. "If I knew I was going to spend my summer in the everglades, I would have brought more than a couple of bathing suits. Plus, I want to dress more," she paused trying to choose the right words, "more appropriately—like a lady not some slut."

WD wrinkled his forehead. "Sounds like you've been talking with Miss Winnie."

She smiled. "She is a very wise woman."

He wiped his hands on a greasy rag. "Yes, she is."

Chloe crossed her suntanned arms across her chest. "Dinner is about ready. Are you hungry?"

"Hangry is more like it. What's on the board today?"

She jammed her hands into her back pockets and swirled a tight circle. Her feet were bare and calloused from walking through the swamp barefoot. "Same thing we've been eating for the last two weeks. The catfish, hush puppies, cheese grits, sweet tea, and homemade potato chips, which I made," she said proudly.

"Which one? The sweet tea or the hush puppies?" he asked, rubbing his stomach.

She looked up at him with a smile in her eyes. "The homemade potato chips, G-Diddy. Miss Winnie has been teaching me how to cook."

He continued to wipe the grease from his hands. It wasn't working. "That's a skill you'll need someday. Let's eat. My stomach thinks my throat's been cut."

Chloe chuckled, wrapped her arm around her granddaddy and guided him to the picnic table.

***

After dinner, WD sauntered back to the shed.

His greasy shirt was stretched tight from eating too many fish, but he was happy. He couldn't remember the last time he felt that way. He blamed it on being outside working with his hands. In reality, he knew God was working on the inside of Chloe's heart as well as his own heart.

Underneath a grinning moon, Chloe appeared. She had finished cleaning up after dinner and stood with a bowl of banana pudding in her hand.

"Want some?" She offered him a spoon.

"Give me a minute. First, let's see if she runs. Take the key and try starting the engine."

A broad grin parted her lips. "Me? Fur rel? I don't know how to drive."

"Not asking you to drive, just crank the engine."

"English please," she said in a playful tone.

Hand raised, he said, "Okay, okay. I get it. Just turn the key."

"Right, turn the key, and don't touch the gas pedal."

She complied and to their amazement and delight, the engine sprang to life and purred like a kitten. WD offered her a broad smile.

"See, I ain't no dummy," he said.

Chloe returned his smile which sent his heart skittering. She reminded him so much of her grandmother.

"No G-Diddy, you're so Hundo P."

"English please."

She shook her head in a womanly way as if to say, don't you get it? "I said, you're one hundred percent way cool."

WD straightened his back and tossed the oily rag onto a pile of rags. "Well, someday, this car will be yours."

Her face beamed. "That's cray! Fur rel?"

"For Real. Now climb out. I need to pull this car out and check the tire pressure."

Pooching her lip, she got out. "That car is way cool. Much better than that old truck."

"Hey, wait. That pickup's got us this far. It would have taken us all the way."

"All the way to where?"

WD put the Mustang in gear and eased it from its cocoon. "All the way to Oklahoma."

Her mouth fell open. "No way," she squealed.

WD got out and began to inspect the tires. Leaning on one knee, he began to check the tires with an air pressure gauge. Satisfied, he straightened and looked at his granddaughter.

"Yes, way. We wouldn't have gotten ten miles in that pickup truck before the cops pulled us over. This baby is our best bet."

"Awe-some," Chloe said as she came around and took her place in the passenger's seat. "Oklahoma where the wind comes sweepin' down the plain." She sang out, her arms flailing wildly. Her lilting voice carried deep into the night and was joined by a cacophony of crickets. Suddenly, the singing stopped, and her face took on a curious expression. "What's in Oklahoma anyways, G-Diddy?"

He dragged his eyes from the parade of stars marching across the sky. "There's someone very special living on the outskirts of Oklahoma City I want you to meet."

"Who G-Diddy?"

"I'm taking Miss Winnie's advice. I'm going to take you to meet your great-grandfather…my dad!"

Chloe's forehead wrinkled. "You've never talked about your father. For all I knew, he was dead-dead. Not dead like something is really funny."

After retaking his place behind the steering wheel, he revved the engine, and pulled to the front of the cabin. "That's because we haven't spoken in years."

Crossing her arms over her chest, Chloe grew sullen. "I wish I had a dad."

WD got out and gave her shoulder a gentle squeeze. "Oh, you've got a dad all right, just not one you'd like very much."

Eyes rounding, Chloe held his gaze. "So do you know who he is?"

Lying was not an option, but neither was telling her the truth. It would crush her. "We all have our secrets, honey. That's all I can say right now. Let's go inside. We need to get a good night's sleep. Tomorrow morning comes early."

Chapter Twenty-Five

Parting is Such Sweet Sorrow …

The morning of April 18th broke clear and sultry.

It had been two weeks since WD left Richmond Hill and he and Chloe had grown to love living as a couple of Swampies. But it was time to go.

As usual, Miss Winnie had already been up for an hour and had breakfast waiting by the time WD awoke. Chloe soon emerged from her bedroom wiping the sleep from her eyes. She was fully dressed and quickly joined Miss Winnie in setting the table.

"Sleep well, child?"

Chloe smiled. She liked being called, 'child.' It made her feel cherished.

"Like a baby. I'd roll over and cry, then fall asleep. Then do it again."

Miss Winnie offered her a sad smile. "Oh child, I'm gonna miss our little talks."

Chloe reached out and pulled her into a gentle embrace. "I'm going to miss you too." The dam behind her eyes broke and tears scalded her cheeks. Fighting back her tears, she finished setting the table and took a seat.

As was her custom, Miss Winnie extended her hands and took Chloe's and WD's before lifting her eyes heavenward and offering a prayer of thanksgiving. When she finished, there was the soft rustling of wings.

Miss Winnie smiled.

***

Just outside the mortal dimension, Prince Azrael bowed his head and listened.

He had grown to love hearing this dear saint pray and made it his mission to see to it that nothing hindered those prayers from reaching the Almighty's ear.

"She did it again," Azrael said in a low tone.

Princes Leo, Cassiel and Haniel, who'd been guarding WD and Chloe through the night, glanced at him with amused expressions.

"Did what?" Leo asked.

Prince Azrael's smile broadened. "She touched the hem of the Almighty's garment."

The three heavenly warriors nodded knowingly. "We need more saints like her," Prince Leo admitted. "Sadly, they are a dying breed."

"It is appointed unto men once to die," Prince Cassiel added. "But I'd like to think her work on earth is far from over."

The angelic guard retook their positions while the mortals carried on a light conversation.

***

After breakfast, WD stood and began to collect his belongings.

"Chloe, when you have finished cleaning up, I'd like you to pack your things. We're leaving as soon as possible. I wouldn't want Miss Winnie to think we've taken up permanent residence here."

The girl's eyes saddened. "That would be all right by me," she said in a low tone.

Miss Winnie came alongside her. "Girl, you've got a whole world out there just waitin' to be experienced. It's time you sprout yo wings and fly," she said with awe in her voice. "I sho do wish I could go wit'cha. But I know I'd just slow ya down."

WD reached out and gave her a hug. "It would be such fun, but I understand. Your place is here in the swamp with your chickens, your fishing pole and your memories."

Her eyes took a distant expression. "Ah those memories. Some good, some not so good, but memories all the same. Now go on girl. Get'cha stuff," she said as her throat closed around a tearful sigh.

"I'll never forget you Miss Winnie. You're a good friend," WD added, his tone husky. "I'll probably not be coming through here anymore."

The thought of him never seeing her again pained him more than he would admit. Eyes misting, he swallowed the lump in his throat.

She eyed him plaintively. "Then I'll see ya in the rapture."

He repeated the words. "See ya in the rapture," he eked out as he hugged her one last time.

"Ah, now don't go a gettin' soft on me," she said, glancing at the bedroom door. She smiled, "She's a good girl with a tender, teachable heart. She reminds me of ya wife. Any chance at reconciliation?"

His face gave way to a pained expression. "That's a road yet untraveled. Not saying I'm not willing to go down it, but first I must complete the task God has set before me."

Winnie patted him on the shoulder. "I understand. I'll fix ya something for the road. At least that way ya won't need to stop and eat for a while."

WD smiled at the thought. "I'd appreciate that. Thanks."

As he spoke, Chloe emerged from the bedroom and set her backpack on the floor. "I heard you, G-Diddy. You were talking about finishing a task. What task?"

Giving her a wan smile, WD said, "Many years ago, my dad, as punishment for my disobedience, told me to put up a fence all the way around our family garden to keep the sheep out. It was hot, dirty work."

"Did you do it, G-Diddy?" her interest clearly piqued.

WD lowered his eyes and shook his head. "Nah, you see, I was a rebellious, strong-willed, hard-headed young man. I put up all but one."

Disappointment registered on Chloe's young face. "Oh. What did he do? Did he give you a beating?"

"He didn't do anything. I didn't give him a chance. As I told you, I left home the next morning and haven't been home since. I have no illusions as to the kind of reception I'll get, but I'm determined to finish what my father told me to do. Only then can I have the kind of relationship with him that I should have."

Winnie gave WD's hand a gentle squeeze. "And I'm doin' what the Good Lord told me to do. Sellin' you that car for a penny was one of the best deals I've ever made. It isn't gettin' any younger sittin' out there in the garage."

"Neither am I so I'd better make things right with him while I still can."

As the old rooster crowed the morning into existence, WD, Chloe and Miss Winnie gathered on the porch for one last time.

"So, this is good-bye," WD said, leaning down, he kissed her weathered cheek. Salt from a single tear stained his lips.

"Ouch," her fingers touched the place where his lips touched, and Chloe smiled.

Then it was Chloe's turn. "Miss Winnie—" she said through tangled vocal chords.

"Now, now child. You obey your granddaddy and do what's right. He's a good man."

Chloe nodded and looked up at her grandfather. "Yes, he is." Then she leaned down and kissed Winnie's other cheek.

Hand to her cheek, Winnie smiled. "Ouch!"

Chloe smiled, "Oh Miss Winnie, you're so funny."

She gave her a gentle shove in the direction of the Ford Mustang. "Don't get lost. Ya know how confusin' these back roads can be."

WD stepped down from the porch. He took one last glance at the cabin before climbing in behind the steering wheel. Turning the key, he said, "She runs like a new car. Thanks for everything. Now don't worry, I know these roads like the back of my hand," pointing to his palm.

As he pulled his arm back inside the car, he took note of the time. It was 6:30 in the morning. If they were lucky, they'd be in Alabama by early evening.

She smiled and took her place on an aging rocking chair sitting next to the door.

With one final wave, he and Chloe left.

***

Perched on the roof of the cabin, Prince Camael, Cassiel and Haniel watched the vehicle round the corner.

He, Prince Uriel, and the others had maintained a close vigil ever since WD and Chloe entered the swamp.

"I'm sure glad that's over," Prince Uriel quipped.

Camael arched an eyebrow. Oh? Why did you say that?"

Shifting slightly, Prince Uriel eyed the old cabin then sniffed his shimmering garments. I'm not sure I'll ever get the smell of frying fish out of these," he said, fanning his vesture.

Prince Camael released a chuckle. "Perhaps keeping up with that old car will air them out. Let us be going."

Chapter Twenty-Six

Madeline Dawson ...

It had been two weeks since Chloe and WD disappeared, and the lack of news was driving Madeline Dawson crazy.

It was bad enough that her ex-husband had escaped from the mental hospital, but the thought that her granddaughter possibly planned his escape blew her mind. *Why would she do such a thing?* The question plagued her day and night.

Stabbed by guilt, she saw Chloe as a carbon copy of herself—wild, rebellious, street-smart. She was young, pretty and wild. As a physical therapist in a military hospital, she had many opportunities to meet men and she found herself quite popular. For a time, she had forgotten her Christian roots. All the Bible teaching, the church services, the youth camps were a blur in the frenzied life of a nurse.

Finally, she came to realize how empty her life was, and she repented of her waywardness.

When she met WD, he was in rehab suffering from multiple gunshot wounds. He and his crew were on patrol in a Fast-boat when they came under heavy attack from the Viet Cong. Had he not called in for air support, none of them would have survived.

For weeks his life hung by a thread. When he came to, he was in a military hospital with little memory of what had happened on the battlefield. Then the pain and the memories began. As his physical therapist, she spent hours nudging him, prodding him, motivating him. Finally, after months of rehab, he regained enough function of his legs to walk, then run. His release was celebrated throughout the hospital wing.

A few months later, they married.

In her opinion, he was the most handsome, funny, intelligent man on the planet, and she wanted to spend the rest of her life getting to know him. As it turned out, he really was all she expected. He was a good husband, a church attender; hard working, devoted; just not a Christian. She had hoped her love would win him over.

It didn't.

Because of the injuries he'd sustained while serving his country, he'd fallen back on opioids. When the pain got worse and the VA doctors refused to up his meds, he turned to alcohol.

Divorce was never her first choice, but when his drinking jeopardized their family, she knew she had to do something. Over the counsel of her pastor, she made the decision. She tried to convince herself that it was for the children's safety, but in reality, it was her pride which drove her to such a desperate act. Over the years she had grown weary of hearing the whispers behind her back, and seeing the condescending looks of the other ladies at church.

Church people could be so cruel.

If only we hadn't divorced, things might have turned out differently, she often told herself.

Although she still loved WD, she knew it was for the best. It grieved her to no end to know after all she had sacrificed, all she had suffered, her sons turned out exactly like their father. After finishing college, and over her protests, they both went to work for him. Joyce was the only one to remain out from under his influence.

Out from under her influence as well.

Always a rebellious child, Joyce gave her mother constant trouble. Then, at sixteen, she found herself pregnant with two years left before her high school graduation. Rather than dispose of the child in her womb out of convenience, she courageously went full term and delivered a sweet baby girl. In order to give Chloe a stable home Madeline took an early retirement to raise her while Joyce finished high school.

Sixteen years later, Madeline saw the pattern repeating itself in her granddaughter. "The sins of the mothers," she would often say. For all intent and purposes, Chloe had run off with two boys. She hoped she didn't do something stupid.

***

Madeline couldn't count the number of years since she had a heart-to-heart talk with the Lord.

Sensing the prompting of her Lord, she found a Bible tucked away in a shelf and opened it. Not knowing where to begin, she opened to Psalm 91. After reading it several times, she closed her eyes and began.

Heavenly Father, it's been a while since I did this and I repent of my own disobedience and laziness. Restore a right relationship with your wayward child. She paused to collect her thoughts. *And now, Lord, I thank you that Your Word is true. I have sown to the wind and reaped a whirlwind. Like Naomi I have gone out full and returned empty. My adult children are following the same bitter path of my husband. Alcohol is the bane of their lives. The love of money has corrupted them. Bitterness and rebellion mark their steps. My daughter, though hardworking has no time for You and now my granddaughter.* Words failed her. Weeping uncontrollably, she poured out her heart to the Lord.

When her mind cleared, she pressed on; *Oh Lord, I declare Psalm 91 to be true over my shattered family—that even though a thousand fall at our side and ten thousand at our right side, let no harm, no evil, no sickness, no disease, no pestilence and no plague come near our dwelling places.*

Restore Chloe to her mother and Lord, if it is possible, bring WD back to me. Let him know he is loved by You and me.

Another wave of tears spilled from her eyes, and she closed the Bible. Peace swept over her like a wave. Immediately, the old hymn, *It is Well* bubbled up in her chest and she began to hum. That night, she slept better than she had in years.

***

High above Madeline's house, a battle raged in the night sky.

Her prayers had ascended only so far when they were met by an ancient foe. His power was that of doubt and unbelief. Throughout her prayer vigil, he had been whispering in her ear, You are unworthy. God will not hear you. It's too late for you or your children.

But Prince Raphael and a host of shimmering warriors wielding flaming swords and silver shields had beaten him back before he had a chance to plunge his talons into her heart. Now the battle rose as her prayers ascended heavenward. Like the prayers of the prophet Daniel, it would take weeks for those words to reach the throne room of the Most High.

"Prince Ariel, gather this saint's prayers in a bottle and protect them at all costs," Prince Raphael commanded.

With the aid of his fellow warriors, Prince Ariel scooped up every word uttered from Madeline's shattered heart and carefully placed them in a silver flask.

Immediately, he and his fellow angels fell under a withering assault. "Lord God," he cried, "Send Your Spirit or all is lost."

A deep throated thunder echoed from afar and grew in intensity until it shook the heavens. A thousand bolts of lightning flashed across the night sky illuminating the warriors of God, emboldening them, empowering them, enabling them. In the brightness of God's Spirit, the evil spirits of fear, doubt, and unbelief screamed, writhing in pain.

"Don't send us into the abyss before our time," they cried.

Ignoring their plea, Prince Raphael and his hosts tightened their circle around the shivering spirits and sliced them into pieces. As a cheer arose among the victorious, the mighty prince lifted his sword.

"Silence," he declared. "The battle is not over. It has just begun."

Looking at Prince Ariel's slumping shoulders, he knew what had happened.

While they fought throughout the night, in the small hours of the morning, the evil spirit of anxiety had crept in and stole Madeline's joy. She sat at her dining room table, a bevy of whispering spirits buzzed around her like angry bees; the spirit of apprehension, the spirit of despair and the spirit of dismay.

"Prince Ariel, go and remind this saint that God has not given us a spirit of fear, but of power, and of love, and of a sound mind. Remind her of the promises of God and guide her fingers across the pages of His Word."

Like a dove, he descended through the realm of the spiritual and touched her shaking shoulders. "Be strong in the Lord and the power of His might," he whispered.

Chapter Twenty-Seven

Richmond Hill Police Department …

Fourteen days had passed since Tramp and Boomer had gone missing and Sheriff Wooten was under tremendous pressure to find them.

Calls for his resignation filled his email box. Phone calls from the mayor, the governor and even state senators were a daily occurrence. He was about to quit when one of his deputies stepped into his office.

"Sir, this may not be of any significance, but we got a ping from one of the two missing boy's cell phones a few hours after they disappeared."

The sheriff was on the phone with the State Patrol, "Say what? Hold on Captain." Hand over the phone, he repeated his request.

His deputy closed the door and took a seat. "We didn't take it serious at the time since it only lasted a few seconds, but now—"

The sheriff slammed the palm of his hand on the desk making the pens and pencils dance. "Why in Sam-Hill am I just now hearing about this? Did you get a location of the ping?"

The deputy nodded. "Not quite. Apparently one of the young men tried to call his mother, but the call ended suddenly."

"Which mother?" he dreaded the answer.

"Boomer's mom; Mrs. Pauley."

The sheriff groaned. "Heads will roll if we don't get ahead of this." He punctuated his statement with a few choice expletives.

Returning his attention to the captain of the State Patrol, he said, "Look, Captain, I just got word that the Pauley boy tried to contact his mother the day he went missing. If I give you the number, do you think you can trace it to its last location?

A moment ticked before the captain responded. "We can sure try. Give it to me."

***

An hour later, Sheriff Wooten's phone rang. Captain Greenwood with the State Patrol counted the seconds waiting for the sheriff to pick up.

"Sheriff, I got a location. It was somewhere in the Okefenokee Swamp."

The sheriff repeated the words. "The Okefenokee? What would they be doing in the Okefenokee Swamp?"

"You got me," the captain said. "But to set your mind at ease, I've dispatched a couple of troopers to check it out. They should be arriving there soon. I'll keep you posted."

"Okay, thanks," Sheriff Wooten said and slammed the phone down. He hated the State Patrol beating him to the punch. This was his case, and he didn't like sharing the limelight. He just hoped they didn't find bodies rather than boys.

***

Being unfamiliar with the back roads of the Okefenokee Swamp, it took the two officers longer than they expected to find the fish camp.

When they did, it was deserted. All that remained were some deep tire tracks and a hat belonging to one of the boys.

"Well at least we know they were here," Officer Newton said to his partner.

Deputy Phelps began a room-to-room search looking for any notes the boys might have left.

There were none.

"Okay, let's go," Newton said. "There's no point in us wasting our time here."

Phelps removed his cap and mopped his brow. "Let's cruise around and see if any of the locals noticed anything."

Deputy Newton harrumphed. "The locals? Not on your life. These Swampies live by one rule. Don't trust outsiders, especially if they are wearing a badge."

"It's worth a try."

"Suit yourself," Newton added grimly.

After an hour of U-turns and getting stuck in the porous sand, they arrived at a lone cabin. A slender woman holding a shotgun guarded its porch.

"That's close enough," her voice rang out across the space between them.

Shielded by his car door, Newton called out. "Would you please point that thing in another direction Ma'am? We just want to ask you a few questions."

"I don't know nothin' about nothin,'" she said, still pointing the gun in their general direction.

"We haven't asked you a question yet," Phelps yelled.

"The answer's still the same. Now git," she waved her hand menacingly.

Not easily derailed, Newton pressed on. "Have you seen any strangers around here? We are looking for a couple of missing teens."

"People go missing every day in these parts. Eaten by the alligators, no doubt."

"How about an old man and a young girl? Have you seen them?" Deputy Phelps called out.

"Can't say."

Newton chuckled. "See? What'd I tell ya. Let's go."

Retaking their seats, Newton put the patrol car in gear, and slowly backed away.

As they weaved their way to the main road, Officer Newton cleared his throat and said, "Did you notice the footprints and tire tracks in the sand?"

Phelps' forehead wrinkled. "As a matter of fact, I did. What do you make of it?"

Officer Newton slowed at an intersection, checked both ways and accelerated on the blacktop highway. "I'd say the old coot had company; one wearing sneakers and the other wearing street shoes. And did you happen to catch a glimpse of the pickup truck sitting behind that shack?"

Phelps nodded, "Sure did, and I got a partial tag. Should I call it in just in case it doesn't belong to the old lady?"

"Yes, by all means. And while we're at it, let's make a run to the nearest town and do some snooping around."

Newton nodded as he called in the information.

A few minutes later, they pulled to a stop at the only light in a town no larger than a postage stamp. Seeing an auto parts store, they parked and got out.

Inside, sat a leathery old man smoking a pipe. Its aromatic smoke filled the small shop as he watched the occasional car pass through town.

"Hello officers," he said as the two men entered. "How can I hep you this fine day?" They were his first customers since WD finished working on his car and he looked forward to the chat. Just not with a couple of cops.

Holding up a picture of WD and Chloe, Deputy Newton asked, "Have you seen anyone fitting this description?"

The older man squinted. He knew from listening to the news who they were and what they were wanted for. But he had no compunction to help the police, reward notwithstanding. "Can't say, officers," he said and took a long pull from his pipe.

Deputy Phelps scuffed the bare wood floor. "How's business these days?"

The shop owner glanced sideways. "Not bad. Why?"

Pushing his hat back, he said in a relaxed tone. "I've got an old Chevy Blazer I'm looking to restore," he lied. "Where would I look for parts?"

The man's face brightened. "That would be either my shop or the junkyard. They stock lots of old parts."

Phelps nodded, "Thanks, I'll check it out."

After pulling a business card from his pocket, he handed it to the old man. "If you run across those folks, give me a call, would you?"

The old man eyed him without speaking.

Back in the cruiser, Deputy Phelps put the car in gear and headed in the direction of the junkyard. "Maybe we'll get lucky," he said to his partner.

***

Thirty minutes later the two officers climbed into the cruiser and left the junkyard.

"So he's driving a restored '68 Ford Mustang," Phelps said as he and Deputy Newton sped back to headquarters. "That guy back there was more than happy to spill his guts; anything to keep his illegal operation off the authority's radar. I'd better call it in."

After speed-dialing his captain, he said, "The guy at the junkyard said the last time he'd seen Mr. Dawson was a week ago."

Captain Greenwood cursed under his breath. "A week ago! They could be anywhere by now. Did the guy at the junkyard have any idea where WD was going?"

"No, sir. Just that he wanted the car road worthy."

"Ok, thanks guys. Come on back. I've got to call Sheriff Wooten and let him know what we've learned."

Chapter Twenty-Eight

A New Man ...

Once the Ford Mustang reached the blacktop highway, WD pressed the gas pedal.

The engine revved and took off with grace and speed. As the wheels hummed along the highway, Chloe broke the silence.

"Back when you caught me, Tramp and Boomer in your garage, I said some awful things to you. I'm really sorry," her puppy-dog eyes reflected true repentance.

WD reflected on that night. "You were planning to steal my truck weren't you?"

She searched the floorboard and nodded sullenly. "Yaas. But we would have brought it back. Had you not gotten out of the hospital, you probably wouldn't have even known."

He reached across the space between them and took her small hand. No longer were her fingernails painted black. Sometime during the two weeks she'd scratched it all off. And with all the fishing, chopping wood, and cooking she had managed to chip most of her nails back to nubs.

"All is forgiven. I couldn't stay mad at you even if I wanted to."

She faced him with a quizzical expression. "G-Diddy, you're different. You used to cuss, and drink, but I haven't heard you say one bad word since we left. What suh?"

He knew from past lessons what she meant and didn't press the issue. "Like I told Miss Winnie, I had a come to Jesus moment. I no longer crave booze. I no longer want to lie, or cheat, or any of the old sins. Jesus is making me a new man."

Her eyes rounding, Chloe asked. "So does that mean you're never going to *sin* again?" she feigned air quotes.

WD shook his head. "Nah, but it does mean I don't want to sin again. I still live in this old body with all its old habits. But by God's grace, I can live like Jesus."

"That sounds so unnatural, so spiritual."

"You got that right. It is unnatural and yes, it is spiritual. Not by might, not by power but by My Spirit, says the Lord," WD said, quoting Zechariah 4:6.

"Is that why you're going to Oklahoma; to see your dad? To preach to him about Jesus?"

"Not exactly. I'll be happy if he doesn't shoot me. All I want to do is see his face and tell him how sorry I am for my rebellion."

"At least you have one…a dad that is. I never did."

WD's mind flashed back sixteen years. Sixteen hard years, years of drunkenness, years of secrets. He could never wash away what he'd done. Perhaps the blood of Jesus could. The promise he'd made between Joyce, Chloe's mother and the man who had gotten her pregnant still haunted him. He should never have made that promise. Now, sitting next to him was a hurting, shattered soul who needed a father, a role model, someone to love her, someone who she could love back.

Finally, he spoke. "We all have our secrets, our regrets."

She pierced him with two black orbs. Orbs which bore far too much pain for a sixteen-year-old girl.

"Why? What do you mean?"

As they merged into I-75 traffic a small, white Toyota suddenly cut him off and he let a word fly.

"Sorry. Like I said, I'm still growing."

A soft chuckle sounded from Chloe's corner of the car.

Nearing Atlanta metroplex sprawl, an information sign flashed; BE ALERT FOR A STOLEN 1968 FORD MUSTANG. CALL …

They sped past the sign lightning fast, but not before it sent a surge of adrenaline through his nervous system.

"Uh oh," he whispered. "We need to get off this highway."

Chloe glanced over her shoulder. "Why? Are you speeding?"

"No. Did you see that info sign?"

She shook her head. "No."

Maybe it's better you didn't. The authorities know I'm driving a Ford Mustang."

Chloe's mouth fell open. "Do they know the license plate or color?"

WD considered her question for a moment. "No, but how many '68' Ford Mustangs are there on the road?"

***

As traffic thickened, WD glanced down at his gages.

"Uh oh. I need to stop and get gas," he huffed. "There's nothing worse than getting lost in downtown Atlanta, especially on an empty tank."

After making several lane changes, he took the next exit and ended up in East Point. Not being familiar with the area, he turned right and entered a residential street. Slowing, he swerved between a row of parked cars. Some vehicles had seen better days; others were in various stages of disrepair.

Suddenly, a small child darted out from between cars chasing a ball. Instinctively, WD jammed on the brake and the Mustang skidded to a stop. Chloe threw her hands up and caught herself before her head hit the dashboard. A moment later, the child scampered from sight.

"That was close," WD whispered.

Chloe glanced around looking for the boy and his ball. They were gone. "Yeah, too close. I don't like this area of town. Can we get outta here?"

Squinting ahead for a sign directing them to the main street, he paused, hoping to see something, anything which would help him get his bearings.

He saw nothing.

Beads of sweat formed over his eyebrows and he swept them aside. With pressure mounting, he made another sharp turn and nearly ran into a wall of youths playing basketball. Their baggy pants hung so low that even Chloe averted her eyes. The vulgar jabber of rap music blared from a boom box drowning out all other sounds. As WD brought the car to a stop, the group ceased their game and gathered around the car.

"I don't like the looks of those boys," Chloe said under her breath.

***

Prince Uriel, his senses on high alert, said, "I smell trouble."

His hand instinctively grasped his spear.

Prince Leo's fingers found the hilt of his sword. "Those hoodlums are filled with legions of demons. Shall I attack?"

Uriel lifted his hand. "Wait. Let's see what the Almighty has prepared for those who love Him, who are called according to His purposes."

Holding their positions close to the car, the two angels remained vigilant.

***

"What up!?" a tall, slender youth called out, his baggy pants revealing his undergarments.

"Looks like we got us some fresh meat," said a pigtailed youth with a red bandana tied around his head. His lust-filled eyes strafing Chloe.

For a moment, WD considered throwing the car in reverse, but the group had gathered so close that he couldn't back up.

"Hey girl," one of the boys said, reaching through the open window.

She instinctively slapped his gripping hand. "Hey watch it! G-Diddy, I don't like this place. Can we get out of here?" Her voice shook with tension. "This is not cool."

"Hey old man, whatcha doin' with that pearly white chick? Are you her sugar-daddy?" the first guy mocked.

WD felt his blood-pressure spike. The urge to punch him in the face was palpable. Hands closing around the steering wheel he took several deep breaths. *Lord, this would be a good time for you to help us.*

To his surprise, Chloe popped her door open. WD's hand immediately reached out to stop her, but she avoided it.

"I got this G-Diddy," she said in a low tone.

Exuding more confidence than he had seen in her, she puffed her chest and approached the closest guy.

"Hey dude! Don't cha be giving' my old man a hard time." She got right up in his face and poked him in the chest. "Bruh! Yo messing' wit dah wrong guy. Alls I have to say is one word and he gonna whip yo—"

The blast of a horn interrupted her before she said too much.

Suddenly, the crowd parted.

Hands raised in surrender the guy backed away. "Hey babe, ahz jus havin' a little fun. Don't go full animal on me."

Chloe gave him another shove before retaking her seat. "Drive!" she whispered between pinched lips.

Needing no encouragement, WD put the car in gear and slowly pulled away. "Nice work. How'd you learn to talk like that?" He gave her an appraising look.

She shrugged. "In school, and not in English class. Everyone talks that way. If you want to survive in the halls of a public school, you either blend in or get canceled. Plus, it's common knowledge that no guy wants some mouthy white girl pushin' his buttons."

Clever girl, he thought.

In another block a street sign appeared with the words Peachtree Street emblazoned in green and white. He cut his wheels and turned down the street.

A few blocks later a gas station and convenience store appeared. Its windows were covered with advertisements for beer, cigarettes, and lotto tickets. Releasing his breath, he pulled in and turned off the engine.

"I don't want to use a credit card so I'm going inside to prepay for the gas. Is there anything you want?"

Shielding her eyes, Chloe appraised the situation. "Are you sure you want to go in there? It's like walking into a lion's den."

WD stared at the advertisements. Suddenly, his jaw went slack, his hands started to shake. His head slumped against the steering wheel as he fought the urge to go in and purchase a six-pack of beer.

The tension was palpable.

Lifting his head, he whispered, "You know, you're right. It would be a mistake to step inside that store. Would you mind?"

Her face brightened. "No prob, G-Diddy. I gotta go to the restroom anyways."

He handed her a crisp one-hundred-dollar bill as she opened the car door. She took it and got out. "Thanks, but I might spend it all. I'm hangry." Then she scampered from the car.

He knew what she meant. "Get a bag of peanuts and an RC Cola for me," he called as she yanked the door to the convenience store open.

Ten minutes later, she emerged carrying a sack. After he finished topping off the tank, he replaced the gas cap and climbed in behind the wheel.

"The change?" his hand extended.

She popped a bubble filling the air with the sweet scent of double-bubble gum. "There wasn't any."

"Say what?"

"Yep, I spent it all and then some."

"On what?" A twinge of anger began to bubble up, but quickly subsided as she offered him a disarming smile.

Reaching inside the bag, she said, "On gas, and these." As she spoke, she handed him the soda and bag of nuts along with a package of cheese crackers and a tube of beef jerky. "I didn't know what flavor you like so I just got the regular kind."

He nodded his thanks, lifted the tab on the can and took a sip. "Ah, that hits the spot."

After opening the package of crackers, he shoved one in his mouth and resumed their journey.

Chapter Twenty-Nine

Back at the Circle D Ranch …

The soft rubber soles of a nurse's shoes squeaked lightly as she pushed an elderly man in a wheelchair to the veranda of his palatial ranch-style home.

It was morning in Yukon County, Oklahoma, and a light breeze stirred the air making the tops of the tall pine trees sway gently. A robin sitting atop a telephone wire greeted the day with a song and was answered by its mate a hundred yards away. Squirrels sprang to the nearby trees as a young girl dashed across the lush green lawn chasing one of the dogs which called the Circle D Ranch home.

"Is this suitable, Mr. Dawson?" the nurse asked.

The older man cocked his head trying to see his nurse. "Whatcha say young lady?" his voice gruff.

The nurse leaned close to his ear. "Is this suitable? We could go to the backyard, if you like?"

"No, not the backyard. That garden plot is so overgrown; it brings back too many bad memories. Take me to the east porch. I like watching that girl run across the lawn."

The nurse stayed close. "That's your great-granddaughter, Rosie, Mr. Dawson. Don't you remember? Your granddaughter Virginia and her husband, Neal arrived yesterday. They will be spending a couple of weeks here. Truman arranged it. He gave them the key to the guest house and said they could stay as long as they wanted. We are planning a big supper tonight."

Blaine nodded absently. "More likely they're here to spend my money. But she's certainly very pretty."

"Yes she is; pretty, that is." After locking the wheels to the wheelchair, she tugged the Afghan higher on his legs. "Will there be anything else?"

He shook his head. "No, that will be all."

***

As she stepped away, the crunch of tires on gravel echoed in the distance.

The late-model car, driven by his attorney, came to a halt in the large parking lot and a slender woman in her mid-thirties extracted herself. With a spring in her step, Ms. Taylor approached the place where her client sat.

"What a lovely day to sit and soak up the sun, Mr. Dawson." she said in a light, airy tone.

He cocked his head and narrowed his eyes. "Ms. Taylor, any day that I can put my feet on God's green earth is a lovely day. What is it this time?" he asked in a level tone.

She reached into her attaché and withdrew a stack of papers bound together with a wire clip. "I have the latest changes on the lease of the property. All it needs is your signature. I'm sure it will be a big relief off your shoulders knowing your family's future is secure."

She took a quick glance at the shadowed figure standing just out of Blaine's peripheral vision and winked.

He sighed heavily. "This ranch has been in my family for generations. My father's grandfather came over from Scotland and settled this valley when the Indians still roamed the countryside. He fought them, cattle rustlers, the railroad and who knows who else to keep it. I can't count the number of kinfolk buried out in the lower forty."

A light breeze rustled her free-flowing auburn hair causing a few strands to fall across her eyes. She brushed them aside and smiled. The thought of the millions she would make from the lease of this property caused her heart to stumble. *If only I could convince the old man to sign the documents.*

Taking a pen from the pocket of her well-tailored suitcoat, she laid it next to the stack of papers.

"If you are ready—"

"—I was thinking, have you had any contact with WD? It seems like an eternity since we've spoken."

"Mr. Dawson, you and WD haven't spoken in years. Remember? He ran away from home when he was nineteen and you haven't heard from him since; no apology, no card, no phone call…nothing. You're not thinking about—" She shuddered at the thought of WD's name remaining on the Will. Getting it removed was the next thing on her agenda.

She took a calming breath and nervously tucked a strand of hair behind her ear. "No, this is the right thing to do. After all, it was Truman who kept this ranch going. And it was Truman who discovered the oil deposits sitting right under your feet. It is only fitting he be rewarded for his labors. Your leasing it to the oil company will insure the family's security for the next one-hundred years. Plus, if that alcoholic son of yours were to get his hands on the deed to this property, who knows what he'd do with it; probably sell it to the highest bidder. So please, Mr. Dawson…Blaine, sign the lease and be done with it."

Blaine straightened. "Don't speak of my son like that. I won't stand for it."

"Yes, sir," Taylor said demurely.

Movement caught Blaine's attention and he turned. His secretary, Dawn Melson stood behind him, a cell phone in her hand. "Excuse me ma'am. There is a call for Mr. Dawson. It's rather urgent."

Ms. Taylor, clearly frustrated by the interruption, said, "Of course, I'll give you some space." Backing away, she stood close enough to hear the conversation. She hoped it didn't involve WD.

Chapter Thirty

Bad News ...

After handing him the phone, Miss Melson stepped a safe distance away.

"Hello?" the senior Dawson said in a shaky voice.

"Blaine, it's Madeline. How are you?"

The older man focused his eyes as if by so doing, he could hear better. "I'm fine, honey. How are you?"

Despite the divorce, Madeline had kept in contact with her father-in-law. He was the only real family she had since her natural parents had died.

"Fine, well, not so fine. Have you heard about WD?"

He shifted and took a quick glance in the direction of his lawyer. "No, no I haven't. What's he gotten himself into this time?" His voice turned hard.

Despite his lawyer's best efforts to keep him in the dark, Madeline was faithful to keep him apprised of WD's life.

"Well, for starters, over a month ago someone set fire to the company warehouse and WD is the primary suspect. The fire and rescue team found him drunk and unconscious in the office when the fire broke out. They think it was either arson or a suicide attempt since they found a gun lying next to him. It landed him in a mental hospital for six months."

"A mental hospital? Why?"

"For his own protection. But that's not the latest. A couple of weeks ago, he disappeared from the facility, and they think he took Chloe with him."

"Chloe?"

"Yes, Chloe, Joyce's daughter, and your great-granddaughter. She is sixteen and the authorities think he took her with him." She intentionally left out the part about Tramp and Boomer.

"Why? Why would WD do such a stupid thing?"

Madeline sighed into the phone. "I don't know, but we haven't heard from them in over two weeks."

The cell phone nearly slipped from his grasp. Using the other hand, he pressed it closer to his ear. "Where did they go?"

A beat passed. "I don't know Blaine. But the authorities are scouring the area. They've put out an Amber Alert and the state patrol is on the lookout for them, but so far, nothing."

***

Beth Taylor stood to leave.

She could see the news had shaken her client to the core. She also knew she was not going to get his signature on the lease today; and probably not tomorrow. Not as long as WD was on the lam. Movement caught her attention and she glanced in the direction of the shadowed figure. It was Truman. She excused herself and stepped closer.

Clearly agitated, Truman asked, "Beth was that Madeline on the phone with Dad?"

She nodded angrily. "Yes, and she was telling Blaine all about your brother."

"What's he gotten himself into now?"

She summarized the one-sided conversation.

"Is there any chance you could get him to sign the lease?"

She shook her head. "Not now," she said dejectedly. "Perhaps with all the negative news about WD kidnapping his granddaughter he'll relent and sign it. After all, if WD is in jail what's the use in him holding out?"

Truman glanced over the demure woman's shoulder. Blaine's back was to them, and he pulled her to his chest. "Just get that signature. Then we'll work on getting WD's name off the Will. Do that and you'll make both of us very rich."

As he tried to kiss her, she pulled back. "I'm doing the best I can without raising his suspicions. You might try talking to him."

He gritted his teeth. "I'll try. We've got a big dinner planned tonight. Maybe after getting better acquainted with Rosie, his great-granddaughter, he might change his mind."

"Let's hope so" she quipped.

Chapter Thirty-One

A Stalled Investigation …

Sheriff Wooten's office walls reverberated with angry voices.

He had just received word that the two officers, who followed the lead at the fish camp, had come up empty.

"Did they ask any of the locals," Wooten demanded.

Greenwood, the State Patrol captain huffed. "Yes, and what they got was old news. WD and his granddaughter had flown the coop. On the bright side, they did get a partial plate from a vehicle sitting behind the old woman's cabin. I'm having it run as we speak. Hold on, Sheriff," Greenwood said cutting off Wooten's next question.

The sheriff drummed his fingers on the desk and listened to a muffled conversation.

Finally, Greenwood's irritating voice filled the connection. "Sheriff, I just got confirmation that my men found WD's truck behind that old lady's shack. The problem is, it's there and WD isn't."

Wooten colored the air purple. "So, you're saying they slipped through *your* fingers." He enjoyed getting underneath Greenwood's skin.

"It wasn't *my* fingers to start with," he fired back. "But I have it on good authority that your guy may be driving a vintage Ford Mustang."

Wooten's interest piqued. "Oh? How so?"

A wicked chuckle percolated through the telephone. "You know I don't have to tell you this, but—" he waited for the sheriff's response.

"Okay, okay. I give up."

A satisfied sigh preceded, "A man fitting your guy's description was seen in town buying parts for a Ford Mustang. Looks like *your* guy may have left the area long before *my* men arrived. He could be headed *your* direction."

Wooten didn't believe that for one minute. "Or he could be heading anywhere. Would it be too much trouble to have your department put out a full alert for Mr. Dawson? He is wanted for questioning in connection with the abduction of three under aged teens. One of them is his granddaughter."

"Already done," Captain Greenwood answered succinctly. "Anything for a fellow peace officer."

No sooner had Sheriff Wooten hung up when his phone buzzed. It was his secretary. "Sheriff, I have the fire chief on the line. Can you take his call?"

Wooten breathed a curse and lifted the phone. "Hello?"

"Sheriff? Olson here. I've got some good news and some bad news. Which do you want first?"

Sheriff Wooten sighed into the phone. He hated playing word games, especially when it came to an ongoing investigation. "Does it matter? I think I'm going to regret hearing whatever you're going to tell me."

Olson chuckled. "You got that right. Here's the good news. All the evidence from the warehouse fire points to either an accident or an amateur, not a trained arsonist."

"So that doesn't rule out WD, does it?"

A beat passed as Olson rustled through the report. "No, not exactly, but…and I repeat, it doesn't conclusively implicate him either. Remember, he was stone-cold drunk in the front office and the fire emanated from a small storage room all the way in the back of the warehouse. In my professional opinion, I'd rule it faulty wiring or sloppy handling of a flammable substance. Either way, ol' WD's off the hook as far as I'm concerned."

The sheriff let out an expletive. "What's the bad news?"

"The bad news is, we found a couple of fingerprints, but no matches yet. Whoever left them is not in our system, meaning, they're probably teens."

More expletives.

"All right, I'll inform the Dawson family that WD is no longer a suspect for arson. But make no mistake; he sure as heck is on the hook for kidnapping."

***

The alarm clock sprang to life and Joyce Dawson's eyes fluttered open like a pair of window blinds.

Muttering, she slapped the snooze button and prayed for fifteen minutes of sleep.

They didn't come.

No sooner had she closed her eyes than her phone jangled. Frustrated, she rolled out of bed and stared blearily at the device. Releasing a sigh, she punched the green button.

"Hello?" her voice not quite awake. She cleared it and repeated the greeting.

"Hello, Mrs. Dawson," said the sheriff. His voice was edged with fatigue. "I'm sorry if I—"

"It's fine, I had to get up anyway. What's up?" she asked as she headed to the bathroom.

"I've got good news and bad news. Which do you want first?" Repeating what the fire chief said.

Joyce twisted the shower tap to cover up the other sounds. "Give me the bad news first."

The chair squeaked before the sheriff answered. "Well, the bad news is, they found some fingerprints at the scene of the fire but are unable to identify them."

"Meaning?"

"Meaning, whoever set the fire isn't in our data base; could be their first brush with crime, could be a transient, it could be just about any law-abiding citizen."

Joyce reached into the shower. *Too hot.* "No. Law abiding citizens don't set warehouses on fire. And the good news?" her voice lifting slightly.

"The good news is the fire inspector has ruled out WD as a primary suspect."

Stepping from the bathroom, Joyce plopped on the bed. "Oh really? Is that so? How did he come to that conclusion?"

She waited as the sheriff rifled through his notes. "Well, according to him and the men on the scene, the fire started in a back room of the warehouse and WD was found on the floor in the front office. That much we know. He concluded that he was in no condition to hike from the front of the warehouse to the back, set the fire and then make his way back to the front office."

"What about him having a gun? Why did he have it?"

Wooten cleared his throat before answering. "Yes, he had a gun. If you recall, it was a .22 caliber revolver. My guess is that it was late at night and perhaps he heard something, maybe he heard the intruders. I don't know, but what I do know is, your father is not being investigated for arson."

Relief and frustration swept over Joyce like the incoming tide. Switching the phone from one ear to the other, she brought the call to an end. "Well thank you sheriff. I guess I'm relieved, sorta."

He snickered. "Yes, Mrs. Dawson, it's a bit of a mixed bag. Have a nice day."

She ended the call, her mind whirling. *If he didn't start the fire, then who did and why?*

Chapter Thirty-Two

From the Target to the Hospital …

Having missed the exit around Atlanta, WD joined the mid-day traffic flowing north on the I-75, I-85 corridor.

He hoped no one had paid attention to the Amber Alert signs. *At least this time.*

Seeing the exit to the west-bound I-20 ramp approaching, he made a lane change and rounded the curve leading from the city. Once he had cleared the downtown traffic, he tried to relax, but it wasn't easy. Foolish drivers raced around him like it was the Indie 500. White knuckled, he gripped the steering wheel harder and focused on the road ahead.

As the traffic thinned, his thoughts turned to other things: things like Chloe not knowing who her dad was.

He had been sworn to secrecy the day she was born and had carried that burden ever since. But now that she was asking the hard questions, he found it increasingly more difficult to avoid telling her.

"Those crackers and beef jerky I ate a while ago are long gone, but I don't like the idea of eating in a restaurant either," he said, trying to get his mind off his problems. "How 'bout we stop someplace and stock up on some supplies."

Chloe pushed herself up from her slouched position and glanced at her watch. It was nearly noon. "Yeah, you're right. That Powerade ran right through me, so please hurry."

WD took a deep breath. He too had the same sensation.

A few minutes later, she pointed at the exit rushing toward them. "There's a Target. Let's stop there."

He signaled and followed the signs to the sprawling parking lot. After finding a spot as far from the front doors as possible, he shut the car off and handed her a hundred-dollar bill. "Here, don't spend it all in one place," he chuckled.

"I'll need more than one of those to buy what I'm thinking about buying."

He gaped at her. "What are you planning on buying?"

She pulled two more one-hundred-dollar bills from his fingers with an impish twinkle in her eyes. "You'll see."

He waited for a few minutes before exiting the car and then made a beeline to the men's room. By the time he returned, a small gathering of car enthusiasts had gathered admiring his vintage Mustang.

"Hey mister, that must have cost you a pretty penny to restore that," a man wearing a pair of overalls and a straw hat, said.

WD guessed it was all innocent banter, so he let the conversation play out.

Thirty minutes later, Chloe reappeared. WD caught her attention and waved her off until the inquisitive group dispersed. Once it was safe, he motioned for her to join him. Carrying a package under her arm, she retook her seat in the car.

As they moved into traffic, she pulled a container of yogurt and some energy bars from the bag. "I figured since you chunked my old phone in the swamp, you owed me this." She produced a new plastic sealed cell phone.

WD's eyes widened. "A burner phone? What are you thinking?"

She ignored his question and began peeling back the stubborn plastic packaging. Once she had gotten it out, she skimmed through the activation instructions.

"I certainly hope you're not thinking about calling your mother."

Her forehead wrinkled; innocence masked her features. "And why not? It's been over two weeks. I'm sure she's worried about me, and frankly, I'm worried about her."

"Yeah, she's worried about you, worried enough to call the police and have every peace officer between here and podunk on the lookout for us. That phone could land me in jail and you in juvie."

"No way."

"Way." He reached for the phone, but she pulled it from his grasp.

"Are you sure about that?" he asked, clearly displeased.

"Yaas. It's totally secure."

WD released a defeated sigh. "I guess we'll find out."

She smiled. "G-Diddy, you're so lowkey. I thought you would really be mad."

"And who says I'm not? And what in heaven's name does *lowkey* mean?"

She powered up the cell phone and punched in the activation code. "It means you're relaxed—cool. You know, lowkey."

He smiled at her attempt at breaking the Gen-z language down to plain English. "I'm glad you think so."

"Oh, and I found this," she lifted a wrinkled one-dollar bill she had snatched up from the parking lot. "I found it just…laaayingg…on…th-the groouund." Her words slurred.

WD watched in shock as Chloe's face paled, her eyes rolled up and her head lulled. Slumping to one side, she nearly knocked her head on the gear-shift.

"Chloe!" WD hollered.

***

Despite his best efforts, Prince Cassiel could not fend off the attack of the enemy.

The snarling half-wolf, half-vulture-like creature had its claws embedded in Chloe's chest and was squeezing it.

"No! You can't have her," bellowed the mighty prince.

Drawing back his broad ax, he swung with all his might. The blade struck firmly along the bony spine of the creature but did nothing to stop the beast from sucking the life from its victim.

All at once, Prince Leo joined the fray, with one swift move he drew his sword and sliced off the wolf-like creature's paws. It whimpered and whined, but Leo was not through. He drew back once more and decapitated it before it had a chance to do any more damage.

"Prince Haniel, minister grace to the young lady lest she succumb to whatever was on that dollar bill."

In a flash, he reached through the ethereal curtain and touched the wound where the beast had penetrated her chest. A moment later, Chloe sucked in a sharp breath, but the damage was done.

She slumped back in her seat shaking violently.

Chapter Thirty-Three

Shocked …

WD stared helplessly as his granddaughter fell into a coma.

He'd seen the same kind of reaction when his buddies mixed booze with drugs, but this was Chloe, not some junkie.

"Chloe!"

Getting no response, he checked her breathing.

It was shallow and labored.

This is bad, really bad. Something on that dollar bill sent her into an anaphylactic shock.

He knew instinctively what he had to do. Despite the risks, he put the car in gear and sped in the direction of the nearest hospital or urgent care unit. Seeing a blue sign with the letter H, he followed the arrow and reached the emergency entrance of the Wellstar Hospital in Douglasville in less than five minutes.

"Hold on, Chloe," he said as he scooped her in his arms and rushed her inside. "Help!" he yelled. "I've got an unconscious girl. I think she's been poisoned."

Within seconds, a trauma team moved into action. A male nurse took her from his arms while a female nurse began to check her vitals. Others joined them in an attempt at restoring her breathing.

"Sir, we'll take it from here," one of the trauma team said as they whisked her away.

A minute later, WD found himself standing alone, helpless, and confused. *Had I done the right thing? Did I just lose the only person who really cared for me? Oh, God. What have I done?"*

He slumped into a rigid chair and bowed his head.

As he began to pray, a warm hand touched his shoulder. "Sir," it was one of the nurses. "Are you a relative?"

Nodding, he said, "Y-yes. I'm her grandfather."

The nurse handed him a clipboard. "If you would fill this out, we need some information about your granddaughter."

He took the proffered clipboard with a trembling hand. "Is she going to be okay? I mean—"

"—She's in good hands, sir. Do you know what happened?"

He blinked absently. "I'm not sure. She was telling me about a dollar-bill she found on the parking lot at Target—"

In a flash, the nurse bolted through the doors leading to the triage unit. He could hear her calling for the doctor. Finally, after nearly an hour, the admissions nurse returned. Relief marked her features.

"Sir, your granddaughter is resting comfortably in room D. You can see her now. Don't be alarmed if she doesn't respond. Whatever was on that dollar bill really had a kick to it. She is one of the lucky ones."

"Lucky ones? Has this happened before?"

The nurse bit her lip and glanced from one side to the other. "More times than we'd like to admit. By the way, where is that dollar bill?"

WD considered her question for a minute. "It's in the front seat of my car. Do you want me to go and get it?"

"No!"

Her sharp response startled WD.

"I don't want you to touch it or the same thing will happen to you. I'll send someone wearing gloves out there to retrieve it. What kind of car were you driving?"

WD's heart jackknifed. His palms grew slick and his breathing shallow. "I-I."

"Sir are you all right?" asked the nurse, clearly concerned.

Taking a sip from a bottle of water the nurse handed him, he waited for his mind to clear. "Yes, I just had a nervous reaction. May I go and see my granddaughter now?"

Seconds ticked before she spoke. "Yes, if you're up to it."

"I think so," WD said, pushing himself up on wobbly legs.

With her help, he stood, thanked her, then followed her to examination room D. Chloe lay with a warming blanket covering her from her neck down. After taking a seat next to her, he reached under the cover and took her hand.

"Lord, thank you for sparing my granddaughter. She doesn't know you, so help her to come to faith in You. Quicken her and restore her to full health. In Jesus' name, amen."

For the next four hours, he watched the nurses and doctors come and go. His only break was when he left to retrieve the infamous dollar bill. Wearing a pair of rubber gloves, he placed it in a plastic bag and returned it to the nurse's station.

At last, the doctor entered. Looking at the chart, his eyebrows hiked up an inch. "Sir, we've analyzed the substance from the dollar bill. It was laced with fentanyl, a highly addictive drug."

WD felt his face go slack. "Will she be okay?"

The doctor closed the clipboard. "Yes, but there are some police officers who would like to ask you some questions. They'll be here in a few minutes. Please wait here."

***

As the doctor left the recovery room, Chloe roused.

"G-Diddy?" She sounded groggy. "What happened?"

Her question echoed distantly in WD's mind, but he was too preoccupied with trying to figure out what to do next to answer her.

"Honey, do you think you can walk?" He didn't wait for her answer. He quickly tossed her clothes on the bed and drew the curtains. "You need to get dressed."

"But—"

"No time to explain, honey. We need to get outta here. I'll explain later. Now hurry."

He stepped from the room and checked to see where the police were. They were at the far end of the hall talking with the attending physician. Seeing an unattended wheelchair with a half-dozen balloons tied to the armrest, he commandeered it and reentered the examining room. Chloe stood, leaning against the bed railing. Her face was the color of milk and she looked like she might double over.

"Here, let me help you." He carefully got her seated in the wheelchair and slid her feet into her tennis shoes.

"Hold on," he said and casually rolled her down the hall. With the balloons obscuring her identity from the close-circuit camera, he headed to the emergency exit. They had almost reached the car when an alarm sounded.

Doubling his speed, he reached the car and swung the door open.

"Quick, get in," he said, breathing hard.

Within minutes, he had strapped her in. Then he ran around to his side, got in and started the engine. A moment later, they were racing from the emergency room parking lot.

"G-Diddy, why did you rush me out of the hospital? I feel like a criminal." She was pale as a ghost and her hands shook.

He checked the rear-view mirror to see if the police had given chase. "Because honey. If the police questioned me, I'd have "contributing to the delinquency of a minor" added to my growing list of crimes."

***

Wings flapping wildly, it was all Prince Uriel and Prince Leo could do to keep up with the fleeing Ford Mustang.

Were it not for Prince Leo's quick thinking WD and Chloe would not have made it to the hospital. As it was, he chided himself for not seeing the drug-laced dollar bill before she picked it up.

"I am truly sorry for not—"

Prince Uriel waved his companion into silence. "Don't blame yourself, my friend. This was all in the Creator's plan."

Leo's face registered shock. "I will never understand the Almighty's ways. Why would He allow such evil to pervade this world?"

Racing to catch up to WD and Chloe, Prince Uriel placed his hand on his friend's shoulder. "Surely the wrath of men shall praise the Almighty and the remainder He will restrain. Meaning, God will work all things for good to those who love Him, to those who are called according to His purposes."

Prince Leo took up a position in front of the Ford Mustang. "As I said, I shall never understand the Almighty's ways, but I love watching Him work."

Chapter Thirty-Four

A Port near Fernandina Beach …

The captain throttled back on the commercial fishing trawler's engines, and they belched black diesel smoke in protest.

It was the end of another long day, and he was glad to see it nearly over. With skill, he glided the ship past the no-wake zone and into the harbor.

Overhead, seagulls squawked before dropping into the surf in search of their next meat. Sandpipers played a game of chase with the incoming waves hoping to snatch an unsuspecting minnow for supper. Old men strolled along the shoreline with metal detectors and children skipped the worn-out waves. The air was pungent with salt, and the stench of rotting fish.

Like two experienced fishermen Tramp and Boomer stood along the gunwale of the boat waiting to cast the lines to the dock. They had been on the commercial fishing boat for two weeks and were relieved to see Fernandina Beach again.

"I'm going to be sick," Boomer said, clutching his stomach.

Tramp gaped at his friend. "C'mon man, get a grip. We've been doing this for two weeks. I'd think you'd have gotten used to it by now."

"I don't think I'll ever get used to that smell."

"You two, tie us off," Jimmy barked.

Anxious to have something firm under their feet, Tramp and Boomer scrambled up the ladder and began to tie the ropes to the deck cleats.

"Okay boys, get busy emptying the hold,"

Boomer and Tramp joined the other men and within two hours of intense labor the job was finished.

"I don't know what smells worse, me or you," Tramp said, pulling his shirt to his nose.

Boomer swiped a greasy hand across his face. "Tramp, look." He produced an old cell phone from his pocket.

Tramp lowered his voice. "Where'd ya get that?"

Boomer glanced in both directions. Seeing their crew mates assembling at the end of the dock, he led his buddy around to a dark corner.

"I swiped it from one of the men when he wasn't looking. I'm going to call my mom."

Tramp took a peek around the corner. "You'd better hurry before they catch you or we might find ourselves swimming with the sharks tonight."

Boomer was already punching in the numbers. "Hello mom?" he said in a raspy voice. He waited for her to catch her breath.

"Where are you? Are you all right? Are you safe?" Her questions flew at him in rapid succession.

"Mom, settle down and listen. I don't have much time. Me and Tramp are in Fernandina Beach. There's a fishing port nearby. Can you come and get us?"

She pummeled him with more questions, but all he wanted to hear was that she was coming to get them.

"Look, I don't know where we'll be spending the night. Just send someone to get us. We'll probably be leaving to go back out on the boat before dawn. Come quick—"

"Hey! You there. Give me that phone." The owner of the phone yelled. And he was none-too-happy.

"Who in blazes were you on the phone with?" he demanded.

"I-I was just ordering pizza, man. Chill dude!"

He yanked the phone from his hand and pocketed it.

Boomer bit back a grin. "At least he didn't check to see who I called," he whispered as the man sauntered off.

"Boomer, Tramp, you guys come over here," Jimmy called from across the wharf.

Dreading the tongue-lashing they knew they were in for, Boomer and Tramp hurried to meet their ship's captain.

"Yes sir, Mr. Jimmy, what do you need?" Tramp asked in a respectful tone.

Jimmy eyed them appreciatively. "Nothin'. I just wanted to say, you guys did a heck of a job this week; it being only your first real job and all."

Handing each of them five hundred dollars, he said, "If you want to call your folks, that's all right by me. But if you want to work another week or so, I'd really appreciate it. It's hard to get good help these days."

Boomer and Tramp exchanged knowing glances. "Yes sir, Mr. Jimmy. Can we borrow a phone?" Tramp asked.

He nodded. "I thought you just did," he said, chuckling.

The two boys' mouths fell open like a marlin.

Tramp was the first to respond. "Well, if they don't arrive before you head out tomorrow, we'd be glad to work for you. Right Boomer?" nudging his buddy in the ribs.

Boomer sputtered, "Yeah, I mean, yes sir."

Jimmy slapped them both on their backs. "Good, now let's load up in the van. I'll take you to the motel where you can wash up. Then we'll head to a place where they serve the biggest steaks in the county. Is that all right?"

"Yes, sir," they said in unison.

***

The phone buzzed sending Boomer's parents into a frenzy.

"Hello?" Edith Pauley said, breathlessly.

Ron, her husband, leaned close trying to hear the conversation. It had been over two weeks and lack of news was wearing on both of them.

"Mom, it's me again." His voice sounded stronger, more confident.

"Son, where you are?"

"Like I said, it's a fishing port on the east coast of Florida called Fernandina Beach. We're fine, but I really want to come home." His voice broke and he fought back tears.

Ron snatched the phone from his wife's hand. "Son, is Tramp with you?"

"Yes, Dad, and thanks for asking how I am." Their frayed relationship had not gotten any better since his disappearance."

***

The moment he finished the call with Boomer, Ron called the sheriff's department.

After filling Sheriff Wooten in on the details, he made one other call. It was to his law partners Bob Grayson, Ellis Grayson, and Tony Estes.

"Guys," his voice boomed through the speaker phone, "a few minutes ago I got a call from Boomer."

"Yes, we know," interrupted Tony. "Tramp called me just after Boomer called you."

Bob Grayson cleared his throat. "Did either of you guys think to call the sheriff?"

"Yes, Bob," Ron said to his father-in-law, "I just got off the phone with him moments ago. He's convinced WD is no longer in Florida, so he's amped up the Amber Alert to a national level."

"So where have Boomer and Travis been for the last two weeks?"

"A place called Fernandina Beach. There's a—"

"I know where it is," Bob cut in. "I've gone deep sea fishing out of that port. There is a small airport not too far from there. You guys want to use the corporate jet to head down?"

A unified yes echoed through the connection.

"Good, Ron, why don't you call my pilot first thing in the morning and schedule a flight to Florida?"

"Yes sir. Thanks. Tony, you with me?"

"You bet," he answered enthusiastically.

"How about you, Ellis, are you with us?"

There was a moment's pause.

"No, I'm afraid not. I've got so many irons in the fire; I can't afford to miss a day. By the way, did either of the boys say anything about Chloe?"

An uncomfortable silence filled the connection.

"I'm sorry man. We were so excited to hear Boomer's voice, we didn't even think about asking…"

"That's all right. You guys fly down there and get your boys. I'm happy for you."

***

With a pianist playing mood music in the background, Joyce, Madeline, Stephen and Ben sat at a round table trying to enjoy an evening out, but it wasn't going so well.

"If you took greater interest in your niece, perhaps—"

"Greater interest?!" Ben demanded. "Joyce, she doesn't even speak normal people's language. Maybe you should have taught her some respect—"

Joyce glared spikes at her brother.

Stephen leaned forward. "Joyce, you know Chloe is as wild as a hare. If you didn't work so much, maybe you could have kept her from ruining her life."

Hands raised, Madeline tried to calm the growing storm. "All right you two. Let's keep it down.

"Hold on, mother. I'm getting a call from Sheriff Wooten." The table fell silent as Madeline, Stephen and Ben strained to hear what the sheriff had to say.

"Yes…okay…I understand…all right…thanks."

"That was informative," Stephen snarked. "What'd he say?"

Joyce released a pent-up breath. "He said they found where Tramp and Boomer have been for the last two weeks."

"Where?" they said in unison.

She sighed. "A place called Fernandina Beach. It's in Florida."

"But what about Chloe? Did he say anything about her?" Madeline pressed, clearly irritated.

Joyce shook her head. "No, nothing. Just that they are widening the search to a national level." Clutching her stomach, she stood. "I gotta go. Mother, will you drive me home? I'm not feeling too well."

Madeline's face darkened. The news of finding the boys and not finding her granddaughter had left her feeling ill too.

"Yes, of course." She stood and helped Joyce to her feet.

After placing a one-hundred-dollar bill on the table, she eyed her sons. "Don't—"

Hands held in surrender, Stephen said, "I know, I know. Don't spend it on booze."

"Right, and you could show a little compassion for your sister. She's going through a lot."

Ben lifted his wine glass. "We'll drink to her," he laughed.

Giving him a frustrated huff, she pivoted and stomped from the restaurant.

Once they were in the car, Joyce began to root in her purse. "I need to call Ellis."

Madeline's eyes bulged. "You what?"

"Mother don't start. Ever since Chloe went missing, I…we have been meeting together for coffee. It's nothing serious. No sparks, no expectations." She lied. "But we do share a common interest."

The silence between them stretched until Madeline reached Joyce's apartment.

"Look honey, I just don't want you to get hurt again."

"Thanks Mother, but I'm a big girl. I think I can handle it," she said as she exited the car. "Good night and thanks for the encouragement." Then she slammed the door and marched straight-legged up the sidewalk.

Chapter Thirty-Five

A Flurry of Activity …

As the Ford Mustang raced for the emergency parking lot exit, the emergency room doctor, followed by three Rn's, burst through the sliding glass doors waving their arms wildly.

"Stop! Someone stop them!" the doctor yelled.

It did no good. There was no security, no police presence, no exit gate.

"Someone call the police! Either that guy just kidnapped that girl or he's her pimp and he overdosed her," the nurse hollered.

"It doesn't matter. He needs to be stopped!" The doctor said, blistering the air with vulgarity.

One of the nurses threw her hands up. "That girl is in no condition to be taken from this hospital. She might relapse into an anaphylactic shock," she spat as she speed dialed 911.

"Hello, dispatch. What type of emergency do you have?" the dispatch officer asked in an even tone.

"This is Nurse Connelly with the Wellstar Hospital in Douglasville. A man in a reddish Ford Mustang just abducted one of our patients. She's a minor and we think he is either part of a human trafficking ring or he's her pimp." Her words flew out in rapid succession.

"Please calm down ma'am. Can you give me any better description of the suspect or his victim?

The nurse took a deep breath and related as much information to the dispatcher as she could without violating any HIPPA laws. Once she'd finished, she ended the call and stomped back into the emergency room.

Within minutes, a call was placed to the headquarters of the State Patrol, who in turn called the sheriff of Richmond Hill.

"Sheriff Wooten," Captain Greenwood gloated, "I think we've just had a break in your kidnapping case."

Wooten, whose feet had been propped on the corner of his desk, suddenly shot upright. "What? When? Where?"

Chuckling, Greenwood continued, "They're in a reddish Ford Mustang; last seen leaving the parking lot of the Wellstar Hospital in Douglasville."

"Which way were they heading?"

"Beats me. All the dispatcher said was an eyewitness observed the fleeing car leaving their parking lot at a high rate of speed heading for the freeway. But the description of the man in question fits the picture we've been circulating."

"And the girl? What about her?" he demanded "Why was she in the hospital?"

Greenwood paused to look at his notes. "All the nurse could say was that she had been taken in suffering from an overdose of a highly addictive drug. She was vague, but that's about the gist of it."

Wooten's mind raced with a dozen possible scenarios. Was WD pimping the girl? Was he taking her across the state line for immoral purposes? Was she a willing participant, an accomplice or was she being taken against her will?

"Thanks Captain. I dread my next phone call."

"I don't envy you, buddy. I'll let you know if any of my patrolling officers spot them."

Wooten was about to hang up when he paused. "Hey, look. We don't know what we're dealing with here, so if your boys spot them, be very careful. This man is extremely unstable. We don't know what he might do."

Greenwood leaned into the phone. "Don't tell me how to run my department Wooten."

***

Feeling thoroughly upbraided, Sheriff Wooten replaced the phone and immediately picked it back up.

After dialing a number he had called so many times he couldn't count, he waited for the usual breathless response.

"Sheriff...any word?" was the same question Joyce always led with.

He breathed heavily into the phone. "Yes, Joyce, we do. But you're not going to like what I have to say."

He heard the phone clatter to the floor and could only guess what had happened.

A moment later, someone picked it up and said, "This is Madeline Dawson, Joyce's mother. Is everything all right?" She could have asked the question any number of ways, but this was probably all she could think to say.

"As a matter of fact Mrs. Dawson, everything is not all right." Then he went on to describe the latest news.

He ended the call with the promise to keep the family informed if there were any new developments. He just hoped the next call to the Dawson family would be that of Chloe's safe recovery and WD's arrest.

Chapter Thirty-Six

Heflin, Alabama ...

WD had only been on I-20 headed west when the sickening thought occurred to him.

Someone may have gotten a description of my car.

Taking the next exit, he ramped off on Highway 5 which took him to US 78. He turned left and entered the sleepy town of Winston, Georgia. Ahead, was a Walmart Super Center with a carwash in an adjoining parking lot. After taking the car though the car wash, he pulled around to the back of the store.

While Chloe slept in the backseat, he made a quick decision. He either needed to get a different car or one that looked different. Entering the store, he weaved his way to the isle where they sold automotive spray paint. He grabbed five cans of high gloss black enamel auto paint, a couple cans of clear coat sealant, and a couple of rolls of masking tape.

Fortunately, there was a self-checkout lane. With his hat pulled low to avoid the in-store video camera, he paid, then dashed back to his car. Glancing inside, he released a tense breath. *Good, Chloe is still asleep.*

Three hours later he stepped back and admired his work. His formerly rust colored vintage Ford Mustang was now a shiny black vintage Ford Mustang.

As he collected the empty cans, Chloe roused, lifted her head, then sagged back down. By the time WD had completed the transformation, the sun was retiring, and a field of stars had come out. Suddenly, the adrenaline rush faded, and he was overtaken with fatigue.

He slumped into the driver's seat and waited. With his stomach rumbling, he remembered he'd not eaten since the morning. It seemed decades ago since he, Chloe and Miss Winnie shared a meal, and he missed her company deeply. He needed a hot meal and a good night's sleep.

Neither seemed likely.

Getting back on US 78, he tried to keep his eyes open but the long day, the stress and the miles had worn him down. His eyelids fell and refused to reopen. As his car crept over the yellow line, the sudden blast from a truck horn jolted him upright.

"Sorry," he said as the annoyed driver zipped past him.

Chloe shifted her position and leaned forward. "What happened?" rubbing her eyes with the palms of her hands.

WD squinted at the speedometer. "I blinked out. We'd better find a motel and rest. I'm beat."

"What's that funny smell," she asked, her nose wrinkling.

"Paint. I'll tell you about it later."

She nodded, half asleep.

Twenty minutes later, Chloe pointed ahead. "Look, Heflin has several motels. Hopefully they will have a room."

"Two rooms."

"Say what?"

"Yes, I want two rooms. For one thing, I snore terribly and secondly, I don't want the authorities to stumble over us and find you in my room."

"Oh, I never thought of that. Can we at least eat together? I kinda like hanging out with you even though you're old enough to be my grandfather." A wan smile danced in her eyes.

He chuckled. "I *am* your grandfather."

"Yaas, my only grandfather," she added smiling.

Growing serious, WD said, "Actually, I need you to put on your ball cap and stay out of anyone's direct line of sight. Even though it's dark, I'm going to wear these sunglasses which I found in the hospital and the baseball hat I got from Walmart. With any luck, no one will notice us."

"Don't you think wearing shades when it's dark outside is a little bit sus?"

Rubbing the back of his neck, WD said, "Yeah, I guess you're right. I'll ditch the shades and hope for the best."

She nodded somberly. "Okay. There's a motel with a diner coming up. Let's try that one."

WD slowed and pulled into the parking lot. Seeing an unlit corner, he backed the car into it. "First, we eat, then we get a couple of rooms. As empty as the parking lot is, I'm guessing they'll be glad to rent us a couple of rooms."

After tugging the baseball cap over her now raven-colored hair, Chloe lifted the collar of her jacket. "There, maybe no one will recognize me."

WD did the same. Stepping inside the diner, they found it nearly full. "There's one," WD said, pointing to a table near the back.

"Take a seat anywhere," a waitress called out.

They did as instructed and found a seat near the back. After a beat, the harried waitress rushed up and said, "Whatcha drinkin'?"

WD bolted upright. With nearly everyone sitting around him drinking beer, it never occurred to him the danger he had exposed himself to.

"Two sweet teas, please," Chloe interjected before he had a chance to speak.

"Thanks, for a moment I—"

"That's all right, G-Diddy. I knew you were going to order soda, but I wanted some good ole fashion sweet tea." An impish twinkle danced in her eyes.

After the drinks arrived, the waitress took their order and dashed to the next customer. Twenty minutes later, the woman returned and slid two plates across the table. WD's meal was a cheeseburger and fries, Chloe's was a house salad.

"Mind if I pray?" WD asked, taking Chloe's hand.

Shock registered on her face. "Pray? Like out loud?"

He nodded. "I told you, I'm a changed man. I give God all the praise for getting us this far and I'm trusting Him to get us the rest of the way."

"Wherever that is," Chloe quipped.

"Let's pray while the food's hot, or cold in your case."

Glancing nervously from side to side, she lowered her eyes and waited.

"Lord," WD began. "Thank you for preserving Chloe's life and giving us traveling mercies. We ask You to bless the food and give us a restful night's sleep. In Jesus' name, amen."

They looked up and found the waitress standing next to them, her eyes closed and two more large glasses of iced tea in her hands. "Amen," she added. "That's so sweet. Is this granddaughter date night?"

Chloe's face pinked.

WD felt the blood drain from his face. *Great, I've drawn attention to myself.* "No, I'm just—"

Suddenly, the crash of dishes broke the moment.

"Excuse me. I think I am needed in the kitchen," the waitress said, and dashed to someone's rescue.

For the next thirty minutes, WD shared a few anecdotal stories of his days in the Navy; at least the ones he hadn't shared already. When they finished, he paid with cash and left without any other disasters.

Across the parking lot from the diner sat an aging one-story motel. Its VACANCY light blinked intermittently. When they entered the office, the night-desk clerk bolted upright.

"How can I help you?" he asked, eyeing Chloe.

The tattoos on his arms and the amulet around his neck sent a clear message; he was deeply involved with the occult.

She tugged her hat lower and kept from making eye contact.

"We need two rooms, preferably close to each other," WD said, pulling out a couple fifty-dollar bills.

The clerk's eyes shifted from Chloe to the money. "Hmm, let's see here. I've got two adjacent rooms on the far end. It'll be two hundred a night."

Chloe wrinkled her nose, "I don't like this place. The clerk gives me the creeps," she whispered.

WD leaned close. "Look, I'm beat. It'll only be for one night."

She crossed her arms and moved further from the clerk's watchful eyes. WD laid the money on the counter and fished another out of his pocket. "I don't suppose you serve breakfast."

The clerk shook his head. "Yeah right. The diner across the way will give you 15% off when you show'em your receipt."

WD nodded and took the keys from the clerk. "Thanks."

Back outside, he said, "Look, I'm really beat, and you still look a bit shaky. Why don't we lay low for a day or two until you get to feeling better."

The whites of her eyes were etched in deep concern, but she nodded. "Okay, but I got a bad feeling about that counter dude."

Looking over his shoulder, he noticed the guy peering at them through the dingy blinds. A cold chill ran the length of his back, and he quickened his pace. "You could be right, or you could still be feeling the effects of that drug. Either way, you need to get some rest."

Under the weight of her backpack, she struggled to keep pace with him. "I think that's a great idea. Wake me when you get up and I'll see if I'm hangry enough to enjoy a 15% off breakfast."

WD smiled, unlocked the door to her motel room and swung it open. Stale air assaulted his nostrils. "It smells like a smoker's room. You want to swap rooms?"

Chloe shook her head. "Nah. Who knows, yours might be worse. Good night." She took the key from him and started to close the door when he stopped her.

"I haven't said it as much as I should, but I want you to know I love you, Chloe. You're one special girl." Then he leaned down and placed a kiss on her forehead.

"Ouch!" she said with an impish smile.

WD pinched back a grin. "Wherever did you learn that?"

Finger to her chin, she rolled her eyes. "Oh, from some old codger who abducted me."

He handed the backpack to her. "Good night, sleep tight, and don't let the bedbugs bite—literally," he said as he backed away.

***

WD's room wasn't much better.

But at least it was quiet, and the water heater worked. After a long hot shower, he dressed in a pair of shorts and stretched out on the bed. Despite the urge to fall asleep, he found a Gideon's Bible in the drawer next to the bed and began to read.

After fifteen minutes, his eyes began to wander off the pages and he laid his head back. *Lord, thank you for your provision, and protection. Guide us on our journey and bless—* his mind caved in and he slumped on the pillow. Soon the room was filled with snoring.

Chapter Thirty-Seven

Chloe calls Home ...

Steam billowed from the bathroom as Chloe stepped out, towel-drying her short hair.

Wearing a soft pair of pjs she'd purchased at the Target store, she yanked the covers down and checked the sheets.

Much to her relief, there were no bedbugs.

After climbing under the covers, she tried to relax, but her mind was filled with the day's events. She couldn't believe that she and her grandfather had been on the run for over two weeks. In a way, she imagined what it must have been like to have been Bonnie and Clyde, the famous bank robbers.

Her thoughts wandered to her mother. *I wonder what must be going through her mind. Was she worried? Did she even care that her daughter was missing? Was it she who called the police? Or had she gone about her life as if her daughter never existed?*

Knowing she had deceived her mom, and her grandfather, left her feeling dirty, empty, unwanted. The dam behind her eyes broke and tears began to fall.

"I don't even know why I'm doing this, but here goes," she said through knotted vocal chords. Blinking back her tears, she picked up the burner phone and dialed home.

"Mom?" she said in an uncertain tone. "It's me, Chloe."

She barely got the words out.

"Oh Chloe. I've been so worried. Where are you? Are you safe? Did your grandfather kidnap you?"

Unprepared for the barrage of questions, Chloe pulled the phone from her ear. "Mom, mom, slow down. "I'm fine, and no, G-Diddy didn't kidnap me. We sorta," she paused searching for the right words. "We sorta took off with mutual goals."

"Mutual goals!? What's that supposed to mean?"

Just like mom…right to the point.

Frustration had replaced the initial concern in her mother's voice. "Well, the authorities have an APB out along with a warrant for your grandfather's arrest. They are charging him with arson and insurance fraud along with kidnapping you and those two boys."

That was only half true.

Where's the, 'I've missed you so much' and 'I can't wait for your return.' Chloe bit her lower lip. "Mom, it's not like that. G-Diddy is a changed man. He's not drinking, or cursing, well, except one time, but that can be explained. He even prayed over our meal, and I've never seen him pray before—"

"—Chloe look, you're in danger. And what's this about you being in the hospital?"

Chloe gaped at the phone. "You heard about that?"

"The sheriff told me all about it. He said an eyewitness saw your grandfather abduct you from the hospital and race off in some beat up old Ford Mustang. Is that true? Why were you in the hospital?"

The longing to set the record straight was palpable, but her mother's questions kept her off balance. Plus, her mind still had not completely cleared from the drugs.

"Where are you and we'll come and get you," she heard her mother asking.

"Mom, you don't understand. G-Diddy is not going to hurt me. I'm fine, really."

Joyce huffed into the phone. "Chloe, you're not listening to me. Your grandfather is not thinking straight, he's unstable. He dropped Tramp and Boomer off in some God-forsaken fish camp in the middle of a swamp to rot and die. Now he's got you and—and—" words failed her.

"Mom! It's not like that. I was there. G-Diddy didn't just throw those two knuckleheads out in the middle of nowhere. He left them in very safe hands."

"I don't care," she said, refusing to accept her daughter's explanation. Breathing deeply, Joyce's voice grew hard. "Chloe, I'm ordering you to tell me where you are."

Hesitating, Chloe considered her options. She knew what Miss Winnie would say. Speaking slowly, she began, "Mom, G-Diddy is on a mission and I'm going with him to see it through. Good night, I'll call you in the morning after you've had time to calm down."

And the phone went silent.

***

The green digital lights from the clock glowed three o'clock and Chloe stirred fitfully.

Scary dreams had invaded her sleep. Finally, she gave up and stared at the cell phone. *At least they hadn't traced the call.*

Taking a shaky breath, she dialed home.

"Hello?" her mother answered groggily.

"Mom, are you up?" The rustling of covers told her she wasn't.

"I am now."

"Mom, I've been thinking—"

"Good. It's about time you came to your senses—"

"—No mother. I'm not telling you where I am so stop asking. I want you to tell me who my father is."

Silence filled the connection. Chloe waited, and stared at the flickering light from the neon sign outside her window as it penetrated the curtains.

"Hello!? Mother, are you still there?"

Another long pause.

More flickering, more counting.

"Honey, you wouldn't understand—"

"—What's not to understand? Look Mom, I'm not a child. I'm sixteen and I have the right to know who my father is. Is he still alive? Does he live close by? What's his name?"

Her questions were answered with soft sniffling.

"Mother, are you crying?"

Seconds ticked.

"Y-yes," she said shakily.

"Why?"

"Because Chloe, I want to tell you. I've wanted to tell you for years but—"

"But what?"

"But I've been sworn to secrecy."

Chloe punched her pillow, slid off the bed and began to pace the floor. The icy tile chilled her bare feet. She flopped on the bed fighting back the tears. "That's what G-Diddy said. Why? Why can't you tell me?"

More sniffles filled the distance between them. "It's complicated."

"Make it uncomplicated."

"I can't!"

"Can't or won't?" Tears soaked Chloe's pillow. "Forget it. I'm sorry I brought it up. But I will find out even if it means traveling half-way across the country with G-Diddy."

Sobbing, she ended the call and tossed the phone across the room. Pillowing her head, she cried herself to sleep.

***

"We cannot allow this girl to learn who her father is," said the spirit of wickedness.

"Yes, that would definitely undo all our plans," muttered Legion, the spirits of fear, doubt, and confusion. "We must keep her fearful, doubting the Almighty's love, feeling unworthy…dirty," they continued. "Let us move quickly while she is still vulnerable and descend upon her with our full might."

A fearsome, lizard-like creature called Scar-Face, grinned wickedly. "And I know just where to attack her. She has exposed her mind to supernatural influences by reading a series of books involving a young boy and his magic wand. Then she started going to movies extolling the virtues of the occult. That was why she dressed in black. She had almost crossed over to the dark side before her grandfather intervened. Let us see if we can use them against her.

Chapter Thirty-Eight

Dreams and nightmares …

As sleep closed in around Chloe's mind, the residue of drugs in her system took over.

In slow motion, she saw herself running through what at first appeared to be tall grass, but then it shifted to bamboo. Miss Winnie ran behind her carrying two cane poles yelling, "Stop! Hold still so I can stick a hook through you."

Next, she was dancing wildly in Boomer's house. It was a graduation party which had gotten out of control. Boomer's parents were out of town, and he had broken into their stockpile of booze. The guy from the inner city of Atlanta stood at a console playing Rap music with its inane rhythm, and vulgarity laced lyrics. The room throbbed. Her classmates gyrated. Guys and girls moved in frenzied motion, their hands raised above her head, jumping up and down. She saw herself spinning, weaving, and bobbing as if she were a marionette. She felt totally out of control like someone or something gripped her by the wrists.

She tried to free herself but couldn't.

She tried to run, but her feet were mired in the floor.

She tried to scream, but nothing came out.

Suddenly, she found herself struggling against a pair of handcuffs. They were attached to the bedposts. Her feet were tied to the footboard. Loud music drowned out her cries. No one paid any attention. Faces came and went.

Then the scene changed abruptly.

Rather than being handcuffed to a bed, she felt movement. Florescent lights flashed overhead, as she was being wheeled on a gurney. She fought against the restraints, but the leather straps bit into her flesh. The gurney jolted to a stop inside a brightly lit room. The smell of anesthetic assaulted her nostrils.

Glancing around, she realized she was in an operating room. Only this time she wasn't high on an overdose of drugs. Her belly was swollen.

She was in labor.

Oh no! This can't be happening. I'm sixteen. I'm too young to have a baby.

Pinching her eyes closed, she tried to shut out what was happening. It was all too fast, too real.

Again, the scene changed, and she lay in a hospital bed. Two babies wrapped in blue blankets snuggled close to her chest. They turned their faces toward her, and she gasped.

Tramp—Boomer! "Oh No!

Reality struck her like a bullet-train.

Anger boiled up in her bosom, not only at what the boys had done to her, but at herself for allowing herself to be the bait. "What a fool, I've been," she heard herself muttering.

She bolted upright, drenched in sweat and panting.

"Shoo," she whispered.

Feeling dirty, she stood on wobbly legs, rushed to the bathroom and emptied her stomach. Then she turned on the shower.

It didn't help.

Worthlessness hung on her like a wet blanket. She changed into some dry night clothes and returned to bed. Sleep was out of the question.

Staring across the room, she sensed a presence.

"G-Diddy?" she whispered, staring at the swaying curtains.

Suddenly, the temperature in the room dropped. Chills covered her arms, and she yanked the covers close.

"G-Diddy, if you are playing a prank on me, it's not funny."

Eyes wide, she pulled the covers to her chin.

"G-Diddy, you're scaring me!"

A low chuckle sounded from across the room.

Burying her head, she pinched her eyes shut. Soon her heavy breathing softened, and she returned to her dream-world.

She saw herself dressed in a long white gown. Soft music played in the background and a large crowd was seated in an open field. Overhead, birds sang, and the aroma of roses wafted through the air.

It was her wedding day.

Standing behind rows of expectant guests, she waited for her bridesmaids to take their places. Finally, a young, handsome man flanked by a robed preacher and an older man with grey salt and pepper hair, took their positions.

The preacher lifted his arms and said, "All rise."

As the music swelled, heads turned, and she took her first step. Women covered their mouths with their hands; men smiled, and young girls squealed with delight.

This was the day she'd waited for, saved herself for. She was going to marry the man of her dreams; the one whom God had planned for her. Although his face was obscured, she felt she knew him. She felt a kinship, a oneness with him.

"Who is he?" her mind screamed.

He turned toward her, but there was no face, just a gaping hole. A voice echoed from the phantom's throat. *"You are unworthy."*

***

In the gray fields between the celestial and the physical, Prince Leo stood, his hands gripping the hilt of his sword.

Whispers echoed through the haze. Dark figures came and went, not taking shape or form. Had they done so, Leo would have sliced them open, but no. The evil one was too wily. He knew how to cast doubt, create fear, cause anxiety in the hearts of mortals.

"Show yourself!" Prince Leo commanded.

"Never!" came the whispered reply. "I have planted the seed of doubt in the heart of this weak-willed girl. She is mine, all mine." His wicked chuckle echoed through the gloom.

Zeroing in on the source of leathery wings, Leo swung his sword. It sliced through the fog, striking something solid.

Diablo cursed and cast a fiery dart in his direction.

Holding his silver shield up, Prince Leo felt the impact of the dart as it struck. It nearly knocked him off his feet.

"This is no small spirit," he said, gritting his teeth. "On guard!" he cried, springing to his feet.

With another swipe of his broad sword, he caught the creature behind the knees slicing its legs out from under it.

"Curses!" the demon bellowed and slung another dart, striking Prince Leo's breastplate.

"In the name of the Almighty God before whom you will one day bow, and the power of His shed blood, I command you to release that girl."

"I will not!" Diablo roared.

Breathing hard, Leo lifted his blade and brought it down hard across the monster's neck. With a shriek, the demon of fear and doubt released one last curse before collapsing into an inky puddle. Leo yanked the dart from his vesture.

After checking on his charge, he saw Chloe sleeping fitfully. He just hoped none of the poison the demon had injected had taken hold.

"Lord God, send your ministering spirits to heal this child's mind," he cried out.

In a flutter of soft wings, two angels appeared in the girl's motel room and touched her. Instantly, Chloe's body relaxed.

Two hours later, as sunlight peeked around the heavy curtains, Chloe's eyes fluttered open. It was morning and she was hungry.

Standing next to her bed, she realized someone was pounding on her door.

Chapter Thirty-Nine

Joyce calls Ellis Grayson …

Dawn could not have come soon enough for Joyce Dawson.

Thankfully, it was not a workday. After two mugs of black coffee, she felt awake enough to make the call. Since Chloe's disappearance, she and Ellis had been meeting at various times. Sometimes they would meet for lunch, sometimes for coffee, never dinner. That would be moving too fast.

"May I speak with Ellis Grayson," she said hopefully.

"Who may I say is calling," the receptionist answered in a professional tone.

"Joyce Dawson."

A moment pause filled the connection before the receptionist responded. "It's been a bit of a madhouse around here, Mrs. Dawson. What with Mr. Estes and Mr. Pauley leaving first thing this morning," she added. "Mr. Grayson is swamped, pardon the pun. He is trying to juggle the other two attorneys' cases on very short notice. Could I take your number and have him call you in—"

"—In what, about three days?" she interrupted curtly. "No, I won't give you my number. I want to speak with Ellis immediately or my next call will be to the press."

"Oh. I see. Well, let me see what I can do," she said in a less-than-professionally tone.

A minute later, Ellis's deep baritone voice filled the connection, "Hello Joyce."

She guessed his receptionist had given out her name. "Ellis, we need to talk," she said without preamble.

Papers rustled. "Of course, but this is really a bad time."

"Is there ever a good time? Look Ellis, Chloe called me last night—"

"Is she okay? Where is she?" Concern etched his voice.

Joyce gripped the phone tighter. Speaking to the father of her daughter brought back a flood of memories. She could not count the number of times she wanted to tell Chloe who her father was…is. Perhaps now would be a good time.

"I don't know. She wouldn't say, but I got the impression she was using a cheap phone so we couldn't trace it. She didn't sound scared or hurt, but I detected a hint of sorrow in her tone. Perhaps she regrets what she'd done."

"Well, she should," he snapped. "Sorry, I didn't mean that. Look, it's a madhouse here. Tony got a call from his son Boomer and he and Pauley are flying out this morning to meet them. It's somewhere down in Florida."

Joyce's heart skipped a beat. She knew what Chloe told her. Perhaps she was lying. Chloe was known to prevaricate when it suited her. "Did they say where the boys were?"

There was a pause before Ellis answered. "Tony said it was somewhere near Fernandina Beach. It's a fishing port."

"Good," she said unenthusiastically. "I'd like to see you. Can you break free around two? We can meet near your office if that's more convenient?"

Another pause.

"Yes, I think that should work. Let's make it two thirty at Mick's. It's a bistro just a couple blocks from my office." He sounded less professional, more human.

Interested? That was too much to ask, Joyce thought.

She fanned herself as heat crept up her neck. "I know where it is. I'll meet you there." She ended the call with more hope in her heart than she had had for years; sixteen years.

Chapter Forty

A 15% off Breakfast …

A light breeze stirred the cool morning air while birds greeted another day in Alabama.

Trucks heavily ladened with fresh-cut logs rumbled along the highway belching diesel fumes. A fire-engine, with its sirens blaring, rushed past the diner headed for a column of smoke.

"Good morning. Sleep well?" WD said trying to sound chipper.

He stood outside her motel room dressed and ready to go.

Chloe eyed him narrowly. "If you thought what you did last night was funny, it wasn't. You scared the living daylights out of me." She stood barefoot in her nightclothes with a blanket clutched tightly around her.

"Chloe, you look like you haven't slept a wink."

Two bleary eyes pierced him. "I haven't, thanks to you."

Hands extended, he said, "What have I done. I was in my room all night—"

"Except when you were not."

"What's that supposed to mean?"

"Admit it." Her voice turned cold. "You were in my room. You moved the curtains, you laughed in a creepy way. It was you I know it and don't appreciate it."

Taking a cautious step inside, he looked behind the curtain. The window unit hummed quietly, blowing cool air.

"I think this is your presence."

Chloe slumped into a chair and pulled her knees up. "I feel like such a nerd."

A soft chuckle escaped his lungs. "I think *nerd* comes from my generation."

"Not funny."

"Funny. Now get dressed. I'm hangry."

A few minutes later, Chloe emerged from her room dressed in holey overall jeans, a tee-shirt and sneakers appeared next to her granddad and waited for the traffic to thin.

"And you paid good money for those?" WD asked, eyeing her quizzically.

She glanced down at herself. "Nah, it was bad money," she chuckled mischievously. "I got them from Target—"

"I know, before you picked up that tainted dollar bill."

She nodded sullenly. "That's the last time I'll do that."

He smiled. "It's a hard lesson to learn. Now let's enjoy our 15% off breakfast."

Hand in hand, they crossed the highway and entered the diner.

"Take a seat anywhere. I'll be with you in a minute!" the waitress' voice sliced through the din of laughter, loud conversations.

"It will take longer than a minute," WD whispered as he guided Chloe to an empty booth near the back of the diner.

With her ball cap tugged low on her head, Chloe followed her grandfather through the crowd.

Taking a seat, she said, "I called mom last night."

WD glanced up from his menu. His face gave nothing away. "I guessed as much."

The waitress appeared next to the table with two mugs and a pitcher. "Coffee?" she asked expectantly.

Keeping his head down, WD said, "Yes, please."

"And you?" directing her question to Chloe.

Not having acquired a taste for the black brew, she said, "I'll just drink water. Perrier if you have it."

The waitress fisted her sizable hip. "Ma'am, this ain't the Waldorf. It's regular water or nothing."

Chloe gave her a frustrated sigh. "Water will be fine," not looking up.

The woman harrumphed and slid a tall, sweating glass of water across the table.

As the waitress disappeared into the crowd, Chloe glanced up just as WD took a sip from his mug.

His nose wrinkled. "It's stale," he said pouring more sugar into the mug.

"What are you having, G-Diddy?" Chloe asked as she stared at the menu.

"The usual. You?"

She shrugged, "the same."

He smiled.

She frowned.

"Tired of oatmeal and whole wheat with no butter?"

A sigh escaped her throat followed by a slight nod.

"You could try eating real food."

She pierced him with a pair of black-orbs. "Or not."

"You ready to order?" the waitress asked, interrupting their banter.

Knowing Chloe's dislike for any kind of meat, WD ordered a full breakfast for himself and oatmeal with a side order of whole wheat toast, no butter for his granddaughter.

Fifteen minutes later, the waitress arrived with their breakfast.

"Let's see, yours was the eggs, and ham with a side of corn beef hash," looking at WD. "And yours is the oatmeal with a side of wheat bread, no butter, right?" the waitress intoned.

They nodded, keeping their faces turned down. "That's right Ma'am, thank you," WD answered.

Giving them a loud huff, the woman turned and headed to the kitchen, the rubber soles of her shoes squeaking like a mouse in a trap.

***

As they returned to the motel, she asked, "G-Diddy, do you think we could spend another night here?

I just don't think I'm up to a road trip yet."

"I thought you didn't like this motel."

"I don't, but—"

"—Still feeling loopy, hmm?" he asked, sipping his morning cup of coffee from a disposable cup.

She nodded. "Something like that. You're not mad about me messing up your travel plans, are you?"

His shoulders rose and fell. "What's another day added to forty-five years? We'll get where we're going exactly when we should and not a day sooner. Plus, I'm still a bit tired from yesterday's drama. That trip to the hospital was nerve wracking. We can resume our journey tomorrow if you're up to it."

She leaned over and placed a light kiss on his cheek.

"Ouch!"

She giggled then stopped. "Hey, where's your car," scanning the parking lot.

WD fought to keep the grin off his face. "It's right over there," pointing toward the parking lot.

"There where? All I see is that black—"

"Ford Mustang?"

"No way."

"Yes way."

"What'd ya do? Sell the other one?" She eyed the vehicle with curiosity.

"Nope, it's the same car. While you were sleeping off those drugs, I stopped at a Walmart Super Center, bought paint and sprayed it all black. But don't look too close. I messed up in a few places and the paint ran."

"That's totally radical, G-Diddy. You're the bomb."

"I take it you like it."

"It's way cool. By the way, did you get our big 15% off when you paid for breakfast?"

He smiled. "Yes dear."

Chapter Forty-One

Chloe calls her G-Ma ...

The moment Chloe entered her room, she checked behind the curtain.

A tense breath escaped her lungs. *What a twit.*

Despite eating her usual vegan breakfast, her stomach complained. She ignored it and threw herself across the unmade bed. Hoping the discomfort would subside, she pulled the burner phone from her pocket and punched in her grandmother's cell phone number.

On the third ring, she heard the woman's gravelly voice. "Hello?"

"G-Ma? It's me—Chloe."

"Oh child, do you think I don't know your sweet voice? Of course it's you. And you're calling me to tell me what? That you're okay, that you want to come home?"

Her grandmother's directness always bothered her, but she let it pass without comment. "I'm fine, G-Ma. And no, I'm not calling to tell you I'm ready to come home. I told mom the same thing so don't ask. What I called to tell you is this, G-Diddy is a different man."

A moment of silence filled the line.

"Oh? How so?" She sounded guarded.

Chloe pinched her eyes closed. She longed to see her grandparents get back together; even though they had been divorced longer than she had been alive. She saw the love in her grandfather's eyes whenever he spoke of her. She knew her grandmother still loved him as evidenced by the pictures on the mantel and the twinkle in her eyes whenever his name was mentioned.

"I don't know. He says he had a come to Jesus moment, that's all."

"A come-to-Jesus moment, hmm? A lot of drunks say that."

Chloe sighed. "Yes, but this seems real. I've been with him for over two weeks, and he hasn't even tried to take a drink of alcohol or even curse. Well, he did, but it wasn't his fault. Some guy cut him off in traffic." She chuckled mischievously. "Other than that, he's really different. He even prays over our meals in Jesus' name. That's totally rad."

Another long pause filled the space between the two. Finally, Madeline spoke with a catch in her throat. "Child, I've waited for years to hear this news. You don't know how many nights I soaked my pillow with tears praying for my lost husband. This is like cool water for a thirsty soul, but my question is, how long will it last? I've seen your grandfather go through AA programs, treatment centers, and counseling sessions all to no avail. How do you know it's real?"

Chloe held her breath trying to think of something to say that would convince her G-Ma that her grandfather was truly a saved man, a changed man. After a beat, she said, "G-Ma, do you know a woman named Winnie?"

There was a long pause and Chloe regretted the question.

A weak "Yes," echoed between the two phones. "Why do you ask, child?"

The tone in her voice sent a chill down Chloe's back. "Hypothetically, if we happened to have run across her and she told me about the change Jesus made in her life, and how she saw the same change in G-Diddy, would that convince you?"

Sniffing back her tears, Madeline said, "Yes, I suppose so, hypothetically, that is."

"Well, believe me. She's right."

More sniffles.

"Look, G-Ma, I gotta go. But pray for us. Don't tell anyone, but G-Diddy and I are traveling to Oklahoma to see his father. He wants to make things right. Pray that his dad doesn't shoot him. Gotta go, bye."

She ended the call before her grandmother could ask any more questions. Feeling better, she pillowed her head, closed her eyes and fell into a deep sleep.

***

"You talk with your G-Ma earlier today?" WD asked.

It was nearly five o'clock in the afternoon and Chloe had slept through lunch. Rather than risk driving around town looking for another restaurant, they had settled on the one across the street from their motel.

"How'd you know I talked to G-Ma?" she asked, fingering her water glass.

"'Cause, you're of the more talkative species. I figured you were bustin' inside to tell your mother all about Miss Winnie and our little excursion in the swamp."

She shook her head endearingly. "Nope, I didn't say a word about Miss Winnie."

"Then what'd ya talk about?"

WD took Chloe's hand. "Let's pray. Dear Lord, thank you for Your watch care and Your provision. Bless this food and give us traveling mercies. It's in Your sweet name I pray, amen. Oh, and thank you for preserving Chloe's life. Amen."

Chloe released his grip. "That's what we talked about; your changed life. You're a different man from the G-Diddy I grew up knowing."

He smiled at her description. "That's what Jesus can do. He makes all things new." He chuckled at his rhyme.

"I'm happy for you, G-Diddy. I really am."

"But it's not for you. I take it."

She dug into her oatmeal. "I didn't say that."

"But you thought it."

"What? And you're a mind reader?"

He shrugged. "No, but I know how the human mind works. We think we know better than God when it comes to eternal matters. Remember, He's eternal, we are temporal. The Bible says, 'harden not your heart for you know not what a day may bring forth,' something like that. Just think what might have happened had I not gotten you to the hospital as quickly."

Chloe stared down at her meal. "Yeah, I guess you're right. But I'm just not ready. I had some terrible dreams last night and they left me feeling fearful, dirty."

He nodded and sent up a silent prayer.

The rest of the meal was spent in silent contemplation as each of them considered their future. He thought of roads, bridges, and towns. Her thoughts were about her mom, her grandmother—and God.

Chapter Forty-Two

On the Road again ...

A shaft of silver light peeked around the curtains, stabbing Chloe in the eyes.

Someone was pounding on her door.

Groggily, she rolled out of bed and stumbled over her backpack. An expletive escaped and she slammed her hand over her mouth.

Where did that come from? She knew the answer, Miss Winnie told her on one of their long fishing excursions. It came from a black heart. She swung the door open and blinked against the bright sunlight.

"What time is it?" she asked, fisting her eye sockets.

WD glanced into her room. "It's nearly noon. You slept through breakfast and would have missed lunch had I not started pounding on your door. How are you feeling?"

She wandered back to the bed and flopped on it. "I feel numb. How should I feel?"

WD held his position, not wanting to enter the room of an underage girl, even though she was his granddaughter. "About the way you do. Now you know how a drunk feels after a night on the town. The only difference is the heaving and the shakes."

"Thanks a lot. Now I know what not to look forward to."

WD stepped out of the way as one of the housekeeping staff pushed a cart passed him. They nodded, not speaking.

"Not if I have anything to say about it," he continued. "Now get dressed. I've got a box of vegan donuts with your name on it. We leave in fifteen minutes."

She wrinkled her nose. "Vegan donuts? I wasn't aware they made such things."

WD crossed his arms. "Neither am I, but I thought it would get your attention."

"Why the hurry?"

He stepped aside to let the same woman push past them.

"Good morning," he said with a smile.

She returned the greeting in broken English and kept going. Once the woman had entered the room next door, he said in a low tone, "As I ate my breakfast, alone I might add, the television was on and they were holding a press conference. Sheriff Wooten was saying that there is a manhunt going on for an escapee from a mental hospital. That's me, if you were wondering."

Chloe feigned shock.

"He went on to say that I am dangerous, and on the run, that I have abducted my granddaughter, that's you."

Another shocked expression.

"And I took two teen boys across the state line without their parent's permission. I am wanted for kidnapping, arson, and a host of other crimes. And here's the kicker, the law firm of Grayson, Grayson, Ellis and Pauley is offering $40,000 of matching funds for information leading to my arrest and your safe return."

Another expletive escaped Chloe's lips. "Oops! Sorry, is that all I'm worth? A lousy 40K?"

"Watch your language, young lady. They're just doing what they think is right. Anyway, it's only 20K if you split it 50-50."

"It's not fair. I called mother and told her that I went with you of my own will and volition."

"Doesn't matter. You left with an escapee from a mental hospital without her permission. In the eyes of the law, I'm guilty of kidnapping. And if Travis's and Boomer's parents press charges, and I'm arrested, you'll be visiting me in some maximum-security prison for the rest of my natural life."

"It's still not fair."

He nodded. "Life isn't fair, but God is just, and I'm trusting Him to see me through." He swung the door closed, grabbed his suitcase and trudged to the old Ford Mustang.

Chapter Forty-Three

Motivation …

Madeline rushed through her morning routine and made a beeline to her daughter's home.

Ignoring the speed limit, she weaved through the morning traffic. She was a woman on a mission. She brought her car to an abrupt halt along the curb, got out, and dashed up the steps.

After ringing the doorbell several times, she began to knock feverishly.

"Mother, what brings you to—"

Madeline rushed past her daughter. "Turn on the television," she said without explanation.

Joyce, still in her robe, flicked on the large screen television and Sheriff Wooten's weathered face appeared.

Gritting her teeth, Madeline stood next to her daughter and listened as he listed crimes against her ex-husband.

"The law offices of Grayson, Grayson, Estes and Pauley have set up a $40,000 dollar reward fund for information leading to the arrest of Mr. Dawson and the safe return of his granddaughter."

"What about the two boys?" a reporter hollered.

Hands raised to quell the barrage of questions flying at him, the sheriff leaned closer to the bank of microphones. "We received an anonymous tip and thankfully they have been reunited with their families."

"I can't believe it," Joyce said, her arms wrapped around her waist. "I told the sheriff emphatically that Chloe was not abducted, that she and her friends simply went with WD of their own will and volition."

Madeline began to pace the floor. "And from what I've heard, even the boys said they didn't hold any ill against WD. It's their money-grubbing lawyer fathers who are out for blood."

"Then why is the sheriff announcing an additional $40,000 dollars in reward money for information leading to Dad's arrest?"

Joyce stopped mid-stride. "Oh, that. It was Ellis' idea. He wanted to get the ball rolling, but now that Ron and Tony have their sons back, they want to keep the pressure on. They claim Dad kidnapped their boys and want him arrested for that and a host of other crimes. Ellis is as mad as a wet hornet for what they've done."

Joyce slumped to the couch and hugged a pillow against her chest. "Why don't we set up a GoFundMe account?"

"A what?"

"A GoFundMe account. It's like CrowdFundMe, only it's for special causes. We could call a press conference and tell them the truth; that WD is trying to reconnect with his father before he dies and to make things right with him. We could call it, Run WD Run or Help WD go Home. Kinda like *E.T. Call Home*, referring to the movie which struck a nerve across America.

It would be like the Prodigal Son story." Eyes wide with excitement, Joyce waved her arms animatedly. "We could ask the public to contribute to WD to help him reach his destination."

Madeline watched her daughter march from one end of the living room to the other. Though not one to seek the limelight, Joyce always rooted for the underdog. And in this case, WD was the underdog.

"I'll ask the doctors and nurses from the hospital to contribute. And if this thing goes viral, who knows how much money we could raise. Maybe even enough to hire an expensive attorney to defend him against all those spurious charges."

Madeline smiled at the thought. She liked the way Joyce thought. If anything, this ordeal had brought this family together; at least her and her daughter. Her two sons were another thing.

For the next two hours, the two women strategized, organized, and mobilized. With the hospital's backing, Joyce had scheduled an impromptu press conference complete with a bank of her fellow nurses and doctors. She then started the process of setting up a GoFundMe account.

"Mother, how soon can you get an appointment with your hairdresser?"

"Already arranged," Madeline said with a grin. "I've had to pull a few strings, but we've got an appointment for a complete make over at eleven o'clock, so grab your things.

"Good, that gives us just enough time."

"Time for what?" Madeline asked as they hurried to her car.

"For the press conference. I've got one scheduled for 2:30 on the steps of the hospital."

***

District Attorney Richard Waterman's daughter, Aimee was no stranger to controversy.

A social activist, twenty-two-year-old Aimee Waterman had already gained a huge following. Her Blog posts, Twitter, Instagram and Tik Tok accounts numbered in the tens of thousands. When she heard what Grayson, Grayson, Pauley and Estes were doing, she knew she found a cause she could sink her teeth into.

Standing in the back of a crowd of ravenous reporters, she watched Joyce Dawson state her case. It was exactly 2:30 p.m. and the sun bore down upon the hastily called press conference with a vengeance. In spite of the heat, the two women standing on the steps of the hospital appeared as cool as a dog's nose.

Flanked by a team of doctors and nurses, Joyce spoke in a commanding voice. "My father, WD, is not the monster the press and media made him out to be. He is a good man. He fearlessly served his country during the Vietnam conflict and was wounded in action. Suffering from his injuries, the corrupt and bloated Veteran's Administration pumped him full of pills.

After the drugs stopped working, he fell between the cracks suffering from drug and alcohol abuse. Years later, he got his life cleaned up and started a successful business. Most of you know WD's Parts Supplies. That company was started by my father. It was burned to the ground, to no fault of his own. But the lazy police department and fire investigators are trying to pin that on him."

She stared into the eye of the camera unblinkingly. "And as you all know, my father and my daughter, Chloe and her two friends took a trip to Florida as a reward for completing another year of high school. Nothing nefarious, just kids having a little fun under Chloe's grandfather's watchful eyes. Yes, it was poorly thought out, and yes, they took off without getting written permission from any of their parents. But how many of you when you were a teen did the same thing, and worse? You know how the saying goes; 'It's easier to get forgiveness than permission.' So today, I am announcing the launch of a GoFundMe account called 'Go WD Go!'"

Suddenly, a bevy of hands shot up.

"Mrs. Dawson, isn't your ex-husband still an alcoholic?" one reporter demanded.

Another voice in the crowd yelled, "Did the Pauley's and Estes' give him permission to take Boomer and Tramp across a state-line?"

Obviously, someone wasn't listening.

"I heard he was going to Oklahoma! Can you corroborate that?" Someone else called out.

Aimee Waterman stood in the back of the crowd, her arms crossed, a smug smile tugging the corners of her mouth.

Heads snapped around. Microphones were suddenly trained on her.

"Aimee, where did you get that information?" one reporter demanded, clearly annoyed he'd been scooped.

She ignored the questions and focused on Joyce. "Your answer, Mrs. Dawson?"

The crowd parted as Joyce and her mother stepped from the podium. "You look younger than I expected," she said when she came within a foot of the younger woman.

Aimee, not missing a beat said, "You're prettier than I thought. Can we meet in private?"

Joyce stepped back and her gave a once over. "My car or yours?"

"I walk or take public transit," she said pertly. "And I'm a vegan, so let's make it a non-red-meat restaurant."

A smile parted Joyce's lips. "Okay, I know just the place. Chloe eats there all the time."

The three ladies made an abrupt about face and walked from the crowd leaving them standing with their mouths hanging open.

***

After placing their orders of crispy cauliflower with warm chickpea salad and pickled pepper tahini drizzle, the three women settled into a private booth in the back of the restaurant.

"So, tell me, where did you find out where WD is headed?"

Aimee shifted slightly in her seat. "I have my sources, which I am not at liberty to disclose."

For that, Madeline was glad. Though not tech savvy, she did know how to text.

Joyce took a sip of her lemon water and set the glass down. "Okay. Can you at least tell me this? Can you garner enough support for my father to sway public opinion?"

Aimee's eyes brightened. "Oh, absolutely—totally."

Setting her elbows on the table, Joyce smiled. "Okay, let me tell you a story—"

Chapter Forty-Four

Go Big or Go Home …

Taking US 78 west, WD saw towns like Oxford, Lincoln, Pell City and Lees come and go taking little interest in them.

Within sixty-five minutes, they were entering the outer limits of Birmingham, Alabama. After stopping for gas, and a restroom break, they pressed on. Highway 78, though slower, proved to be less traveled, and he saw only a few local police cars.

Fortunately, the authorities were looking for a rust-colored Ford Mustang, not a shiny black one. By six-thirty they had crossed the Alabama-Tennessee state line and were entering the late afternoon traffic of Memphis, Tennessee.

Chloe had been quiet throughout most of the three-and-a-half-hour trip; only commenting on the change of scenery. Other than that, she'd kept to herself. For that, WD was grateful. He had run through several scenarios as to how he'd approach his father. But no matter how he played it out, he knew it would be ugly. The last time they spoke, they each said some terrible things. His Father's voice still echoed in his ears.

Why God? Why did you lead me on this, this crazy idea?

It was not the first time he questioned God. Ever since Miss Winnie talked him into making things right with his father, he knew this was God's will. But as he fleshed it out, he found it increasingly more difficult to do.

"Are you getting hungry?" Chloe asked.

Sitting upright, he blinked. "Why? Are you?"

She stretched. "No, but I do need to use the restroom," she said, giving him a deep yawn. Checking her breath, she wrinkled her nose.

WD considered it for a minute. "Come to think of it. I could use a break too."

"There's a Welcome Center coming up in a few miles. Let's go there."

She nodded and pinched her knees tighter together.

"Hurry."

He sped up and quickly exited the highway. As he pulled into an empty slot, he said, "Be sure to pull your hat down and don't look at anyone in the eyes."

Then he placed a ball cap on his head. After adjusting a pair of sunglasses, he popped the door open and got out. Standing next to the car, he stretched.

"I'm glad we stopped. I didn't realize how cramped that thing is until I got out." Glancing around, he noticed Chloe was already halfway to the front doors of the Welcome Center.

Following her lead, he paced the distance and entered the center without garnering any interest. The refrigerated air prickled his skin sending shiver-flesh up his arms. He rubbed them away and headed to the men's room. A few minutes later he returned to the center. One wall was lined with literature and maps of Tennessee's state parks. On another wall was a large-screen television.

As WD watched the scene unfold, Chloe came up alongside him. "What's going on?" she asked in a low tone.

He glanced around to see if anyone was looking at them. Scores of moms and dads guided anxious children to the restrooms ignoring the older man and teen girl.

"It's the nightly news and they're replaying a press conference from earlier in the day. The reward has risen to 45K."

As they turned to walk away, the images on the screen changed and the face of a young lady appeared.

"Hey, I know that girl!" Chloe exclaimed.

WD paused and glanced over his shoulder. Chloe had stepped closer to the television, listening intently.

"This is Aimee Waterman. Hi guys," she said in a playful tone and waved to the invisible host of followers. "Aimee-you-can't-tame-me, here with another story of abusive parents verses independent children. In this case, it's about a Navy Veteran trying to go home." A picture of WD flashed across the screen. It was a much younger version of WD in full Navy uniform.

"That's Woodrow Dawson, better known as WD. He's trying to return home after years of rejection by his abusive father."

In the background a mummer of "Go WD Go," began to swell. Hastily drawn posters with the words *Go WD Go* appeared. "I know what you're thinking because I was skeptical too, but then I met his daughter, Joyce Dawson."

All at once, Joyce stepped forward. Her makeover made her look twenty years younger. To her left, Madeline Dawson stood looking much younger as well.

Among the group gathered behind Aimee was a rather handsome man wearing a flashy red tie and three-piece suit. His jet-black hair glistened in the sun, and he appeared to have spent many hours playing golf or tennis.

Despite the sobriety of the occasion, the man wore a Pepsodent smile, and Chloe wondered if he was some politician trying to get in on the show.

"Hey look!" Chloe said enthusiastically pointing at the television. "It's mom and G-Ma."

Heads turned as passersby slowed to catch a glimpse of the action on the TV.

WD grabbed Chloe and tugged her back. "Be quiet, you're drawing attention to yourself."

"But—"

"Hush! Let's go," he said, tugging her arm.

Chloe's feet remained fastened to the hardwood floor.

Aimee's voice had hypnotized her. "We are here because an injustice has been done to Mr. Woodrow Dawson, better known as WD."

Between noisy children and loud parents, some of what the young lady said was obscured.

"As a result, he fell between the cracks in the bloated system and got hooked on drugs and alcohol," the young woman was saying.

WD lowered his head and tried not to be conspicuous. "Let's go, the crowd is gathering. Someone might recognize us."

"Wait, I want to hear what she has to say," Chloe said, her hands jammed in her pockets, her legs slightly apart. She was not leaving until she heard the truth.

Aimee continued, "The government should have placed this man on disability and given government assistance, but no! He has been framed for arson, kidnapping, and unjustly held in a mental hospital."

It was only partially true, but the crowd of activists wasn't interested in the gory details of his life. All they wanted was another cause to rant and rave.

Joyce Dawson stepped to the microphone, cleared her throat, and spoke in a level tone. "Today, we are setting up a

GoFundMe account and are asking you to contribute to help WD get home to his father."

Cheers rose from the enthusiastic crowd.

All at once, a number appeared at the bottom of the screen with the GoFundMe account flashing the running total. As they watched, the amount began to grow exponentially.

"That's awe-some," Chloe cried.

Feeling watchful eyes, WD gently, but firmly took her by the hand. "Let's go," he said with urgency.

This time, her feet began to move, and they pushed through the front door.

"Hurry, I think someone saw us," WD said over his shoulder.

Chapter Forty-Five

The law offices of Grayson, Grayson, Estes, and Pauley..

The conference room reverberated with Bob Grayson's booming voice.

"How dare you betray us!"

Ellis, not intimidated by his father's bravado, stood his ground. "Betrayed? You think going around behind my back is not a betrayal? It certainly is. Remember, Chloe is my daughter. It was your idea not to let me do the right thing and marry her mother—"

"You were young and stupid—"

"And you stepped in to save me from my stupidity. Right?" Sarcasm dripped from every word. "You pulled me out of public school and sent me to a fancy private school because you were embarrassed. Then you paid off the Dawson family in exchange for their silence."

"It was for your own good—"

"It was for your good, Dad, your reputation and the family name!" His voice shook with emotion. "And now that it might come out, you convinced Tony and Ron to help you."

"Hey wait a minute!" Ron Pauley protested. "WD took Boomer and Travis without our permission, if you will recall."

"Yes, but those boys are not interested in bringing charges."

"Ellis, you know as well as me, they don't have any say in the matter. We, their parents, do and we want him charged to the fullest extent of the law."

Tony Estes nodded in agreement. "You know he's right Ellis. We didn't betray you. It was your idea to set up a reward fund in the first place."

Arms extended, he lifted an envelope from his side of the mahogany conference table and shoved it across its smooth surface. "Dad, fellas, it's been a pleasure, but I think it's time for us to part company—"

"Son—"

Ellis waved off his father's protests. "Don't try to stop me, Dad. You have interfered, and intervened in my life ever since I was a child. It ends here…now! Today, I am resigning from the firm and will start my own practice."

"No!" Tony, his long-time friend, and brother-in-law shouted. "You can't leave us. Not now, not in the midst of all this." He waved his hands at the large screen television on the wall displaying the rally.

"That's where you're wrong, old buddy. This is my fight, my chance to correct a wrong which I should have sixteen years ago. And possibly help another struggling fool correct a wrong in his life. This is my chance at redemption and I'm going to take it." Fire burned in his eyes.

"Son, if you do this—"

"What…you'll cut me out of the Will? There you go again, trying to control my life. I've been thinking about opening up my own practice for years. But rather than encouraging me, you offered me a junior partnership even though Ron has more seniority. Is that fair? I submit to you, that's a betrayal. It's a stab in the back!"

All at once, the room burst into loud voices as both Tony Estes and Ron Pauley launched into the fray. While the three attorneys argued, Ellis quietly slipped from the room, collected his belongings and left the law offices of Grayson, Grayson, Estes and Pauley.

Within minutes, the GoFundMe account grew by another ten-thousand dollars.

***

"I want to thank you for opening my eyes," Ellis began as he pulled the chair back for Joyce to take a seat.

The clock on the wall of the bistro read seven o'clock and the restaurant buzzed with activity. The flat screen television screamed for attention as the news station replayed the rally.

"It's weird seeing myself on TV," Joyce said as she ducked her head to avoid inquisitive eyes. The press conference turned rally had gone on for over an hour with Aimee's supporters chanting 'Go WD Go.'

"I had no idea my little speech would cause such a stir," she said amidst stares and finger pointing.

"You want to leave and find a less conspicuous place?"

Joyce shook her head allowing a few strands of frosted hair to fall across her eyes. She brushed them behind her ear, revealing a small diamond earring. She caught him staring. "Don't stare, you're making me nervous."

He smiled. "You were never one to seek the limelight."

She took a sip of her water. "No, that was you…always the big man on campus, stealing girl's hearts and—"

He touched her arm. "Joyce don't go there. What's in the past, stays in the past. We've got to think about Chloe and what's good for her—for us." Without giving her a chance to respond, he continued. "I resigned from the law firm."

Joyce nearly spilled her water. Gasping for air, she said, "You what?"

"I quit, kaput, done. I'm tired of my father manipulating me. You know back then, it was dad who forced me to leave the public school. I wanted to do the right thing, but—"

As eloquent a speaker as he was, the muscles around his throat cramped and words failed him. He took a halting breath; his eyes bore the sorrow he felt. His heart screamed for mercy, though he knew he didn't deserve it.

Joyce reached out and clutched his forearm. "I thought we weren't going to talk about the past."

He forced down the lump in his throat. "That's right," he croaked out.

Smiling through her tears, Joyce continued, "Then let's."

"Let's what?"

"Let's talk about the future—our future. Is there one for us?"

Eyes glistening, he nodded. "Yes, I certainly hope so."

"You know it will take some doing to convince mother that you're on the level."

He nodded. "I'm pretty good at swaying an antagonistic jury. I think I can convince your mother."

"And then there is Chloe. She's been asking questions."

He waited a moment for the waiter to place their meals in front of them before continuing. "Such as?"

"Such as who is her father? She may very well hate you."

He rubbed the back of his neck, a nervous habit he had never quite learned to disguise. "I'm a big boy—and a lovable one. I'm willing to give it a try if she is."

That brought a smile to Joyce's face. "Me too."

Chapter Forty-Six

Friday Night All-You-Can-Eat Catfish …

Little by way of scenery had changed in the nearly four hours since they sped from the Welcome Center.

Pride welled in WD's heart over the way his refurbished Mustang performed. Laying rubber and fishtailing from that parking lot reminded him of his wilder days. *Ah, those carefree days in the rodeo,* he mused.

With the air whipping through his thinning hair, he let his mind wander. Why had he run away in the first place? It wasn't like his father had asked him to do some monumental task. Putting up a fence was nothing compared with some of the things he'd had to do in the Navy, or even in recent years. Guilt stabbed his heart. *What a fool I've been. All those wasted years.* His heart ached. He'd missed his mother's funeral. He'd missed seeing his younger brother graduate from both high school and college. He'd left the ranch to in the hands of an aging father and a brother who had no interest in ranching.

What was I thinking?

After another hour WD's frustration abated and he finally spoke. "I wish your mother and G-Ma would stop meddling in my affairs. All I want to do is to finish the task dad had given me and be done with it. If he doesn't shoot me, my mission will be a success."

Chloe uncrossed her arms. The wind swirling in from her open window had whipped her short hair in a frenzy making her look like a wild woman. "G-Diddy, they're just trying to help."

"I don't need their help. I just want to be left alone and finish what I started."

"But you're not alone. You've got me to think about."

"You volunteered to make this trip."

"G-Diddy, you need me."

"Need you? You're just slowing me down," he shot back. He didn't mean half of what he said. But he said it anyway.

"G-Diddy, I've never met my great-grandfather. Heck, I don't even know who my real father is. You're the closest thing to a father and now you want to disown me." Her words cut his heart like a knife.

Biting his lip, he kept his eyes averted. If he looked into his granddaughter's eyes, he knew he would certainly break his vow and tell her who her father is. Perhaps he would do it anyway.

He released a tired breath. "Look Chloe. I'm sorry for speaking so harshly. I shouldn't have. Will you forgive me?"

He took a hopeful glance and saw the fire in her eyes had cooled.

"Yeah, sure." She didn't sound too forgiving, but he didn't push his luck.

"Look, it's been over four hours since we left Birmingham and I'm getting hungry. Plus, I need a break." Glancing at the fuel gauge, he said, "This car is sitting on empty."

Chloe pulled herself up to a sitting position. "Yeah, me too. What are you hungry for?"

WD considered the question. "I could use a good steak and baked potato."

Her nose wrinkled. "I could use a good catfish like the ones me and Miss Winnie used to make."

A dreamy smile played on his lips. "Come to think of it, that sounds real good. Let's keep an eye out for a catfish place."

A few miles later signs pointing to Uncle Buck's Fish Bowl and Grill began to appear.

"Good, it's on I-40," he said as he sped along the highway. Entering Memphis, he left I-22, and took US-78 into the heart of the city where several major thoroughfares converged.

"Lord, help me not to get lost," he whispered.

Gripping the wheel tighter, he leaned forward squinting.

"There," Chloe pointed. "Take I-69 and stay on it until you see the WB signs to I-40. Whatever WB stands for."

"WB stands for west bound."

He took his eyes off the road long enough to see Chloe with the phone clutched in her fingers.

"What?" she asked, her face a wash of innocence.

"What are you doing?"

"It's Google Maps, G-Diddy. It's how we navigate now-a-days. Quick, get into the far-right lane," she said with urgency.

He gripped the wheel, flipped on the right turn signal and made several quick lane changes.

"Now get off the road…highway…whatever."

He followed her directions and saw a sign which read, Uncle Buck's Fish Bowl and Grill.

"There it is. I just hope it's worth all this finger-pokin' and navigatin'," he said as they pulled into parking lot.

Chloe smiled. "Ask not, want not."

"I think the saying goes, ask and ye shall receive," he added with a crooked smile.

"It's the same thing. Anyways, if it's half as good as Miss Winnie's I'll be happy as a clam." Her smile had returned which made WD feel much better.

By the time they finished eating, both WD's and Chloe's bellies bulged.

"If I eat another bite, I think my stomach will burst," Chloe said, rubbing her pooching tummy.

WD smiled. "That had to be the best catfish I'd ever eaten, not counting Miss Winnie's of course."

She nodded. "It ran a close second. Those hush puppies were to die for."

"And that banana pudding. Now that was a winner. I don't think I can drive with all those fish swimming around inside me. How 'bout we find a motel and sleep off our catch."

Chloe nodded and wobbled to the car. "I'm all for that."

After retracing their tracks, they got back on I-40 going west until the highway split.

"Follow the WB lanes to I-40," Chloe said, pointing at her cell phone.

Forty-five minutes later, signs appeared indicating there were several motels near Forrest City, Arkansas.

"I'm beat. Let's take the first hotel and see if they have some rooms," WD said giving an ample yawn.

Chloe squinted. By now, the sun rode low on the horizon sending narrow shafts of orange light between the trees and the buildings. "Do you think stopping here is a good idea? You being a Most Wanted fugitive and all."

He counted the seconds before answering. "We can't sleep along the road or in a rest area. And as far as we have to go, it's better to get a good night's sleep in a clean bed."

Giving him a shrug, she began to gather her belongings. "Well, it could mean spending the night in some local jail on not-so-clean sheets. But it's up to you."

He grimaced at the thought. After parking in a secluded spot near the back of the hotel, he pulled his hat down and entered the lobby. Its refrigerated air was a welcome relief to the sultry air through which they'd been riding.

"Two rooms, please," he said, keeping his head down.

The concierge, a young female with bright blue eyes, handed him a clipboard. "Fill this out please while I check room occupancy."

Not wanting to give too much information, WD sloppily jotted his name and license plate in the required blanks, then handed it back.

"Can I pay with cash?" he said hopefully as he was unprepared to use a credit card.

The young millennial's eyes widened. "You mean Cash-App?"

Chloe, who had been standing at the greeting card kiosk, stepped closer.

"No, he means cash. You know; real money?"

For a moment, the young lady considered the idea of someone using paper money to pay for something.

"I-I guess. Let me check with my manager," she said and hurried off.

WD waited nervously until the millennial returned with a smile. "My manager said yes. It'll be three hundred dollars for the two rooms per night.

At first, WD wanted to protest, but decided not to make a scene. "All right." Taking out three crisp one-hundred-dollar bills, he placed them on the counter.

Before he could ask for the keys, the young lady snatched up the bills and ran a pen-like device over the money.

"Why'd ya do that?" WD asked.

Smiling, the concierge said, "I was just checking to make sure these were not counterfeit."

"I certainly hope they aren't," Chloe blurted without thinking.

The girl smiled. "Don't worry, they aren't. Here's your keys. Breakfast starts at 6:30."

After taking the keys, WD and Chloe trudged down the corridor in search of their doors.

"Too bad I didn't bring a bathing suit," Chloe said as they walked past the indoor swimming pool.

WD paused long enough to see several young men stretched out on beach chairs. *I'm glad you didn't,* he thought. "I'll call you in the morning," he said. "Are you going to call your mother or G-Ma?"

A beat passed. "You read my mind. What should I tell them?"

WD thought for a moment. "Tell them what I said. We don't need any GoFundMe money. I've got plenty. We just want to be left alone. That's all."

Chloe eyed him a minute. "You sure that's all? Nothing like, 'Thanks honey, I love you?'"

WD scuffed the concrete sidewalk. "Well, you can add whatever embellishments that suit you."

"You mean to say, you don't still love G-Ma?"

He jammed his hands in his pockets and studied his shoes. "Yeah, I guess I still do."

"You guess?"

Shifting nervously, WD nodded. "Yeah, I really do, but,"

"No buts. I'm going to make it my mission to see to it that you and G-Ma get back together."

"After all these years? Forget it. It's too late for me…us."

She pierced him with two black orbs. "You just said, 'Ask and ye shall receive.' Well, I'm asking."

"I think you've got it all wrong. That verse means to ask God, not ask me."

Chloe waved her key over the lock and opened the door. "Well, all the same. I'm going to do my best to get you two back together and that's final." Then she stepped inside her motel room and closed the door.

Chapter Forty-Seven

Rain, Rain, Go Away …

Sometime in the small hours of the night, a storm rolled across the region, bringing with it strong winds and torrential rain.

In the midst of the swirling clouds, Prince Leo and his cohorts battled the forces of evil. With each flash of lightning, mighty swords clashed. At each rumble of thunder, the dark enemy slammed against the shields of light. The effect of the invisible conflict brought violent weather as the spirits of fear and doubt made an assault on Chloe's mind.

"I surmise we have overlooked something," Prince Leo said to his commander, Prince Uriel. "Without the Spirit of God indwelling her, Chloe is vulnerable to the evil one's attack."

"Prince Haniel, guide WD to inspect Chloe's belongings. There could be some evil device hidden in her stuff."

He saluted crisply and descended through the ethereal curtain.

***

Unaware of the spiritual conflict which raged in the skies above them, WD and Chloe rested peacefully in their separate rooms.

The first indication that there was any trouble happened when the lights in the motel room flickered then blinked out. A rumble of thunder rolled overhead and the clock on the stand next to WD's bed flashed zero.

He checked his watch. *Two-thirty-five a.m.*

"Great," he muttered. "That probably means the restaurant's power is out too."

All at once, lightning flashed across the inky sky followed by another deep throated roll of thunder. Then the rain came. Within a matter of minutes, the parking lot was a river of muddy water. Getting to the car was out of the question. Any attempt to leave would be foolhardy.

The storm roamed across the heavens for the next five hours, filling streams, flooding the low-lying areas, and pooling on the streets. Staying close to the building, WD inched along the sidewalk until he reached Chloe's room. With the power out, every room looked dark, ominous. After knocking on the door and waiting longer than he wanted to, the door cracked open.

"G-Diddy?" She sounded scared.

"Who else would be knocking on your door in this weather?"

She narrowed her eyes and stared at the wall of water cascading down from the floor above them.

Pulling himself closer to the door, he said, "Do you mind opening the door? I'm getting soaked out here."

"Sure, hold on, let me throw the chain."

He eased back enough for her to do so and in an instant, nearly fell into her room. "Sorry, but I had icy water running down my back."

"I'm the one who should be sorry. What a klutz. Let me get some towels so you can dry off."

Gathering a sheet around her slender body, she dashed to the bathroom and returned with a stack of motel towels.

"Thanks," and he began to towel dry his hair. "Have you noticed the power is out?" he asked, peering into the mirror and combing his hair.

Without thinking, she flipped the light switch.

Nothing.

"Told ya."

"How long's it been out?"

WD glanced at his watch. "About six hours. It happened around two-thirty. If the power doesn't come on soon, I doubt the restaurant across the street will be serving breakfast."

She slumped on the bed. "Great. I'm getting kinda tired of pop tarts. I was hoping for something a bit more nutritious."

WD peered out the open door at the sheets of rain cascading from the low hanging clouds. "The parking lot is a river of mud too. How 'bout we wait and see if the weather clears before checking out. I'd hate to drive in this mess."

"Sounds like a plan. I dread the thought of dashing across the parking lot to the car anyways. My sneakers would get soaked. By the way, why did you park so far away?"

He glanced in the direction of the Mustang. It was barely visible. "I didn't want anyone to see it."

She shuddered. "I think it's safe to say no one will." As she headed for the small bathroom, she stopped long enough to grab a few essentials before entering. "I hope the hot water heater still works," she said as she closed the door.

A moment later, WD heard, "Uh oh, I can't see a thing," her voice sounded muffled. Cracking the door open, she said, "there, that's a little better." She giggled nervously.

With steam boiling between the cracked door and the frame, WD heard his granddaughter humming an unfamiliar tune.

"At least she's got a happy heart," he told himself.

Rather than risk getting soaked again, he took a seat and watched the rain coming down. It had a hypnotic effect and soon he caught himself nodding off.

Suddenly, the ground shook as thunder rippled across the heavens. He jolted upright and realized he had been asleep for nearly thirty minutes. Trying the light switch and getting the same nothingness, he hollered. "I'm going back to my room."

"Okay," came her reply.

"By the way, what did your mother and G-Ma say when you told them what I said?"

Her muffled voice echoed through the partially closed door. "They said they are sticking with the plan, your opinion notwithstanding."

"And that I still love your grandmother? What did she say to that?"

Her voice took on a romantic tone. "She said if you're willing to make things right with your dad, then she is willing to let bygones be bygones."

"What's that supposed to mean? Does G-Ma still love me?"

Chloe stuck her head out the bathroom door, her short-black hair stood on end, her eyes glowed with an impish twinkle. "Oh Yaas, totally."

WD felt his face warm. "I guess I've got a lot of plannin' to do."

Wrapped in a towel, she stepped from the steaming bathroom and kissed his weathered cheek.

"Ouch," he said, touching the wet spot on his cheek.

She patted his shoulder. "Oh G-Diddy, you're so cool."

As he prepared to leave, he noticed Chloe's backpack had fallen over. Picking it up, a small figurine tumbled to the carpet. It was no larger than a piece from a chessboard but was far different. It had small, emaciated wings, an evil hooked nose and two beady eyes. Its clawed fingers held a trident spear.

"Hmm, I wonder why Chloe would have this in her possession," he said to himself.

Eying the figurine in his fingers, she asked. "Where did ya get that?" her hand extended.

He placed it in her palm. "It fell out of your backpack. I thought it was yours."

Her shoulders rose and fell as she inspected it. "Nope, never seen it before."

"What is it?" WD asked retaking it.

"It's an amulet. It is used in satanic worship."

"Well, what would you be doing with an amulet?"

Her nose wrinkled. "That's just it. I wouldn't. Someone must have put it in my backpack," her face turned the color of chalk.

All at once, WD sat upright. "I remember the guy at the motel in Heflin had something like this hanging around his neck. I'd bet he slipped into your room and put it there."

Clutching her midsection, Chloe slumped into a chair. "I think I'm going to be sick."

He fisted the figurine. "I'm going to burn this before it causes us any more trouble." Taking long strides, he stomped to his room. Once he was inside, he made sure the fire alarm would not go off, then he built a small fire in the trashcan. As he laid the ugly amulet in the fire, faint screams of someone or something echoed in the distance. Glancing through the curtains and seeing nothing but torrential rain, he took a seat on the bed and watched the figurine wither in the fire and wondered.

Chapter Forty-Eight

Time to Go …

Sitting in a motel room for a second morning was not WD's idea of a road trip.

Between him and Chloe, they had ordered enough pizza and Uber-eats that the drivers were getting suspicious. Finally, he made a decision. Picking up the phone, he called Chloe's room.

Silence.

No power.

Worried that something untoward had happened to his granddaughter, he yanked the door open. Chloe stood, dressed modestly, her backpack sitting next to her feet.

"Chloe, I was just calling your room."

She slinked into his room and dropped into one of the chairs. "I'm bored. Can we leave?"

"Yeah, sure." Checking his watch, he said, "I've got an idea. It's Sunday, let's go to church and then hit the road."

Her forehead wrinkled. "Church? Like, organized religion?"

He smiled. "Well, I don't know how organized the churches in Arkansas are, but yes, let's go to church. Then we can continue on our way."

She huffed and lifted her backpack. "What if one of the old ladies of the church recognizes us, what then?"

WD considered her question for a moment. "You make a good point. I guess we'll just have to trust God on that one. Maybe there will be two empty seats on the back row. We can sit in the back and leave when the invitation starts."

Eyes rounding, she asked, "What's an invitation?"

He guided her to the Mustang and tossed their belongings into the small rear compartment. "You mean your mother hasn't ever taken you to church?"

She shook her head. "Only on Christmas and Easter."

WD felt the corners of his mouth turn down. "I'm sure sorry about that. I feel like such a failure. My getting a divorce from your grandmother screwed up my whole family." His shoulders slumped and he leaned heavily on the trunk of the car.

Laying her hand on his back, she said, "It's okay, G-Diddy. Things are going to work out, you'll see. It's like one of those movies where the hero is battered and broken and covered in blood having been beaten down by an ancient foe. But he rises from the ashes one last time and keeps fighting on. Or like the long-distance runner who trips and falls. And then out of the mist, his competitor comes alongside him and puts his arms around him and lifts him up and together they stumble across the finish line.

That's us, G-Diddy. You've been beaten down by alcohol, by the world and the devil. You've stumbled and fallen, but you got up and kept going. And I'm like that guy who has come out of nowhere to help you finish your race. So, you see G-Diddy, it's okay. You're gonna make it, we're gonna make it."

He took a cleansing breath. "You really believe that?"

She nodded. "Hey, if God can change a drunk to a sober man, then He can restore your family."

"Thanks, Honey. I am so glad you decided to make this journey with me. I don't think I could have gotten this far without you." He climbed in behind the steering wheel, stuck the key into the ignition, and waited for her to get in.

Once she was seated, she reached over and touched his arm. "Let's go to church."

Smiling, he put the car in gear and guided it to the highway. As Chloe hummed, he silently prayed and thanked God for what He was doing in his and Chloe's hearts.

*****

As they sped along the highway, Chloe reached out and turned on the radio. At first, there was nothing but static. But as she adjusted the knobs, various stations bled in and out.

"I'm not sure we'll get much out here," WD said, glancing at the dial. "Plus, all I can get is AM. The antenna is broken so I can't get any FM channels."

She gawked at him. "What? No FM.? No Sirius XM?"

He shook his head. "Nope. Remember, this is a 1968 model car. They hadn't thought of all those fancy features. This is just a basic car. Basic meaning stripped down, that is," chuckling.

She flicked the radio off and tried her phone. "Uh," she groaned. "It isn't designed to receive radio signals. This trip is turning out to be way boring." Folding her arms over her chest, she pressed herself into the seat as far as she could.

WD smiled. "It's not that bad, Chloe. You never know what might happen to spice up the trip. Relax and enjoy the scenery."

"I've a better idea. Tell me about your days in the rodeo," her eyes danced with excitement.

It had been many years since he'd thought about those wild days. Some were good, many were unremarkable, but one stood out. Taking a long breath, he plunged ahead. "I did a lot of barrel racing. The rider and his or her horse must act as one as they race around two fifty-five-gallon barrel drums."

"How'd you do, G-Diddy?"

He shrugged. "Sometimes I'd win and sometimes I'd lose. It all depended on how well the two of us cooperated. I was pretty good."

"What other competitions did you do?"

He let a few beats pass. "I tried my hand at bull riding, but got my butt kicked…literally, and bronco bustin.' I was pretty good at that. I actually won a few trophies."

"Fur rel?" Chloe exulted.

"Fur rel."

***

The sun had just broken free from its cloudy prison when WD pulled into the parking lot of a stately white columned church sitting in the center of town.

They had driven as far as Conway, Arkansas and WD's watch read ten-forty-five. Suddenly, the music began to play from the church's belfry which served as a last-minute call for the faithful to gather in.

"Let's hurry, it's about to start," WD said as he and Chloe got out of the car and hastily walked across the parking lot.

Taking her by the hand, he guided her up the brick steps to the front door where a friendly greeter stood.

"Welcome friends. You're just in time. Services are about to begin," he said, handing them a bulletin. "We're glad to have you. Is this your daughter?" he asked, eyeing her with passing interest. "We have a youth service going one in the Family-Life Center, if you prefer to go to that." Lowering his voice conspiratorially, he said, "It's not as stuffy as the service here in the sanctuary," he said with a wink.

The throbbing of drums reverberated across the parking lot drowning out the lofty music coming from the pipe organ.

Chloe's forehead wrinkled, her eyes pleading.

He nodded. "No, thanks. I think we'll just stick with the stuffy traditional service, if that's okay."

The man smiled good-naturedly. "It's fine. I don't like all that drumming and screaming either." Swinging the door open, he let a wave of cool air drift out.

Inside, a number of well-dressed men and women stood talking in low tones. Their eyes cut in the direction of Chloe and her grandfather. Someone harrumphed.

"Why are all those people staring at us? I feel like I'm under a microscope, G-Diddy," Chloe whispered.

He shook his head. "I don't know. Perhaps it is the way we're dressed."

She glanced down at her tattered jeans and plaid cotton shirt. "It looks fine to me."

WD inspected his own attire. He was dressed in a pair of blue jeans and a golf shirt. It wasn't dirty or immodest, just not your typical First-Church Sunday best. "I guess we just didn't meet their level of spirituality. Maybe we should have gone to the rock service."

Her nose wrinkled. "Or not. Maybe the next church won't be so judgmental. I want to leave, I'm not comfortable here."

He leaned down, "Neither am I. I don't think this is the one for us. Let's go."

Taking her by the elbow, he guided her back outside, down the steps and back into the parking lot.

The greeter's voice chased them all the way to the car, but they ignored him.

Chapter Forty-Nine

Sunday Go to Meetin' …

Turning right out of the parking lot, WD guided the Mustang along a tree-lined road.

With the sunshine peeking through the leafy canopy, they cruised at a leisurely speed, not knowing where to go. As they left the city limits a church sign, with the words ALL ARE WELCOME painted on it, appeared in the distance.

"Let's try that one," WD said as he slowed and entered the gravel parking lot. "It looks more like our style."

"And what style is that?" Chloe asked.

WD thought for a moment. "Hmm, that's a good question. I see your point. It's not about style. It's all about God's presence."

"And you didn't feel God's presence," her fingers formed air quotes, "at the last church?"

His shoulders rose and fell. "Not to be judgmental, but with all that drumming coming from one side of the parking lot and the critical looks from that welcoming committee, I felt—" he clamped his mouth shut before he said too much.

As they neared the front doors, a man wearing a crisp pair of overalls, stepped out looking worried. His face brightened as WD and Chloe drew closer. Extending a leathery hand, he asked, "Are you the preacher?" eyeing the two strangers.

WD glanced at his granddaughter. "No, we're just passing through. Why? Did you scare off the last preacher?" he said in a kidding tone.

The man's face belied his concern. "No. Our old pastor died of a heart attack a month ago and we've been gettin' by with guest speakers. One was supposed to be here by now, but he's late. Plus, the old pastor's wife was our only piano player and she's gone to live with her daughter in Mobile. So we're kinda wingin' it."

Chloe tugged her grandfather's sleeve. "Maybe we should leave. There's nothing happening here."

WD straightened. "Hold on a minute. I heard an old preacher once say, 'Something good is going to happen today.'" His musical tone was carried aloft by a light breeze. "C'mon Chloe. Let's go in and see what God has in store for us."

Entering, they were immediately encircled with friendly faces and warm handshakes. "Are you our guest preacher," an elderly lady asked in a shaky voice.

WD waved off her insistent gaze. "No ma'am, my granddaughter and I are just passing through."

The woman wouldn't let go of his hand. "Son, God brought you here for a reason. Now tell us what He's told you." She would not be denied.

Others joined her and pushed him forward toward an old, well-worn wooden pulpit.

An upright piano sat near the front of the sanctuary and WD redirected his steps. "All right then, let's get started," he said reluctantly. "But I'm no preacher. I'm just one thirsty man tellin' another thirsty man where to find the Water of Life." The memory of Arnie brought a lump to his throat.

Sitting on the rickety bench, he cracked his knuckles and began to play a familiar tune. Soon the entire congregation, with the exception of Chloe, was singing to the top of their lungs. When he finished, he transitioned to another key. "All right, everyone join me in singing, *Amazing Grace*," he said, and took off playing and singing.

When he finished, he rose and took his place behind the pulpit. An expectant hush settled over the room as the spiritually hungry saints awaited his opening comments. Feeling unworthy to stand behind the sacred desk, he stepped around it and took his place in front of the communion table.

Clearing his throat, he began, "My name is WD, and I'm a drunk!"

A soft gasp rippled throughout the room. People began to whisper nervously. A few people headed for the exit, but WD lifted his hands beckoning them to take their seats.

"Was a drunk, that is," he continued. "By God's grace I don't drink anymore. Allow me to tell you a story." Then he began to talk about Arnie Winowski. "He was just as broken as I was, but God did a work in his life, and he wanted to share that with whoever came across his path. He told me that God loved me just as I was. That Jesus died for my wicked, drunken soul, and that He rose again and now sits at the right hand of God the Father. And that if I would confess my sin, He would be faithful and just to forgive me of my sinful past, and my uncertain future."

He paused to wipe the tears from his eyes.

"I didn't get saved that day. But that night, ol' Arnie left this sin-cursed world and was greeted by his Savior, the Lord Jesus Christ. At his funeral, I heard a clear presentation of the gospel. With Arnie's picture staring me in the face and God's sweet Spirit tugging in my heart, I prayed." His voice rose. "I prayed, ladies and gentlemen like I'd never prayed before. I confessed my need for a Savior, and I asked Him to save me. I knew in an instant, God heard my feeble cry. From that day to this, I have not even wanted another drink of alcohol or drugs. He has changed my life and given me a desire to make things right with my earthly father."

A man wearing overalls stood and pointed an accusing finger. "Say, aren't you the one that's been all over the news these past weeks?"

WD took a dry swallow. There was no denying it. "Yes, yes that's me. And that's my granddaughter. Her name is Chloe. We are on our way to Oklahoma to see my father— her great-grandfather, whom she's never met."

The congregation stirred nervously.

Mr. Jenkins, the only remaining deacon, stood and lifted his hands quieting the restless crowd. "Now folks, we invited this man to speak. So let him."

WD nodded his thanks and proceeded to unpack the story about the garden plot, iron fencepost and his rebellion. He finished with, "By God's grace, I plan on going to my father's ranch just outside of Oklahoma City and finish the work my Heavenly Father sent me to do."

Tears streamed down the faces of all but a few.

"Now I beg you, if there is anyone under the sound of my voice who has felt the Holy Spirit tugging on your heart, I urge you to say yes. Don't wait. Today is the day of salvation, don't harden your heart and sin away your day of grace."

Movement in the back of the room caught everyone's attention. At first, it was the accusatory man, then others. Men and women from all walks of life made their way forward and began to pray. It was like a praying contest with voices rising heavenward.

While the praying continued, WD pushed through the kneeling prayer-warriors and retook his seat at the piano. Remembering one other hymn, he began to play. Through tangled vocal cords, he sang, "I've wandered far away from God, now I'm coming home. The paths of sin too long I've trod, now I'm coming home."

Soon others joined him.

"Coming home, coming home, never more to roam. Open wide Your arms of love, Lord, I'm coming home."

As the last strains of the old hymn faded, one more soul moved.

It was Chloe.

Head bowed, eyes stained with tears, she wept her way to the front of the church. An elderly woman took her by the hand and spoke softly. "What is it child? Why have you come forward?" her eyes glistening.

"I want what you have…what he has," nodding in the direction of her grandfather. Her throat closed and she took a shaky breath.

The woman guided her to a quiet corner where she opened the Bible and took her through the well-traveled verses which leads to eternal life.

Bowing her head, Chloe began even before the woman finished. "Lord, I'm sorry for the mess I've made of my life. I have rejected You, but now I realize You are my only hope. I want You to cleanse me and come into my heart as Lord and Savior, in Jesus' name—"

And all the church said, "Amen!"

***

Above the din of angry growls from the dark forces, a triumphant cheer arose from the celestial hosts.

Smiling broadly, Prince Leo felt the presence of his commander. "Well, my friend, you now have a personal invitation into the presence of Almighty God and experience what many of us have heard—God singing."

In an instant, Leo found himself surrounded by a myriad of the heavenly hosts. His knees buckled and he prostrated himself before his Creator.

Suddenly, the expansive throne room grew thick with a heavy cloud. The outer walls, though shrouded from sight, began to reverberate as the deep tones of God Himself began to sing. His voice rose and fell in a melody unheard by human or celestial ears. It was a song reserved to the Creator of the universe whenever one of His lost sheep entered the fold.

For those in the room, time meant nothing. All that mattered, all that existed, did so for this one purpose: the glory of God. For uncounted moments, the joyful praise resounded. Finally, the sweet tones faded in the distance.

Rising, Prince Leo stood on uncertain legs.

"See, I told you," Prince Camael said in a reverent tone. "It's like nothing you've ever heard or will hear."

Leo wiped the moisture from his eyes. "Oh, how I long to hear it again," his voice still not clear.

"And you will, my friend. There are countless souls still astray and it is our joy to partner with God in guiding them to safety. Now let us return. The enemy is angry. He roams the wild plains of earth seeking whom he may devour."

In a flash of light, the two warriors took their places over the small church in Conway, Arkansas.

Chapter Fifty

Dinner on the Grounds …

The service ended and the members hastily threw together a potluck dinner.

"We want you and Miss Chloe to stay and eat with us," one of the portly women said, her face beet red as she set the tables.

Mr. Jenkins stepped closer. "Yes, we insist. It is only fittin' that we share our earthly goods with you since you shared your spiritual goods with us."

WD nodded at the comparison. "Well, now that you put it that way." He glanced at Chloe who smiled and gave him a thumbs up.

Jenkins continued, "Then it's settled. Oh, and by the way; the scripture says, those who gladly received the Word were baptized. It would be my honor, as the only deacon of this congregation, to take you and your granddaughter into the baptismal waters and see that you are scripturally baptized. Would that be acceptable?" his smile wide, his eyes expectant.

WD shifted his weight from one foot to the other. "Well, if that's what it means to be a disciple of Jesus, then yes. It would be my honor to let you baptize us."

Chloe dug her fingers into her grandfather's forearm. "What have you gotten us into, G-Diddy?"

WD lowered his voice. "It's all right, Chloe. He wants to baptize us."

"What's that mean? Is it sorta like a college hazing?"

He chuckled at the metaphor. "Kinda. From what I understand, it's a way of identifying ourselves with Christ's death, burial, and resurrection. Like putting on a uniform."

She nodded uncertainly. "Okay, if you say so."

"Wonderful," the elderly man said. "I'll see to it that we prepare the baptismal pool. Mind you, it might be a bit chilly."

While they waited for the ladies to set out the food, Chloe leaned over and said, "G-Diddy, I didn't know you could play the piano."

His smile widened. "There's a lot you don't know about me, but that's one thing I don't mind sharing. Along with all my studies and chores around the ranch, Dad insisted I take piano lessons. At first, I hated it, but once I'd gotten the hang of it and learned a few songs, I began to like it. Actually, I got pretty good." He shook his head at the memories.

"What were some of your favorite songs, G-Diddy?"

Rubbing the back of his neck, he thought a moment. "Well, most of them weren't church songs. Some were Scott Joplin, Ragtime or honky-tonk music, but I did pick up a few hymns as well. I'm surprised I remembered the ones I played today."

She patted his forearm. "You did good G-Diddy, real good."

One of the ladies took her place in the center of the room and tapped the side of a Kerr jar with a large spoon to get everyone's attention. "We're ready. Mr. WD would you mind praying over the meal?"

He gave Chloe a nervous glance. "I've never prayed in public. What should I say," he whispered.

She gave him a gentle push. "You can do it. Just say whatever comes to mind. It will be fine."

He took a shaky breath and began, "Lord, we thank you for Your bounty and blessings. For Your grace and goodness. Bless these dear people and the labor of their hands and this food to the nourishment of this body of believers. In Your name I pray, and all God's people said—Amen."

***

Sitting on plastic chairs at folding tables lined with disposable tablecloths, the church-folks laughed and shared their food.

As Chloe munched on fresh vegetables and non-animal related goodies, a young man slid in next to her.

"Hi, my name is Kyle," he said in an air of confidence.

His dimpled chin and strong jawline spoke of strength. His ice-blue eyes seemed to cut right into her soul.

"Hi back, I'm Chloe, but of course you probably already knew that."

What a twit, she thought.

His smile revealed a perfectly formed set of teeth.

Her heart skipped, and she tried to control her breathing. "Are you from here?"

Another twit question, she chided herself.

Picking up a pickle from her plate, he popped it in his mouth and smiled.

"Hey, did you just come over here to forage my food," she asked kiddingly.

A pair of strong shoulders hiked up. "Nah, I just thought, if your granddad wanted to hang with my grandparents a while, you might want to go roller skating with me and some of the other teens."

Covering her mouth with her hand, she tried to control her nervous laughter. "I-I've never been roller skating. I'd probably fall on my backside and break something."

The color of the young man's face, though tan from working outside, deepened. "Only my heart if you say no." His eyes bore a sincere expression.

"Hey, I don't even know you. You could be some kind of serial woman-slayer."

Palms held up. "Guilty, I admit it. Just ask my friends."

She looked around over his shoulder and saw three girls and two guys smiling and waving back at her. "This is a set-up, right?" she asked, her heart pounding in her ears.

You twit, why are you acting like a junior high school girl? He's just a guy.

"C'mon," one of the girls said. "It'll be fun."

Chloe caught her grandfather's attention. "G-Diddy, how long are we going to stay here?"

WD glanced at his watch. "I was hoping to get on the road by about three."

All at once, Mr. Jenkins, the deacon, spoke up. "My wife and I were just discussing that. We had hoped you'd stay at least through the night. There is a big storm coming our way. It would be foolhardy to venture out on the highway."

WD glanced down at his plastic plate. "There is a piece of cake with my name on it," he said. "But we haven't made arrangements with a motel—"

Jenkins lifted a pair of calloused hands. "I'll hear nothing 'bout no motel, you're stayin' with maw and me. We got plenty of room. Ain't that so?" He looked for approval from Edna, his wife of fifty-seven years. She nodded and gave him a bright smile.

"Then it's settled. Now let's get on with the baptism. If your granddaughter wants to go roller skating, then they can go."

Within fifteen minutes, the church family had gathered outside around a make-shift baptistery.

"It ain't much, but it's all we've got," said the old deacon. "Why don't you go first, Woodrow?"

It had been nearly sixty years since anyone had called him by his first name. And he liked it.

With care, he ascended the short ladder and stepped down into the baptismal waters. The shock of the cold well water took his breath away. "Oui, that's cold," he sputtered.

Herman, the deacon, smiled. "Then best to get with it. My brother, have you received the Lord Jesus into your heart and trusted him as your Lord and Savior?" His words shot out with practiced skill.

"Y-yes," WD's teeth chattered.

"Then I baptize you in the name of the Father, the Son and the Holy Ghost. Buried in the likeness of His death—"

Grabbing WD by the wrists, he plunged him beneath the icy waters and yanked him up sputtering. "Raised to walk in newness of life."

A unified "amen!" sounded from the assembled group as he fumbled out of the pool.

"And now you, young lady," the old deacon said.

"This isn't a joke, is it?" Chloe asked as a women pushed her forward giggling.

"Nope, it's what the Bible calls, scriptural baptism."

She glanced at her grandfather who shook uncontrollably under a stack of towels. "Don't look at me. I'm just trying to be obedient," he said through chattering teeth.

With reluctance, Chloe climbed over the concrete wall and dropped into the freezing water. "That's the coldest water I've ever felt," she said, her lips turning blue.

Herman took her hands. "Then let's get with it. I've been in this tank longer than the both of you."

It suddenly dawned on her that he had, the only difference was, he was wearing waders.

Quicker than a wink, the man took her through the path of obedience and soon she was shivering next to her grandfather.

"Now that we have that behind us," Edna said, "let's get some hot coffee in your system."

She took Chloe by the hand and helped her to her feet.

"I can't feel my feet. How am I supposed to roller skate?" she asked as she stumbled along the path.

"It'll pass, sweetie. And by the way, that nice young man who invited you to go roller skating is my grandson. He's a real fine boy."

Chloe nodded as she and the older woman reentered the church basement. With Edna's help, she dried off while the older woman found a pair of dry jeans and a cotton shirt to replace her wet ones.

Chapter Fifty-One

Storm's a Brewin' …

Back upstairs, the other women hurriedly cleared the tables while the men talked sports and politics.

Having found a mug, Edna filled it with coffee and offered it to Chloe.

"I think I'll pass," she said apologetically.

Edna smiled and took a sip. "Sorry, I should have guessed. You look more like a Frappuccino sort of girl."

Not wanting to be rude, Chloe smiled. "Thanks, but I'm more of a green smoothie girl."

The two shared a laugh as they reentered the room. With Sunday dinner was finished, the excited chatter soon turned to yawns and talk of a Sunday afternoon nap.

"Let's get this place cleaned up," one of the ladies said, ignoring the stain on her buxom chest.

With everyone's help, the room was quickly transformed into a Sunday school classroom again. Chloe enjoyed watching Kyle join in. With practiced skill, he carried tables and returned the folding chair to their right position. When they finished, Kyle and the other teens piled into a large church van.

"C'mon, Chloe, it'll be fun," he said.

Chloe gave her grandfather one last pleading glance and climbed in. A moment later, the van rumbled off, leaving a trail of grey smoke. After the church family said their good-byes, Deacon Jenkins guided WD to the house.

"We don't have much, but it's clean and comfortable," the elderly woman said. "We'll put you up in the guest room. It's at the top of the stairs to the right. Your granddaughter can have the study. It's just down the hall next to the bathroom. There are fresh towels there and plenty of bubble bath."

WD got the impression that it was a bathtub, not a shower. "I'm sure Chloe will enjoy a hot bath when she gets in. By the way, where is this roller rink?"

Edna fingered her chin. "Herman, where's the roller rink?"

He finished putting the leftovers in the refrigerator and took a seat in his rocking chair. "It's not far. Just about a mile back toward town." He didn't sound too certain of its location.

Despite WD's need for a Sunday afternoon nap, Herman and Edna pummeled him with questions. Questions about his relationship to his wife, his children, his job. Answering with as little details as possible, WD kept the conversation away from the real reason for this journey.

Thankfully, Herman yawned indicating it was time for his Sunday afternoon nap. A moment later, his snores filled the living room.

Taking his cue, WD excused himself and headed up the rickety stairs. The bed groaned under his weight as he stretched out on it. A moment later, his eyelids fell and refused to open.

An hour passed and the deep rumble of thunder rolled overhead. Suddenly, the warning signal located near the fire station released a piercing ominous blast.

WD's eyes popped open.

Herman's voice rose up the stairs. "Woodrow, you need to get down here. There's a tornado comin' our way. Get to the basement as fast as you can!" The urgency in his voice left no doubt of the seriousness of the situation.

WD grabbed his shoes and jammed his feet into them,. then he stood, yanked his shirt over his shoulders and headed for the stairs. All at once, the lights flickered. Stumbling, he made his way to the landing. Uncertain which way to go, he fumbled around the corner.

"Hurry, this way," Herman said.

"What about Chloe? Has she returned from the roller rink?"

The two elderly saints exchanged puzzled expressions. "No, she hasn't had time," came his dubious reply.

WD took a step toward the door, when suddenly a large limb came crashing through it.

"Duck," he yelled over the roar of wind.

Herman tumbled backward against the refrigerator. WD grabbed him from a dangerous fall. Then he rushed him down the stairs as the storm crashed around them. Huddled close, Edna prayed while the men listened to what sounded like a massive locomotive rolling through the house.

The structure shook violently sending wisps of dust through the cracks in the ceiling. Suddenly, the lights blinked followed by thick darkness.

Above the crack of timber, the wind shrieked like a wild banshee. Glass shattered, China fell, furniture vibrated across the floor above them.

Then total silence.

Afraid to breathe, WD waited for the others to lift their heads.

"Is everyone okay?" he asked, breaking the eerie silence.

Edna's voice came crisp. "Herman?" she sounded frightened. "Herman?" she repeated. "He's not breathing," she gasped.

All at once the man sucked in a sharp breath. "I-I thought I saw angels," he sputtered.

WD felt his way to where the man lay and lifted his head. "Mr. Herman, can you move?"

Herman blinked. "I don't know. Everything is blurry."

Guessing he'd been struck by something and had a concussion, WD tried to make him as comfortable as possible. "I need to find my granddaughter. Do you think you'll be all right?"

Nodding, Edna held her husband's hand and prayed.

"While you're at it, pray for Chloe and the other teens."

She pinched her eyes tighter and continued to pray.

Taking a cautious step, WD ascended the stairs. The door hung partially open, and a light breeze was the only reminder of the violent winds which had just raked through the community. With care, he pushed the door further open and stepped into what was left of the kitchen.

It, along with most of the house, was gone. All that remained was the table on which an untouched Bible sat.

Sirens echoed in the distance as fire and rescue vehicles attempted to close the distance between their station and the township. But trees, power poles and debris lined the streets making it impossible to get within a few miles.

As lightning brightened the sky, WD glanced around at the destruction. It looked like a warzone. Gone were the ancient trees, gone was the barn and surrounding outbuildings.

Gone was the church.

He tried to imagine the force it took to leave such devastation.

***

An hour earlier, the roller rink hummed with lilting roller skating music.

Laughing uncontrollably, Chloe swung her arms wildly as she tried to keep her balance.

"I'll never get the hang of this," she sputtered between shrieks of laughter and pain from hitting the hardwood floor.

Luckily, Kyle was there to help. With his arm wrapped around her waist, he held her up until she got her balance. Being that close to him, sent a wave of excitement surging through her veins. His manly scent, his piercing blue eyes, his strong arms invited her to linger, to stare.

Feigning imbalance she let him guide her around the rink while waltz music caused them to sway back and forth in a gentle movement. It was the first time she had actually allowed herself to be near a real guy, and she enjoyed it. Her experience with those losers, Tramp and Boomer meant nothing to her.

Now, in Kyle's arms, she felt cherished.

Despite the fact that they'd only known each other less than an hour, she knew he was different. His glances were not filled with lust and desire. They were light and playful.

After a few laps around the rink, she found herself laughing and skating effortlessly. She even joined a long line of other skaters and sped around the hardwood rink totally absorbed in her newfound freedom.

Suddenly, the lights blinked out, the music ground to a halt and the confused skaters were sent reeling toward the protective barrier in the dark. Above the screams of frightened girls, a deadly roar intensified. In the distance, the sirens from the fire station warned of impending danger.

"Chloe," Kyle's voice sounded near.

"Over here," she said, feeling blindly for his hand.

Lightning flashed illuminating the building giving everything a strobe-light effect. In stutter-step fashion, Chloe inched closer until she found his hand. It was cold and wet.

"Kyle, what happened?"

A crimson stream ran down his face from an ugly gash. His unfocused eyes stared blankly.

"I—I hit my face on the iron pipe," he said in a shaky voice.

As they and the other teens assembled in the center of the rink, the building shook with the full force of the oncoming tornado. All at once, the roof was peeled back as the monster tornado ripped the hollow shell of the roller rink apart. Wood, sheet metal and bodies were thrown in all directions.

"Help!" someone cried as they were yanked from the ground and swallowed up in the swirling cacophony.

Chloe felt herself being lifted and slammed against the floor. The jolt took her breath away. Fearing for her life, she clung to a two by four plank. "Help!" her words were ripped from her throat.

"Hold on," Kyle yelled over the shriek of the winds and snapping timber.

Extending his hand, he reached for her. With one arm wrapped tightly around the iron railing, he grabbed Chloe by the waist, and pulled her close.

"Oh, Lord, don't let us die," she prayed.

"My hand is slipping," Kyle yelled with panic in his voice.

A moment later, the walls buckled. Having lost his grip, he and Chloe slid helplessly across what was left of the roller rink floor. They slammed into a pile of debris with a sickening thud.

"Kyle!" Chloe hollered over the raging wind.

In an instant, a wall collapsed where she and Kyle had been clinging.

"Kyle!" Chloe's repeated cries went unanswered.

Finally, as the 'Devil's Tail' moved to more fertile ground, she heard someone moaning.

"Kyle! Can you hear me?"

Another pained groan.

With rain pelting her like giant tears, she thrust aside a piece of sheet metal that had pinned him down. A large gash had been carved across his face, and he was covered with blood. One of his arms was grotesquely twisted behind his back, and it was clear he had a broken leg.

In a near panic, Chloe lifted his head. "Kyle, Kyle! Can you hear me?"

His eyelids fluttered but his eyes remained unfocused.

"Somebody help!" she cried, amidst the moans and cries of the other teens.

***

While the storm raged, the death angel swept across the grey plains seeking yet another soul.

He had already taken three lives and was hungry for more. Clutching his sickle in his hands, he prepared to slice into Kyle's chest when Prince Selaphiel suddenly appeared. In a flash, he swung his broad sword and hacked the sickle in two.

The death angel's empty eyes, like embers glowed with renewed hatred. His long bony fingers released their grip on the handle, and he clawed the air in a futile attempt at ripping the breath from Kyle's lungs.

"Not so fast," cried Selaphiel, and brought his sword down across the demon's scrawny arm. Bones shattered, inky blood spurted, and the arm clattered to the earth.

Breathing curses, the death angel drew a dagger with a pentagram emblazoned on its narrow blade and thrust it toward Kyle's heart. Just before it struck, Selaphiel's sword deflected it, sending the dagger skittering across the misty battlefield. Defenseless, the skeletal creature screaked and dashed into the maelstrom. Rather than give him chase, Prince Selaphiel rejoined the fight for Chloe's life.

Already, a hulking figure with bulging eyes, hunched back and long muscular arms bore down upon her. It was the spirit of hopelessness. Her young faith wavered. Her feeble prayers had gone unanswered, and the evil spirit whispered, "God is not listening."

In her desperation, she had almost come to believe it.

As he prepared to drive a spike into Chloe's heart, a golden arrow ripped the air apart. It struck the creature between in the chest. With a steady hand Prince Leo drew back and let another arrow fly and then another. They plunged deep into the beast's heaving chest with deadly accuracy.

Convulsing violently, the creature collapsed, his guttural cries echoed in the distance as he fell through the ethereal floor and disappeared into the abyss.

All at once, through the billowing darkness, came her grandfather's voice.

God had heard.

God had answered.

Chapter Fifty-Two

WD to the Rescue …

Fearing for Chloe's safety, WD ducked his head and dashed into the storm.

Before he reached Herman's pickup truck, he was soaked to the skin. Through the blinding rain, he could see the truck. It was covered with limbs, but otherwise was undamaged. With each step, he prayed the man had left the keys in it.

Thankfully, he had.

Whispering a prayer, WD threw the limbs aside, climbed in and turned the key. It roared to life, and he released a pent-up breath.

"Thank the Lord."

Gritting his teeth, he put the vehicle in gear and sped from the driveway. He cut the wheels to the right and was nearly hit with a door. "Wow, that was close!" he cried and raised his arm to block the impact. The door swirled, struck the hood of the truck, and kept going. He had only driven a few yards before he encountered a fallen tree. With care, he eased the truck around it and pressed on. Weaving between limbs, chunks of wood, blocks of concrete, and a swing set, he kept going.

As he rounded a bend in the road, he jammed his foot on the brake and brought the truck to an abrupt halt. The once large skating rink had been reduced to a pile of rubble.

"Oh Lord, no!" he muttered.

Tears filled his eyes and he fought to see ahead. Being careful not to slide into the ditch to his right, he got as close as possible to what was left of the roller rink. Gulping air, he jumped out and dashed through the storm.

The cries of injured people stung his ears, and he wondered which ones belonged to Chloe.

Pelted with angry drops of dirty water, he swiped them aside, and plunged into the darkness. With only the headlights from the pickup truck to guide him, he picked his way through the debris field.

Suddenly a familiar voice caught his attention.

"Chloe!?"

"G-Diddy!"

"Where are you?" he strained his ears.

"Over here!"

Movement caught his attention. He turned. She was standing next to a pile of wood, her bloody hands flailing wildly.

"I'm coming," he hollered back.

Lifting a board, he cleared a path until he reached her. Arms extended, he pulled her close to his chest. "Oh honey, I was so worried," his voice broke into sobs.

"G-Diddy, I think Kyle is—"

He pulled her back and gaped at her. "Is what?" having forgotten all about the young man.

She knelt next to Kyle. "He's not breathing."

WD lowered himself to get a better look. Placing his fingers on the young man's neck, he waited—praying.

"He's got a pulse, but it's weak. We've got to get him to a hospital. Help me get him up."

Together, they lifted Kyle from the tangled wreckage and gently carried him to the pickup truck.

"Lay him in the back and let's get him covered."

Grabbing a piece of insulation, WD tucked it around Kyle's broken body.

"Stay with him. I'm going to see if I can help anyone else," he said as he strode off in the direction of the roller rink.

Fifteen minutes later, he reemerged with two injured teens leaning against him.

"Chloe, help me get these two in the back," his breathing labored, his eyes bore a steely determination.

Once they were loaded, he put the truck in gear, made a three-point turn and picked his way to the main road. Taking care not to become the next causality, he brought the pickup as close to the fire and rescue vehicles as possible.

"Over here!" he yelled to a group of paramedics.

Within minutes they reached WD and Chloe. "I've got three young people in the back—"

Before he could finish, the paramedics rushed around him with several gurneys and oxygen tanks.

"We can take it from here, sir," a member of the fire and rescue squad said. "Do either of you need medical attention?"

WD checked himself. With the exception of a few cuts, he was fine.

"How about you, Chloe?"

She glanced down at her bloody shirt and jeans. "This is Kyle's blood. I'm—" her eyes closed, and she collapsed before getting the words out.

***

Princes Camael and Leo surveyed the path of destruction.

"The prince and power of the air, the ruler of darkness threw everything he had against us," Camael said.

"And nearly prevailed," Prince Leo added sullenly.

Prince Selaphiel squinted through the thin veneer between the two realms. "Yes, were it not for reinforcements all would have been lost. Fortunately, Prince Raphael and his hosts arrived in time, or the outcome might have been different."

"True, but the battle is not over." Lifting a silver trumpet to his lips, Prince Camael blew a long blast. In a flash, the hosts of light gathered around them, their weapons at the ready. "Let us take the fight to the enemy," he said as he and the others mounted their white stallions.

Lifting his sword, he cried, "Charge in the mighty name of Jesus, the LORD GOD of the UNIVERSE."

At the name of Jesus, the hosts of darkness writhed in pain as if acid had been poured on them. In a withering assault, the forces of light sliced through the remaining demons.

Finally, as the gentle rays of sunlight peeked over the horizon, Prince Leo slid from his steed and took his place next to his commander. "I'm glad that is over," he said with a weary sigh.

Prince Camael released a weary breath. "This doesn't compare to the first battle. If you will recall, Lucifer, son of the morning, the deceiver had cast his deception over a third of the hosts of Heaven in an attempt at ousting the LORD GOD ALMIGHTY.

Prince Leo nodded. "The memory, though many millennia ago, is still fresh. The LORD GOD cursed Lucifer calling him Satan, the Great Dragon. He cast him out of Heaven along with those fallen spirits, but they refused to leave. It took all of the hosts of light to drive them out and at great peril to ourselves."

"Not to mention the celestial city," Camael added.

Leo sighed. "Thus, the need for a New Heaven and a New Earth. For the former has been polluted by the Evil One."

Prince Camael finished cleaning his blade and returned it to its scabbard. "And we wait that day with anticipation."

***

As dawn brightened the sky, the community learned that the tornado had taken three lives including Herman Jenkins.

Suffering from a concussion and unable to get proper medical attention, he slipped into his Lord's presence.

"I guess we'll not be leaving too soon," Chloe said.

She had been taken to the hospital and released having suffered shock and dehydration.

WD nodded gravely.

Eyeing the destruction left behind by the tornado, and knowing the little church would need someone to officiate the committal service, he said, "Not only are the roads impassable, but my car is buried beneath a pile of rubble. I'll be lucky if it even runs after what it's been through."

Chloe's lower lip trembled. "I was thinking about Kyle. I'd hate to leave him now. He's really hurting. He lost his granddad and almost died."

WD wrapped his arm around her slender shoulder. "I have no intention of leaving these people right now. Let's focus on helping them clean up the mess and getting their lives back together before thinking about our needs."

She smiled through her tears. "Knew you'd say that G-Diddy. You're the best."

He hugged her close. "Can you call your mother and let her know we're all right?"

"No," she said sullenly. "The phone got smashed when I fell. Plus, with the power out, who knows how long it will be before we can contact the outside world," sounding forlorn.

"Yes, you're right. It's like we're in the twilight-zone."

Her nose wrinkled. "The what?"

He shook off her expression. "It's nothing, just an old saying from another time."

Chapter Fifty-Three

The Day After …

News of the tornado's destruction quickly reached Montgomery and beyond.

Within hours, power trucks, tree cutting services, fire and rescue vehicles from all over the South began to gather in the parking lot of a nearby shopping center. Men and women in orange vests and hardhats assembled in small clusters. Smoke from fires hung thick in the morning air giving rise to the apocalyptic scene.

Taking his place on the back of a fire engine, Ward Tomlin, the head of the local FEMA unit, lifted a bullhorn to his mouth.

"Okay, everybody. There are a lot of injured and hurting people all around us and they need our help. Let's get one thing straight, we're not here to prove anything. There are no egos, no big shots, no big me and little you around here."

His firm jawline and deeply furrowed forehead wrinkled into a smile. "With the exception of me."

A chuckle wafted through the group.

He continued in a lighter tone. "We all know our jobs. Remember, we are professionals, so let's roll up our sleeves and get to work."

After meeting with the heads of power, fire, medical, the Red Cross, and the local police, he turned his attention to the media. They were already assembling outside the yellow tape barrier anxiously awaiting word from the authorities.

He and his team stepped to a bank of microphones and waited for the perfunctory camera flashes to subside. After a beat, he adjusted his belt and began in a somber tone.

"Folks, it is clear we are dealing with a real personal disaster. As you know, it is too soon to tell what extent of damage we are dealing with. My team and I have just arrived and are assessing the damage, but let me be clear, it is bad. I ask that you remain outside the cordoned off area until I give the all clear. I don't want to have to rescue some nosy reporter from a live powerline."

His comment was met with a few chuckles.

He continued, "Use your long-range camera lenses to capture any images if you want, but no one, let me repeat, no one is to enter the restricted areas without my permission. That is all."

Suddenly a bevy of hands shot up begging his attention. Giving them a sideways glance, he strode off in the direction of the hastily assembled Red Cross tent.

Within hours the hum of generators filled the eerie silence bringing light and hope to those who'd lost nearly everything. With painstaking care, the tree cutters and linemen worked together to clear the road so the first responders could get close enough to render aide. By the end of the first day, the scene had gone from hopelessness to hopefulness.

***

Her hands clutching a mug of coffee, Joyce and Ellis sat for their weekly meeting and watched the television.

The tornado which had devastated Arkansas played on every news channel.

"I wonder where Chloe and Dad are," Joyce said.

Ellis took a sip of coffee. His new venture had taken off and he found it difficult to focus on much less than his clients and the cases before him. "I'm sure they are all right," he replied absentmindedly.

Joyce pierced him with a pair of glistening eyes. "How can you say that? We have no idea where they are. They could have been driving right through that area when that storm hit. They could be dead and I would never know it—" her throat closed.

Ellis set his mug down and took her trembling hand. "I'm sorry, Joyce. I've been so busy. I promise to make finding Chloe and your dad my first priority. I have some friends out there. Let me make a few phone calls."

She sniffed. "Thanks, Ellis. You're a good friend."

"Friend? I was hoping we'd moved beyond friendship," he said, giving her hand a reassuring squeeze.

Wiping her eyes with a napkin, she smiled. "Yeah, me too."

Chapter Fifty-Four

The Aftermath …

After a long, sleepless night in the basement of the Jenkins house, WD and Chloe left and made their way to the temporary chapel and morgue.

Edna had just finished saying her good-byes to her husband when they entered. She smiled through her tears while the attendants placed his body in a cooler until other arrangements could be made.

"How are you holding up?" WD asked, his eyes wet with tears.

She swiped the moisture from her cheeks. "By God's grace, I'll fight on," her voice strong, her smile radiant.

"Can we get you something?" Chloe asked, keeping her voice soft and low.

Edna gave her a shaky smile. "No dearie, I'm fine."

"Where will you go? Your house is a total loss." WD asked, scanning the broken horizon.

Her slight shoulders slumped. "Some of the church family offered me a place until—" her voice broke as a new wave of tears flooded her eyes.

Chloe drew her into a soft embrace. "We're family now, Miss Edna. If you need anything, you can call on my granddad and me. We are here for you."

She nodded, not speaking.

"Would you like for us to take you over to the triage unit? They've finished patching up Kyle."

The elderly woman's eyes brightened. "Oh yes, that would be wonderful. Would you?"

The load on WD's shoulders lifted. He felt somehow responsible for this woman. He remembered reading in the Bible about caring for the widows and fatherless. "It would be a pleasure."

A tent with the words, Red Cross, painted on its sides and roof sat only a few yards from the morgue. However, it seemed much longer as he and the others trudged toward the entrance. Stepping inside, they were met with much cooler, cleaner air, despite the astringent smell of alcohol.

"Ah, that's better," Edna said, breathing better. "I don't think I'll ever get the smell of smoke out of my lungs."

Chloe lifted her shirt and sniffed. "Or my clothes."

A nurse carrying a clipboard greeted them. "Do you have someone here?" her eyes switching between WD and Edna.

"Yes, my grandson. His name is Kyle—"

The young nurse's eyes brightened. "Oh yes, Kyle. He's quite a character. And you are—?"

"His grandmother. He lives with my husband and—" her words failed her.

WD reached out and touched the shaken woman's arm. "This is Edna Jenkins. Her husband is in the—"

The nurse's smile faltered. "Of course, I can see the family resemblance. Follow me."

As Chloe and her grandfather followed them, she leaned over and whispered, "I think nurse Madi has taken a special interest in her patient."

WD glanced down. "Do I detect a twinge of jealousy?"

Hand to her mouth, she feigned surprise. "Me? He singlehandedly saved my life before I saved his."

A chuckle bubbled in WD's chest. "Nah, it couldn't be. Not you, you're too dead."

Chloe fell silent until they reached Kyle's bed.

"Kyle," Edna said and took a seat next to her grandson. "I had no idea—" her voice faltered.

He lifted his one good hand and patted her heaving shoulders. "It's okay, Ma'Maw," he said, trying to console her. "It looks worse than it is."

Chloe speared him with a glare. "Kyle, you know that's not true," she said kiddingly.

"Hush," WD whispered. "Let's stay positive."

She took a seat opposite Edna and touched his cheek. "I was so worried for you. I thought you—"

"—died? Nah, it would take more than a tornado to take me out," he said, trying to sound strong.

With Edna sitting quietly next to her grandson, Chloe filled the silence with unrelated chatter. After twenty minutes, Kyle's eyes sagged and WD nudged his granddaughter. "I think the drugs are taking over the conversation and Miss Edna looks beat. Let's say we get her situated someplace comfortable and look for something to do."

Chloe squeezed Kyle's hand one final time and stood. Giving him a wishful sigh, she leaned down and kissed his forehead. "I'll visit you every day until you're well enough to be released," she said in a shaky voice.

Kyle forced his eyelids open. "I'd like that."

Edna smiled with a knowing expression. Leaning close to WD, she whispered, "Ah, young love. Isn't it sweet?"

He smiled, not wanting to add fuel to the fire.

***

Standing outside the Red Cross tent, WD waited for his granddaughter and Edna to finish their visit.

Movement caught his eye, and he turned as a dog limped toward him. The animal appeared to have suffered some type of trauma as did many of the residents. Kneeling, WD inspected the dog, looking for a collar, anything which might identify the dog's owner.

As he did, an ominous growl gurgled in the animal's throat.

"It's okay boy, I'm just trying to help."

After feeling for his collar and finding none, he went on to inspect the animal's wounds. His left paw had a nail in it and his right flank was raw and bloody. Guessing the dog had been picked up by the wind and blown from his family, WD gently carried him inside. *Perhaps the emergency doctor can do something about the dog's foot,* he told himself.

"I got an injured dog here," he said to the first person he saw as he carried the fifty-pound dog into the trauma unit.

The doctor peered over his rimless glasses.

"I don't treat animals which bite," he said curtly.

"I don't think he'll bite you. He didn't bite me, and I ran my hands all over him."

The doctor eyed WD for a minute. Letting out a frustrated huff, he said, "You know, we've got a lot of injured people coming here every hour. I don't have time for—"

WD squared himself. Even though he wasn't a dog person, he hated to see the animal suffering. "Look, just treat his paw and give me some salve, and I'll look after him so you can get on with the real patients," he said, not hiding his irritation.

Reluctantly, the doctor led WD to an examination room. "Put him there," he said, pointing to a paper covered table.

WD followed the doctor's instructions and rubbed the dog's grizzled fur trying to keep him calm. He didn't need the dog to bite the doctor after assuring him that he wouldn't.

With a nurse at his side, the doctor inspected the dog's paw. After a moment, he straightened. "I'm going to have to sedate him before removing that nail."

"Why is that?"

"Look, sir, that nail is bent and it's going to hurt like crazy when I try to remove it. I just don't want any surprises."

WD nodded. "All right, just don't overdose him."

The doctor narrowed his eyes. Turning to his assistant, he said, "Rob, muzzle this dog, then get his weight. We're going to knock him out for a few minutes."

Rob glanced at the animal. "I'm guessing he's about fifty-five pounds by the looks of his muscular frame.

"Got any idea what kind of dog this is?" WD asked.

Rob rubbed his chin. "My guess is he's a retriever."

"A Chesapeake Bay Retriever," a nurse interjected. "My neighbor had one almost like him," she added.

"Do you think this dog belongs to your neighbor?" WD asked with rising hope.

The nurse shook her head. "I don't think so, that was a few years ago. That dog is probably dead. He was pretty old."

Returning his attention to WD, the doctor continued. "Once the nail is out, I'll pack it with some antibiotics and stitch it up. That raw place will get infected, so I'll administer some antibiotics there as well. He should be his old self in a day or so. Whose dog is this, anyway?"

WD scuffed the ground. "I don't know. He didn't have any identification when he limped up here."

The doctor slammed his fist into his palm. "You mean to say I'm wasting precious medical supplies on a stray? I knew I should have insisted on putting him down." He followed his comments with a few choice expletives.

WD held his breath, not wanting to let the situation escalate. "I'll just stand out of the way," he said after a few beats.

"No, just wait out in the waiting area," he said gruffly.

Twenty minutes later, the nurse found WD slumped in a plastic chair. He had drifted off to sleep when he felt her touch. "Sir, you can see your dog now."

"My dog? I didn't say—" he clamped his hand over his mouth. It suddenly occurred to him that he had just become the proud owner of a dog…a large one at that.

Chapter Fifty-Five

The First Saturday …

WD finished attaching a collar around the dog's neck and clicked a leash to it.

Then he lifted the dog from the examination table and gently placed him on the ground.

"Let's go," he said to Chloe.

Eyes wide with curiosity, she asked, "What's wrong G-Diddy?" skipping to keep up.

Ignoring her question, he guided her and the dog through the triage unit.

Outside, he released a frustrated huff. "No one seems to know where he came from; probably got blown here with the tornado. Looks like I am now the proud owner of a dog."

She reached down and rubbed the animal's neck. "So, what are you going to name him?"

A crooked smile parted WD's lips. "Toto, like in the movie."

Chloe's eyes rounded. "Oh, I get it. Follow the yellow brick road, and all that."

"Yep, that's about it. Ain't that right, Toto?" When he said his name, the dog alerted. "I guess he likes it," WD added. "Come along, Toto. Let's see if we can make ourselves useful."

***

For the next five days, Chloe divided her time between visits to Kyle and the soup kitchen.

Although she was unfamiliar with cooking, what she lacked in skill, she made up for in enthusiasm. As the work crews took shifts, many of them took special interest in the girl with the purple and orange streaks in her hair.

WD and Toto, on the other hand, spent much of their time riding a tractor. By the end of the first week, he had cleaned away the fallen trees and limbs from the elementary school parking lot. Once he had finished clearing the gravel parking lot, it occurred to him that his new church family had no place to meet.

"Ward," he hollered to a beefy man as he left the mess hall. He and the head of FEMA were on a first name basis, and that was good enough for WD.

"Yeah, WD, what'd ya need?" he asked, one hand holding a Bologna sandwich and the other a Styrofoam cup filled with black coffee.

WD, not one to mince words continued, "Now that I got the church parking lot cleared, I'd like to have a large tent set up so we could have church. Tomorrow is Sunday, ya know."

Ward pushed his hard hat back and mopped his brow. "Wow, is it Saturday already? The days sure have run into each other."

He shoved half the sandwich into his mouth and washed it down with a gulp of black coffee. "Come to think of it, that's a great idea. I'll see what I can do. Where do you want it?"

While he wolfed down the other half, WD scanned the area looking for the best place to put up a tent. Pointing to the east side of the parking lot, he said, "How about over there."

Ward nodded. "Consider it done." Then he strode off with a cell phone pressed against his ear.

"What about a piano, hymnals and all the Church stuff?" Chloe asked sidling up next to her grandfather.

The lines on his weathered forehead wrinkled. "I never thought about that. Let me try something." Taking long strides, he found Mr. Jenkins' pickup truck, got in and headed into town.

A few minutes later, he pulled into the black-top parking lot of the big white church in the middle of town. Getting out, he caught the pastor as he entered his study.

"Preacher?" he called out.

The man's eyes narrowed. "Yes? Do I know you?" He sounded irritated.

WD ignored the rebuff and stepped closer. His jeans were stained with dirt, and his hands were the hands of a working man. "No, but that's beside the point. I'm from the church down the road; the one that was destroyed by the tornado."

The pastor's face gave nothing away. "Yes, terrible thing." He turned to go inside.

"Yes it was, but I've got an idea which may help your church and ours."

"Oh? How so?" his tone flat.

"I'm glad you asked." Pulling a small New Testament from his shirt pocket, WD thumbed through its pages until he found the verse he was looking for. "It says in I John 3:17. *"But whoso hath this world's goods, and seeth his brother have need, and shutteth up his bowels of compassion from him, how dwelleth the love of God in him?"*

The pastor rocked back on his heels, rubbing his narrow chin. "I see your point. And you are?"

"The name's WD and I represent those brothers and sisters who are in need of your assistance."

The two men's eyes locked and WD held his gaze wondering what the man would say.

After a beat, the man relaxed. "What do you need?"

WD did some quick calculating. "We have a temporary place to meet. We just need chairs, hymnals, a piano, electric lights, and some fans if you have them."

The pastor smiled for the first time. "Let me make a few phone calls." Then he pulled his cell phone from his pocket and speed dialed a number. "Bob, I need you to call the men together. We've got a job to do."

His voice boomed into the phone. After ticking off a long list of items, the pastor ended the call and extended his hand. "Brother, I am so glad you stopped by. You can count on us."

WD thanked the pastor and returned to the work site.

Within hours, U-Haul trucks appeared driven by people from the First Church. As they arrived, scores of people, led by the pastor, began to unload chairs, an electric keyboard, a pulpit, song books, halogen lights and fans."

"We just so happened to have all this stored in the basement." The pastor's face glowed with pride.

WD kept his thoughts to himself and accepted the gifts with a glad heart. "We really do appreciate it, Pastor," he said, shaking the man's hand.

"Would you like our worship team or our worship pastor to speak to your people tomorrow?"

WD sent up a quick prayer. Smiling, he said, "No, sir. God has laid a message on my heart, and I'm really excited about delivering it."

It was only half true. God had been speaking to him, but it being a real 'message,' well, that would be determined in the morning.

Chloe, who had been standing next to her grandfather, eyed him suspiciously. "This outta be good," she chided. "I can't wait to hear what the Lord told you."

The lines on WD's face wrinkled into a grin. "Me too," he said with a wink.

Chapter Fifty-Six

The First Sunday …

For WD, the eleven o'clock service couldn't have come sooner.

He had been up nearly all night trying to put his thoughts into words. *Is this what a real preacher goes through every week?* His admiration of pastors and teachers skyrocketed.

As the sun sailed high overhead, he left his sleeping quarters on the far side of the church property and walked into the meeting tent. Wispy clouds skittered across the azure sky. Sparrows winged their way through the open expanse while earth-bound creatures: squirrels and dogs played chase.

Just before he stepped into the tent, he knelt next to Toto and attached his leash to one of the tent pegs. When he entered the temporary sanctuary, he was surprised to see every chair filled and scores of his co-workers standing along the outside of the tent.

Feeling squeamish, he wondered if it was a good idea to have turned down the pastor's offer to have his worship pastor lead the service.

"You can do it, G-Diddy," Chloe's five-word sentence gave him the courage he needed.

After playing the same three songs he played the previous Sunday, a few volunteers passed around a hat for the offering. Having overlooked the offering plates on his list of requests, the hat was the next best thing. By the time it reached the back, it bulged with tens and twenty-dollar bills. *What do we do with all that money?*

Ward Tomlin spoke up as if he had read WD's mind. "I'll see to it that it makes it to the bank."

"Thanks, brother. How'd ya know?"

Tomlin grinned. "I've seen that look before. Now, you don't worry about the offering. You just worry about sayin' what the Good Lord told you to say."

With the preliminaries out of the way, WD took his place behind a rickety podium. He laid his Bible on it and spread his notes. It wasn't that he needed them. *Just in case I lose my place.*

The air was filled with anticipation, and he knew it was time. He began, "As most of you know, Chloe and I are…were on our way to visit my father. You see, not only am I a drunk but I'm a lousy son. Like the prodigal son, I took my leave from my father, ran away from home and I haven't been back. I was rebellious, and bull-headed. My father had asked me to fence in his and mom's garden spot behind the house. I put down all but one of the thirty fence posts. I thought, I'll show him," he said through clenched teeth. "The next day, I left. From there, my life spiraled out of control. I bounced from one job to the next and all the time I heard my father's voice ringing in my ears."

Tears scalded his cheeks as did many in the congregation. Sin-hardened, barrel-chested men found themselves weeping like babies.

But WD wasn't finished. "I hit bottom when I landed in a psycho ward. I knew I wasn't crazy, but I also knew I wasn't thinking straight. Once I got my heart right with God, I made up my mind to get things right with my father. Now I haven't arrived yet, mind you, but I'm on the road to recovery. This is the message God has laid upon my heart to share with you. I'm calling my message, The Road to Recovery or The Steps to Restoration."

Chloe, sitting next to Edna, opened her Bible and took out a pen and note pad. Noticing Kyle fumbling with his Bible, she reached over and opened it.

"Thanks," he whispered.

His smile caused her heart to skip a beat. *Focus,* she chided herself.

"I'm drawing my thoughts from Luke 15." WD was saying. "It's the story of the Prodigal Son." After reading the passage, WD checked his notes. "The first step on the road to recovery is Realization." Reading from the yellowed pages, he said, "'And when he came to himself,' in other words, he came to his senses. I too found myself eating out of a dumpster. Maybe some of you have too."

A ripple of laughter spread like smoke from a campfire.

He continued, "'and when he came to himself, he said, How many hired servants of my father have bread enough to spare and I perish with hunger? I will arise and go to my father.' You see folks, that was me in the pigsty. I was the one craving nourishment. I had spent my life seeking pleasure knowing all the time nothing could satisfy the deep longing I had in my soul. 'I will arise and go to my father.'" His voice rose and fell in rhythmic cadence.

"So, the first step to restoration is realization. The second is Return. 'And he arose, and came to his father.'"

At that, Miss Edna lifted a hand and shouted, "Amen and amen!"

Others joined her. For a while WD didn't know what to do. Finally, the exuberant congregation settled down and he pressed on. "The prodigal got himself out of the miry pigpen and took off in the direction of home. That's me—I'm headed home, but along the way, I ran into you dear folks."

Smiles spread across their faces.

"The next step on the road to recovery is Repentance. Without repentance all we've done is put a bandage over the cancer of sin. That thing in your life needs to be confessed and forsaken. The prodigal said, 'Father, I have sinned against heaven, and in your sight.' You see friends, all sin is against God. It may affect others, but it is an offense to God first. David, when confessing his sin with Bathsheba, said, 'against Thee have I sinned.'"

More shouts of "Amen," and "Glory," filled the air.

WD took a sip of water from a plastic bottle and continued, "'And the son said, 'I am not worthy to be called your son.' That's when the father stopped him. Our worthiness does not depend upon what we've done or not done. It is totally dependent upon who the Father is. You see, the son's relationship with the father had been broken, but nothing could undo the fact that he was the father's child. That is true of me, but it is especially true of my Heavenly Father."

He concluded his comments by returning to the keyboard. Lifting his raggedy voice he began, "I wandered far away from God. Now I'm coming home. The paths of sin, too long I've trod. Lord, I'm coming home."

The congregation soon picked up the theme. Weeping, folks from every background, every level of society, began to make their way forward. Soon there was no place for them to kneel and the overflow went up the aisle and out the back of the tent.

Chloe and Edna joined in, praying with those who asked for it. Finally, the crowd thinned and retook their seats.

WD blew his nose and cleared his throat. "There is one last step on the road to restoration." He paused and scanned the crowd.

"What is it?" someone yelled.

Smiling, WD said, "It's Running."

Shocked expressions filled their faces. "Running?" another person called out.

"Yep, Running. You see folks. The father ran to the son, not the other way around. In those days, fathers didn't run. They were too regal, too august. They didn't run, but this man had been waiting for years to see his son, and he ran to meet him.

Then he said, 'Bring forth the best robe, and put it on him; and put a ring on his hand, and shoes on his feet: and bring hither the fatted calf, and kill it; and let us eat, and be merry; for this my son was dead, and is alive again; he was lost, and is found. And they began to be merry.'"

As if on cue, the congregation spontaneously and began to sing, "*Amazing Grace*."

When they finished, the bells from lofty belfries sounded in the distance.

Edna's face turned ashen, and she fanned herself.

"What's wrong, Miss Edna," Chloe asked as she and Kyle helped her to a folding chair.

"It's the bells of Heaven," she said, looking heavenward.

Chloe gave a quizzical look to Kyle.

"Ma-Maw, it's just the bells from the big church uptown."

She waved off her grandson's comment. "Nope, those fell silent years ago. What we're hearing are the Bells of Heaven."

Chapter Fifty-Seven

Kyle and Chloe …

Throughout the rest of April and most of May, Chloe and Kyle were nearly inseparable.

Their short friendship had quickly blossomed into a deeper bond; one of love and respect. One evening, after they had finished their responsibilities in the mess hall, Kyle led Chloe into the double-wide modular unit which now served as their sanctuary thanks to the county.

Sitting on a folding chair Kyle tried to imagine life without Chloe. He took a nervous breath and let it out slowly. "I know you and your granddad are going to leave soon."

She silenced him with her finger against his lips. "Just because we are leaving doesn't mean it'll be forever. I'll be back, I promise you."

He sighed. "We've only known each other a few weeks, but I feel like I've known you all my life."

She bit back the tears which welled behind her eyes. "Kyle, I'm not the sweet, charming, submissive girl you think I am. There are things I've done; bad things, awful things. Things which hurt the very people I love." Her lower lip quivered, and she buried her face in her hands sobbing.

Unsure how to console an emotional female, he waited, not speaking. Taking her cold, clammy hand, he brought it to his lips and kissed it.

Instinctively, she said, "Ouch," then caught herself.

"Why did you say that?" he asked, clearly confused.

She smiled. "Oh, it just something G-Diddy does whenever I kiss him on the cheek. It's the same thing Miss Winnie did too. I told you about her, didn't I?"

He nodded. "Yeah, but that doesn't explain why you did it."

Her shoulders moved slightly. "Habit, I guess."

"Are you gonna to tell me that deep dark secret?"

Chloe stood: her arms wrapped around her slender waist. "Do you remember G-Diddy's sermon he preached that first Sunday? The one where nearly everyone went forward including yourself?"

He smiled at the memory. "I sure do. What about it?"

She retook her seat, letting a few strands of hair fall across her face. In the weeks since their arrival, she had let her hair grow and washed all the purple and orange out of it. She brushed the strands behind her ear, her fingers trembling slightly.

"Well," she paused to collect her thoughts. "He said, among other things, to make things right with someone you've offended, you've got to go back to the point where the offense started."

"Yeah, that's why he's going home—"

"Don't interrupt me," she snapped.

Hands in surrender, Kyle leaned back. He had not seen Chloe's dark side and wondered if he really wanted her to peel back the layers.

"Well, that's what I've got to do...go back to—"

***

Three pairs of gossamer wings stirred the ethereal air as Prince Leo, Prince Cassiel and Prince Haniel guarded the two young people.

Being alone and unaccompanied added a new layer of temptation to the youths. Their love for each other had grown. So did the natural urges. Even now, in the church sanctuary, the spirit of impatience, whispered its sweet siren call.

"Be on guard," Prince Leo said, his lips stretched tight. "The enemy is near; I can feel his presence."

Prince Cassiel sniffed the air.

"What are you doing?" Leo asked.

His long-time companion's face brightened. "I was trying to do what Prince Selaphiel does, sniff the air for the presence of sulfur. It works for him."

"Did it work?"

Cassiel sniffed again, then nodded.

Prince Leo took a step back and sniffed. "Hmm, maybe you're right." Sliding an arrow from its quiver, he noched it and stood at the ready, while Princes Dina and Cassiel prepared their weapons.

Suddenly, a door slammed and WD entered. In the blink of an eye the shadow which had crept into the modular vanished.

***

"There you are," WD said, breathing hard. "I was beginning to think you two had eloped." His kidding tone did nothing to lighten the somber mood.

Kyle immediately dropped Chloe's hand and stood. "Uh, hello sir. We were just—"

WD and Toto, stepped closer. "No need to explain. I was young once." He smiled down at his granddaughter. "You're having a disagreement, I can see. Perhaps I should leave—"

"No!" the two young people said in unison.

"Umm, no sir, Kyle said. "It's nothing like that. It's just, well. I wish I was going with you tomorrow. There's nothing here for me, not since granddad died. Plus, they're not going to rebuild the roller rink, I've got no job."

WD eyed the two for a moment. "I'm sure a smart guy like you will find work. Or perhaps you don't really want to find a job here. Maybe you're like me. When I was young, all I wanted to do was to sprout wings, see the world."

Kyle forced a weak smile. "Sorta like that."

Laying his hand on the young man's broad shoulder, WD said, "My advice to you is, never forget your roots. You stand on the shoulders of your granddaddy and grandmother. Make them proud whatever you do."

Kyle, squaring his shoulders, received his words like they were his marching orders. "Yes, sir," he said respectfully.

WD smiled and looked at his granddaughter. A lump formed in his throat. He had come to love this little community including the young man standing next to Chloe. Heaving a sigh, he said. "Pack light, honey. We leave at dawn."

Chapter Fifty-Eight

Getting Out of Dodge ...

Beneath a velvet sky studded with twinkling diamonds, WD climbed from his bunk and headed to the wash house.

It was Friday, May 26th and a chill still hung in the morning air. *At least, the smoke had cleared, and the light breeze is fresh*, he told himself as he and Toto padded across the gravel parking lot.

After a quick shower, he shaved and prepared for a long drive. Having snagged a few prepackaged breakfast items, he threw his belongings into the rear of his car and strode to the opposite side of the compound.

"Chloe, are you up?" he whispered through the tent flap. "It's time we get going."

Her disheveled head popped out of her tent. "Yes," she said grudgingly. "You know we still have lots of work to do?"

He surveyed the area. It was true, they had made a lot of progress and yes, there was much to be done.

"I overheard a couple of the new arrivals talking about the reward. It's grown to nearly fifty thousand in the last month. They were thinking about going to the press and telling them about us."

Her eyes widened. "Us? Like you and me?"

He nodded. "I think they've put it together who we are. If that is so, the authorities with be soon to follow."

"But what about these people? They still need us."

He waved her protest aside. "I know, but there are plenty of others here now to fill our place and more are coming every day. We need to leave, or we may not be able to."

She stepped from her tent fully dressed. "I've really grown attached to Miss Edna. She's so alone," she said, handing him her backpack.

He took it and led her to the car. After placing it in the trunk, he turned. "You've grown attached to a handsome young man named Kyle, too."

She nodded glumly.

Placing his arms around her, he pulled her close. "You know, Honey, you've changed so much. You've grown into a woman of God; caring, compassionate, strong, and beautiful both on the inside and the outside. If I don't get you outta here soon, I'll have a line of workmen standing outside my tent asking for your hand in marriage."

She shrugged off his arm. "But Miss Edna needs me."

"Miss Edna has the Lord and a host of brothers and sisters in Christ who are more than adequate to fill the need. Now come on, the sun is about up."

She squinted at the night sky and then at the far eastern horizon. "That ain't happening. We've got at least three more hours of sleep before the crack of dawn. And what about your car? Does it run? Have you checked it out?"

WD waited for her to get settled before closing the car door.

"Get in Toto," he told his dog, then came around and climbed in behind the wheel. He had gained weight and muscle along with a golden tan from working all day in the sun.

Smiling, he said, "Yes dear, I've checked it out. It'll get us to where we are going. I promise you."

She snuggled deeper in her seat. "I'm going to miss this place," she said sullenly.

He sighed, "Me too. How 'bout this, on our return, we'll stop in and see how they are getting along. That way you can say a proper good-bye to Miss Edna."

The suggestion brought a smile to Chloe's face. "And Kyle."

"Then it's settled. Now try to get some rest. We've got a long drive ahead of us and many miles to go before we sleep."

***

Mr. Allen Tate, the chief editor of the local television station, stamped out his cigar and lit another.

It was eight o'clock on Friday morning and he needed a big story to carry the station through the weekend.

"Watson," he barked. "Get in here."

Watson, a cub reporter fresh out of the university, was hungry for his first big break. More zealous than wise, he was willing to sacrifice truth in exchange for prestige.

"Yes, sir." His pink cheeks and fiery red hair made him look much younger than twenty-five.

"What's this I'm hearing about a blogger back east promoting a GoFundMe account in support of that wacko escapee and his slut granddaughter?"

The young reporter, a blogger himself, snapped to attention. "Uh sir, her name is Aimee Waterman, and she has a huge—"

"I don't give a rats rear-end about the size of Ms. Waterman's Blogs. What I want to know is, are those two mysterious people; the old man and young teenage girl working out there where the tornado struck, the same people the country's been looking for?"

Watson's face went slack. "I—I don't know, sir. The authorities have kept the area cordoned off from the media and the locals have been pretty closed mouth as to who comes and goes out there."

Allen lifted his bulk to his fullest height, came around his cluttered desk and jabbed his stubby index finger into the young reporter's scrawny chest. "You're the press, for crying out loud. Use that to your advantage. Get out there and demand access to that poor, devastated area. Tell them the country needs to know what's been going on. Take a camera crew and drive through the barricade if you have to, but I want a story and you're going to get it." He fouled the air with vulgarity.

Shaken badly, Watson made an about face, and nearly ran from his boss's office.

"You there," he said gruffly, pointing to a camera crew, "load up. We're taking the van and heading out to Conway. We leave in five."

"But—"

"No buts, just grab your gear and follow me."

Five minutes later, the van, with the letters of the television stenciled on its sides roared from the station's parking lot. They had only been on the road ten minutes when the front tire of the van blew, sending the crippled vehicle lumbering off the road and into a tree.

"Everyone all right?" Watson asked amidst billowing steam and the stench of burnt rubber.

Three heads bobbed. "We're fine, but I don't think we're going to make today's deadline," the driver said.

Climbing out, Watson surveyed the damage. "I think you're right. Let's call the station and see if they can get another van out here. If not, we'll just have to put the spare on."

After calling the station manager and being told they had the only van available, the crew, three guys and one female technician, set about replacing the blown-out tire.

***

Hovering just beyond the vision of human perception, Prince Camael stood with a small dagger in his hand. "That should keep them busy for a while," he said to his companions.

***

By the time Watson and his news crew got the tire fixed, the sun had burned away much of the morning gloom.

With the sun glaring down upon them he cursed his bad luck.

"Let's go guys, we're burning daylight," he said, glancing in the side-view mirror at his reflection.

He prided himself in his good looks and hoped one day to be an anchorman on some high-profile television station. "Maybe today," he muttered to himself.

Thirty minutes later, he and his news crew entered the city limits of Conway, Arkansas. The streets were still lined with utility trucks. Men in hardhats came and went from the local restaurants and diners.

"Where's the Red Cross station," he asked one utility worker as he walked to his truck.

The man lifted his hardhat and rubbed his bald dome. "Just follow me. I'm headed in that direction."

Following his instructions, the driver of the station van put it in gear and got behind the utility vehicle. A few minutes later, they arrived. Long rows of white tents lined the area. Hastily painted signs pointing to the men's section, the women's section, the mess hall, the Red Cross tent and the chapel, teetered in the breeze.

Seeing a line of workmen entering the mess hall, Watson got out and rushed ahead of his crew. "Sir, can I ask you a few questions?"

"The name's Kyle," the young man stated flatly.

"Sir, I'm doing an expose on how the older generation and the younger generation view disaster, and I was wondering if you knew of a couple of people I could talk to."

Kyle eyed the reporter with suspicion. "I'm young and that guy over there is old, why not interview us?"

Watson stepped back, annoyed with the guy's question. "Uh, well, I'm not exactly interested in your age. I was thinking about a girl with purple streaks in her hair. And an old man…used to be a drunk. Have you seen them?"

Kyle's fists formed into two tight knots. He nodded and said, "Oh that girl. She could be anywhere. As far as her hair is concerned, that changes all the time. You might find her over there," pointing to a line of woman assembling outside the tent marked laundromat.

Watson thanked him eagerly and marched off in that direction.

With any luck, those guys will be chasing their tales all day, Kyle mused.

Chapter Fifty-Nine

Driving Lessons and Making Confessions ...

The road leading to the main highway had changed a lot since the storm had come through.

What had once been an unmarked two-lane road now had a white stripe painted along the shoulder, and a dotted white line clearly marking its center. Luckily, at this time of the day, there were no other vehicles on the road and WD was able to slip away unnoticed.

Traveling west, he watched the dark sky slowly give way to lighter tones of blues. As the sun beat back the night it cast javelins of orange and red into the thin layer of clouds, painting them in a vast array of colorful hues. He silently thanked his Heavenly Father for letting him see the light, both the light of the glorious gospel, and the light of another day.

With his window rolled down, he let Toto stick his head out. A smile tugged the corners of his mouth as Toto's ears and tongue flapped in the wind. They had traveled as far as Russellville, Arkansas when he realized he needed gas. He pulled into a gas station and shut off the engine.

Chloe roused, "Why are we stopping? Is something wrong?"

He got out. "Nope, nothing's wrong. I need to get gas. Plus, I didn't get my daily dose of java," he said as he and Toto headed inside the small station. A few minutes later they returned. In his hand was a large cup of coffee and a donut. Between bites, he sipped the steaming brew and filled the tank. After a few minutes, it clicked off and he returned the nozzle to its place.

Chloe had taken out an energy bar and leaned against the car munching it seemingly in a daze.

"Chloe, catch," he said and tossed her the car keys. "It's time you learned how to drive," he said with a whimsical smile.

Her face brightened. "You mean me? Drive this car? Way cool," she said, coming around to the driver's side.

WD got in the passenger's side and closed the door. "You're proved yourself to be a young woman of worth. It would be an honor to teach you. Now get in and start the engine."

With bubbling excitement, she followed his instructions. After giving her a quick explanation of the gages and pedals, he had her start the engine. In her excitement, she revved the engine too much causing Toto to whimper and her to giggle. Hand over her mouth, she said, "Sorry."

WD smiled.

"First, check your side mirror to see if anyone is coming. Then, if it is clear, put the car in gear, press the gas pedal and ease off the clutch."

The car hiccupped a few times but began to accelerate.

"Not too fast," he cautioned, hand raised. "You don't have a learner's permit. I don't want you to get a ticket on your solo flight."

She grinned broadly as the car picked up speed.

"Let's try downshifting and making a few turns."

After about a half-hour, he had her driving like a pro. "Okay, I think that's about all the lessons for today. Let's exchange places."

Pooching her lip, she feigned disappointment. "You're way cool, G-Diddy. Thanks." She got out and as they crossed paths, she leaned over and kissed his weathered cheek.

"Ouch."

*****

Once they were back on I-40 heading west, Chloe curled up in a tight ball and grew somber.

As the road stretched into long, boring ribbons of concrete, Chloe and her grandfather were left to their thoughts.

With Toto sleeping soundly in the backseat, WD's mind went back to the sermon he preached the first Sunday after the storm. He believed every word he had spoken, but now, with his home only hours away, he wondered if his father's reaction would be anything like that of the man in the parable.

Sensing his granddaughter's dark mood, he asked, "What's wrong, Chloe? You look like the kid whose hand got caught in the cookie jar."

She grimaced. "Guilty," she muttered.

WD shifted to get a better look at her. "Guilty of what, speeding?" he said in a light tone.

She slumped deeper into the seat. "I-I, wah-we,"

"Stop stuttering, girl. Spit it out. I'm a big boy. You can tell me anything."

Her face contorted. The dam behind her eyes broke, and tears cascaded down her cheeks.

"Honey, is it Kyle?"

She waved aside his question. "No, no G-Diddy. Kyle is a perfect gentleman. We didn't even kiss."

She swiped the tears from her face, but still they came. Taking a halting breath, she began, "Me and my Fam, we are responsible for the fire; the one in the warehouse. There, I said it." It was as much a confession as it was an admission.

WD counted the seconds before responding. Finally, he said, "I know."

Her head snapped up. "You do? I mean, you did? I don't get it. Why didn't you say something?" Her hand covered her gaping mouth.

"And get you kids thrown into jail for arson? No way."

"But how did ya know? We were in the back and—"

WD changed lanes to pass a slow-moving truck. Once they did, he returned to the right lane. "I'd noticed a lot of stuff had gone missing from the warehouse and so I thought I'd do a little snooping around. As usual, I'd been drinking. So it took me a while to stagger to the rear of the warehouse. I heard voices. Hoping to catch the thieves red-handed, I carried a small caliber gun with me. I peeked into the window and saw you and your Fam…Boomer and Tramp.

"You were smoking and cutting up. I didn't think too much of it. I'd done the same years ago. I returned to the front office, sat down and poured another drink and began to run the numbers on accounts receivable. That's when it hit me. I discovered your Uncle Stephen had been embezzling from the company.

Shocked, I went off the deep end. I finished the bottle of Jack Daniels looking for the courage to confront him. In my anger, I fingered the gun. I'm not sure what I planned to do with it. I just knew I was mad. As I stumbled for the door, I tripped over the trash can, fell and hit my head."

Chloe listened in silence. "So, you mean to say, you knew about Stephen stealing and still you didn't say anything? Why?"

His shoulders slumped. "He's my son. I couldn't do that. I love him, plus…" He paused, searching for the right words.

"Plus what, G-Diddy?"

"Even though my father was hard to live with, I knew he loved me and my brother. But I rebelled against him, and so I was determined not to make the same mistake with my sons

that he did with me. I'd rather face jail time than see them—"
his voice broke, and he pulled over to the side of the road.

Weeping, he laid his head against the steering wheel and
poured out his heart. "Chloe, it was wrong what you kids did.
You shouldn't have even been in the warehouse. As to the
fire, I know it was an accident, but that doesn't make it right.
Still, it wasn't okay back then, but it's okay now. I forgive
you."

Tears dotted her eyelashes and leaked down her cheeks.
"Oh G-Diddy, I'm so sorry."

He drew her close. "As I said, all is forgiven."

She sniffed back a tear. "Is that why you want to see your
dad, to ask for his forgiveness?"

He nodded and wiped his face. "Yes, that is my prayer."

She straightened, her eyes glistening. "Then what are we
waiting for. Let's get a move on."

He smiled and took a halting breath. "Okay, here we go."
Putting the car in gear, he checked over his left shoulder, cut
the wheels and took off down the highway.

Chapter Sixty

A Picture is Worth …

Sheriff Vincent Case slammed the phone down, and let out a string of expletives.

"I'll be darned if I'm going to arrest a local hero at the behest of some yahoo back east," he said to his secretary.

She moved aside a stack of memos and placed a mug of steaming hot coffee on his desk.

"What if what they're saying about the man is true? He could be dangerous."

The sheriff narrowed his eyes. "Dangerous? Maybe to the shrubs in front of his tractor, certainly not to the folks out there in Conway." Thumping the stack of memos with his forefinger, he continued, "If I go out there and attempt to take that guy into custody, I'll have a revolt on my hands. From what I've heard, that man singlehandedly brought that community together. Why he even went to the First Church and virtually talked them into helping the little country church get its feet on the ground. I've never seen anything like it, and I'm not about to screw things up by questioning him."

His secretary smiled. "I knew you'd say that. But what about the press? They are descending on Conway in droves looking for them."

He harrumphed, "Maybe I should go out there and arrest them for disturbing the peace."

***

It had been another grueling week for Joyce Dawson.

The hospital had her on a four-day schedule. *At least then I'm not thinking about Chloe,* she told herself. *But that doesn't stop me from worrying about her the rest of the time.*

After another ten-hour shift, she left the hospital and headed home. As she neared her apartment, she noticed a car sitting along the curb. She secretly wished it belonged to Ellis.

It didn't.

It belonged to her mother.

She was the last person she wanted to see.

"Have you been following the news?" Madeline asked as she got out of her car and raced up the steps to her apartment.

Obviously, she had been waiting for a while to tell her daughter about some earth-shattering news as evidenced by the empty cup of coffee and box of donuts.

Joyce gave a tired sigh. "No. I've been at work all day. Look, mother. I'm beat. Can this wait?"

"No. Let's get inside and I'll tell you." She sounded more excited than she had in weeks.

Fumbling with the keys, Joyce unlocked the front door and swung it open. "Come in, make yourself comfortable," she said, kicking off her shoes.

Madeline stepped to the other side of the living room, grabbed the remote and flicked the television on. A young, red-headed reporter stood in front of a camera speaking rapidly.

"We are following a lead that Woodrow Dawson, better known as WD and his granddaughter Chloe, whom he allegedly abducted, have been hiding out here in Conway, Arkansas for the last month."

A picture of Chloe wearing an apron and a white head covering appeared on the screen. Despite the change in appearance, it was clearly her.

"She looks so different," Joyce said, plopping on the couch.

Madeline stepped closer. "It's her all right. And that's WD," pointing at a sunburned man riding a tractor.

He wore a tattered straw hat and a pair of overalls. His face was fuller, but there was no confusion, it was WD.

The news anchor droned on about the mysterious couple who had suddenly appeared after the tornado ravaged the area, and who had led the effort to bring order out of chaos.

"Locals are calling him a 'hero,' 'a lifesaver,'" the news anchor added. "But is he a hero or just another desperate man trying to escape the long arm of the law? Back to you, John," said the reporter to the news network anchor.

Joyce flicked off the television, grabbed her cell phone and called the sheriff.

"Is the sheriff in?" she asked without giving her name.

She began to pace the floor, biting her thumbnail.

"Hello Mrs. —"

"—Sheriff have you been keeping up with the news?"

The sheriff let an expletive fly. "Yes, Ms. Dawson. I just heard about it. I've called the local authorities and asked them to check into it. But I'm not too hopeful. There are hundreds of people volunteering for the cleanup effort. It could have been them or it could have been someone who happens to look like them. WD isn't the type to let himself be photographed. And especially not hang out in a disaster zone."

"But what about the pictures? The reporter showed pictures of Chloe and WD. It is clearly them."

"Okay, okay, Ms. Dawson. Like I said, I've called the sheriff of Conway and he promised to check the story out."

"I wonder why he hasn't already done so. The entire area is a disaster zone. Surely there are police and state patrol units combing the area."

"I know Ms. Dawson. But there are a lot of volunteers flooding the place. He could have just kept his head down and blended in."

Chapter Sixty-One

Brothers Grimm ...

Stephen Dawson paced the floor on his newly refurbished office like a caged panther.

Ever since their father's disappearance nearly eight weeks ago, he, Ben and their uncle had been frantic to get Blaine's signature on the lease.

Following the attorney's advice, Truman, Bob Grayson and his two sons-in-law, Tony Estes and Ron Pauley, had set up an off-shore shell-company with interests in leasing the oil and gas rights to the Circle D ranch.

"I can't believe this," Stephen cursed into the phone. His conversation with Ms. Taylor hadn't gone very well. "Why can't you get the old man to sign the lease?"

He stepped to the wet bar, poured himself a drink of Scotch, and downed it. Then he poured a second. He glanced at his older brother who had been listening in silence.

"Because, the old man heard on the news that WD might be heading his way. He doesn't want to do anything without consulting him."

Stephen fouled the air with profanity. "Look, if we don't close the deal by the day after Memorial Day, the contract falls apart. You've got to talk him into signing it. Can't you get Truman to put pressure on him?

"Truman tried, but he and his father aren't getting along."

"So where does that leave us?" Ben asked.

"Out in the cold, that's where it leaves us. So, I need you to get him to sign that stinking contract, do you understand?" He leaned closer to the speaker phone, his knuckles white as he gripped the desk.

Ms. Taylor sighed into the phone. "I've nearly camped on his doorstep for the last month and offered him every incentive outside of my first-born. I don't know what else I can do."

Stephen glared at his brother. "Say something," he demanded.

Ben bunched up his shoulders. "Double our offer. That should do it. What else can we do?"

"Do it," Stephen said, then ended the call. "The profit from that little change is coming out of your pocket, sonny boy. If you hadn't been so greedy in the first place, Dad would have never discovered you were embezzling from the company."

"But I thought the fire destroyed all the records."

"Not all of them. Apparently good ol' Dad downloaded it on a flash drive and placed it in a fireproof safe. If the authorities get their hands on the drive, we, little brother, are the ones going to jail, not dear old dad. And you can forget the land deal."

"Can't you call our lawyers and have them add time to the contract?"

Stephen took a sip of his Scotch and slammed the tumbler on the desk. "I'll try again, but neither Mr. Grayson, nor those two blood-sucking sons-in-law want to touch the contract with a ten-foot pole. To make matters worse, Ellis resigned from the law firm and is threatening to go to the press if we don't stop him."

Ben stood next to his brother and stared out the office window. "And how do you propose to do that?"

A wicked grin parted his lips. "We fight fire with fire."

"Oh? How so?"

"What if we were to call Ellis and remind him of his past; how he'd gotten an under aged girl pregnant and failed to take responsibility. All it would take is one phone call to the press and his new business venture will blow up in his face."

Lifting his tumbler, Ben saluted his brother's evil plan. "I like the way you think."

"Make the call. In the meantime, I've got to call Bob and see if I can put a fire under his tail."

***

Bob Grayson's personal phone rang, and he glanced angrily at it.

He, his two sons-in-law, Tony Estes and Ron Pauley had sequestered themselves at his mountain retreat to discuss what to do with the Dawson situation. They'd been putting out fires ever since Ellis resigned. With WD's picture splashed across every news outlet, this meeting was all out damage control.

"Excuse me, guys. I've got to take this," he said and punched the call button.

Looking nervously at his father-in-law, Estes said, "Should we leave?"

Hand over the phone, he said, "Sit, I want you to hear this." Then he put the call on speakerphone.

Sitting on the edges of their chairs, the two younger attorneys exchanged worried looks.

"What is it?" the senior partner said curtly.

"Grayson!" Stephen Dawson's irritating voice crackled through the speaker. "You know if we don't get an extension, that contract will blow up in our faces. And it will probably come out that you were using a shell company to pose as buyers."

Bob coughed into his fist. "You know I can't do that, not without raising the old man's suspicion. Anyway, he'd have to sign off on the extension, and I don't think he'll do it."

Stephen cursed. "Couldn't you tell him we've run into a glitch on our end? Say, we're having trouble getting our financing together? Something like that?"

Ron and Tony glanced at each other.

"No," Ron whispered. "If we tell him that, we'd be lying. That's a federal offense."

Grayson acknowledged his associate's comment.

"Look Steve, this is your problem. I told your uncle from the get-go this was risky."

"And yet you did it anyway. And you accepted the million-dollar retainer fee we gave you. So, this is as much your problem as it is ours. My brother and I want to submit a new offer, double the price. Now let's get this deal closed or we all will be enjoying our retirement in a state penitentiary."

***

Standing outside the door Tramp and his cousin Boomer, listened to their fathers discuss the Dawson situation.

The day of their rescue, they had insisted on WD's innocence; that it was their idea to go to the beach with Chloe over the Spring break and use WD's pickup truck to get there.

None of that mattered.

Having overheard what their grandfather and their dads were planning to do, they knew they had to stop them.

"Look Tramp," Boomer whispered. "We can't just stand idly by and let them swindle Chloe's great-grandfather out of his ranch. That's just wrong."

"What do you suggest?"

Tramp, having recently turned eighteen, pinched his eyes shut. "I've got a plan. Follow me."

***

Madeline had just set a plate of fried eggs and toast in front of her daughter when her cell phone vibrated to life.

She huffed and dug it from her purse.

"Hello?" she said, uncertainty etching her voice.

Seconds stretched as she listened to someone breathing. "Hello?" she repeated.

Finally, a husky male voice said, "Mrs. Dawson? This is Tramp…uh Travis Estes. Do you have a minute?" He sounded scared.

Madeline bolted upright. Gripping the phone she said, "Why should I talk to you!?"

"Mrs. Dawson, Mrs. Dawson, please. Hear me out."

Eyes burning, she gritted her teeth. "What?"

Seeing her mother's reaction, Joyce laid her fork down and leaned closer. "Put the phone on speaker," she whispered.

Madeline did so and laid the phone on the table.

Tramp was saying, "Mrs. Dawson. I'm really sorry about what me and Boomer did. We were stupid."

"You got that right—" she snapped.

"Please, Mrs. Dawson, I'm trying to tell you that it wasn't our idea to press charges against your…your—"

"WD?"

"Yeah, Mr. WD. He's really a nice man. He treated us real good. Taking us to the fishing camp was the best thing he could have done. Me and Boomer actually loved what we learned. Ain't that right, Boomer?"

His cousin leaned closer to the phone. "Hey, Mrs. Dawson. It's me, Boomer. What Tramp is saying is true. We tried to talk our parents out of pressing charges, but they wouldn't listen."

Travis continued, "Mrs. Dawson, we want to make things right, but we need your help."

Madeline sucked in a sharp breath. "What kind of help?"

There was a moment of silence before Travis continued. "Well, first, we'd like you to ask Aimee Waterman to interview us and give us a chance to tell our side of the story."

"And?"

"And I want you and Chloe's mom to pack your bags."

"What? Why?"

"No more questions, but after the interview, we're going on a trip."

Chapter Sixty-Two

Home, Home on the Range ...

"Sir, do you want me to take you to the back porch or the front?"

Blaine Dawson's personal nurse asked as she wheeled him from the breakfast table. He, his granddaughter Virginia and her husband Neal, and great-granddaughter Rosie, had just finished eating. They had said their good-byes and as usual, Blaine wanted to be left alone.

"No, take me to the front. I want to see the sunrise this morning," he said expectantly.

"Very good, sir. And would you like an afghan? It's a bit chilly in the shade."

"No, that won't be necessary." His voice echoed in the cavernous mansion.

The large ranch-style house had been in his family for generations, but ever since his wife passed away, it was just a staging ground for his own departure. With WD being sought by the law, and Truman acting like a fool, he had little reason to live. And yet every morning, she wheeled him to the east side of the house. There he'd sit for hours, staring at the distant horizon.

As they passed his study, his eyes landed on the lease. His mind reflected on the discussion he'd had with Truman.

"Dad, why don't you sign the Lease and be done with it," Truman argued.

"Because, son, I'd be throwing away decades of hard work. Not that you would care."

"Dad, why would you say that? I have worked my tail off keeping this god-forsaken ranch while you sit in your

wheelchair mourning over your long-lost wayward son. Who, I might add, will never return."

Truman's words cut to the quick.

"Son, this ranch has always been yours. I don't need to sign a lease for you to enjoy the wealth beneath our feet. But instead, you griped and complained over trivial matters," his voice shook with emotion.

"If you really took an interest in this ranch, you should have made it profitable. And I would have left you most of it at my passing. But no, you'd rather let it crumble in around you rather than see a dime go to Woodrow."

Blaine rubbed his temples trying to rid himself of those angry words, but still they haunted him. The rift between him and his son had only gotten worse, and he regretted saying what he did. But it was true. All he really wanted was for his sons to get along and for them to be happy. He realized that wasn't to be.

An engine roared in the distance, and he glanced up. A late model car swept up the long drive followed by a pack of dogs.

Those dogs are too friendly to stray lawyers in my opinion, he thought.

The trail of dust kicked up from the car settled as it came to a gentle stop. Ms. Taylor had the uncanny gift of parking in the exact place where she'd parked 48 hours ago. She got out and carefully picked her way across the lawn. She had been after him for the last two months trying to get him to sign over the rights to the oil deposits. However, being a savvy businessman, his instincts told him not to sign the lease and he always followed his instincts.

Standing at the bottom of the steps, she looked up. "Good morning, Mr. Dawson. How are you this fine day?" she asked, trying to sound chipper.

"Ms. Taylor, I thought I told you I'd call you if I had a change of heart," the older Dawson growled.

She fixed a condescending smile on her face and put one dainty foot on the lower step.

"That's far enough, Ms. Taylor. My mind is made up. I'm not going to sign the lease."

She offered him a poochy lip. "I thought you might say that. That's why I brought with me another offer; a better one."

His eyes narrowed. "I'm not interested."

"You haven't heard the offer," she said, taking another tentative step.

He glared down at her. "You don't take no for an answer, do you?"

"Nope. That's why I get paid the big bucks." Her smile didn't reach her eyes.

Blaine shifted in his chair. He was used to dealing with relentless salesmen, and cagey saleswomen, but none as pretty as she. Nevertheless, his mind was made up.

"Well, you may be making the big bucks, but not from me. The answer is still no!"

"They doubled their offer."

"I don't care."

"And they promised in writing that you can maintain drilling rights for the next one-hundred years."

"What good will that do me if I die in the next year?"

She took another step and offered him a manila envelope. "WD could reap the benefits. It's all there in black and white."

"Don't talk to me about WD," he said with finality.

After handing him the envelope, she stepped back. "Just look it over. But they need an answer by the day after Memorial Day."

He eyed her narrowly. Her shapely legs, well-proportioned form may have swayed others, but it did little to sway him.

"I'm expecting company soon so if you'll excuse me. I'd like to be left alone."

Stepping back she said, "Certainly, I totally understand."

As she sped off, he wheeled himself into his study and tossed the manila envelope in the trash.

"Lawyers," he growled. "Blood suckers."

Chapter Sixty-Three

Detours and Parades ...

The hum of tires on pavement had a relaxing effect on both passenger and driver.

With no air conditioning, WD had rolled down the windows to let the cooler air in. But the further west they traveled, the hotter and dryer the air became. Soon large half-moons of sweat had formed under his arms. Using a soiled paper towel, he mopped the sweat from his face while Toto panted heavily making it seem even hotter.

Suffering in silence, Chloe's face glistened as she let the wind blow through her hair.

They had made it as far as Dora, Arkansas, a border town between Arkansas and Oklahoma on I-40, when he noticed he needed gas. Plus, his parched mouth craved something cold and wet. The silent urge for a real drink edged its way into his mind, but as he quoted a verse of scripture, the temptation evaporated.

He pulled into a gas station and cut the engine. While he refueled the car, he sent Chloe in to pay and buy some cold drinks and a few snacks. After getting back on the highway, they had traveled another forty-five minutes when he began to see detour signs. Sensing another long delay, he said, "Does your GPS show an alternate route?"

She waggled her recently acquired phone between her fingers. "It's dead-dead."

"What good is a phone if it keeps dying?"

She shrugged and returned to her notebook.

The moment he slowed; the temperature gauge indicated the engine was running hot. "Uh oh."

"What suh?"

He sighed heavily. "It's the engine light. I'd hate the idea of breaking down along a lonely stretch of road."

Peering ahead for a gas station, he saw flashing blue lights. He slowed and joined the other slow-moving cars.

"What's happening?" Chloe asked, her face beet-red. She wiped a few strands of hair from her forehead and joined her grandfather's gaze.

He gripped the steering wheel tighter. "I'm not sure. Could be construction, an accident. Who knows."

A wave of concern rolled over him as he approached a State Trooper. His flat-brimmed hat and dark sunglasses gave nothing away. He waved them to stop. Immediately, Toto stood and pranced from one side of the car to the other.

"Put your hat on and act like you're asleep," WD said, pulling on his own hat.

Leaning his elbow out the window, he tried to calm his racing heart. "Anything wrong, Officer?"

The state trooper lowered his head and peered into the car.

Chloe lay curled up in a tight ball.

"Sir, there is construction up ahead and we are diverting traffic through town. I need you to turn around and take the road on your left."

"Does that road happen to have a service station on it? My temperature gauge shows my engine is overheating."

The officer glanced in the direction of the town. "Can't say for sure. I guess you'll just have to find out. Now please, turn around and follow the detour signs."

Irritated at the probable delay, WD followed the officer's instructions and made a U-turn. Within minutes they were cruising along a two-lane road lined with rusting mailboxes and wood-framed houses sitting on cinder blocks. As they neared Webber's Falls, Oklahoma, he noticed a banner stretched across the road.

WD slammed his hand on the steering wheel.

"What's up?" Chloe asked looking surprised.

"I just remembered; this is Memorial Day weekend. There won't be a service station open anywhere."

"Why do you need a service station? The gas tank is still reading three-quarters."

He glanced down at the dashboard. "But the temperature gauge is reading hot, and I'm worried the thermostat or the water pump is going out. Either way, we've got trouble if we can't get to a garage."

The lines around Chloe's eyes deepened. "Maybe we should pray."

It did his heart good to hear her say that. Over the last month he had seen his granddaughter grow spiritually. She even started a small Bible study with some of the young girls whose homes had been destroyed in the tornado.

"Good idea, you pray, I'll drive."

Silence filled the cab and WD gave Chloe a sideways glance. Her eyes were pinched shut, but her mouth moved.

"Out loud," he whispered.

"Oh, okay. Lord, you know where we're going and how important it is for us to get there. Would You help us? The car is overheating, and we really need Your help, amen."

It was a simple prayer, but one of simple faith.

***

Prince Uriel couldn't hide the grin on his face.

"I think that went rather well. Don't you think?" he said as he laid aside the State Trooper's uniform.

"Aye matey," came Prince Leo's Scottish brogue. "Why the Almighty wants them to go through that town, I'll never know."

Prince Camael materialized through the ethereal curtain. "Don't you remember the time when our Lord surprised His disciples and went through Samaria just to meet a woman who had five husbands?"

Leo's eyes took on a distant expression. "Aye, I certainly do. And he told her all things whatsoever she had did."

"Done," corrected his commander.

Prince Leo cleared his throat from the automobile fumes. "Whatsoever she did…sir," he smiled.

"And what happened?" Prince Camael pressed. He enjoyed rehearsing the stories of His Master's exploiters.

Leo squared his shoulders as if this were a test. "She went and told all the men of the city, and they came out to listen to the Savior."

Prince Uriel placed his mighty arms on the top of his spear. "I always love hearing what great things the Lord has done."

"As do we, but that is for another time. Come along my friends. There is yet much to do."

In a flash, the three companions and their hosts spread a net of protection all around the smoking Ford Mustang.

***

The only traffic light in Webber Falls turned red and WD brought the car to a halt.

Steam billowed from underneath the hood and WD glanced around hoping to see a gas station.

He saw none.

While he waited for the light to change, a man wearing an Uncle Sam's hat and a red, white and blue pants and vest, stepped to the side of the car. "Sir, it is my honor to welcome you to Webber Falls. I would like you to take your car through that car wash." He pointed to a coin operated car wash.

"Why?" WD asked slightly irritated at the man's impertinence.

Uncle Sam gave the Ford Mustang a once over. "Because your car is dirty. Why else would you take a car through a car wash? Now follow me."

"But the engine is overheating," WD protested.

"Follow me," Uncle Sam insisted.

WD bit his tongue and cut his wheels.

Taking long strides, the man led them to the entrance and dropped in several quarters. "Don't forget to roll up your windows," he said with a sly smile.

With the windows rolled up, the heat grew exponentially.

"If this thing doesn't hurry, I think I'll melt," Chloe said, not hiding her frustration. Over the roar of spray and blowers, Chloe's voice was nearly drowned out, "I don't understand what's going on?"

"Neither do I, but I think we're about to find out."

Five minutes later, they emerged with a shiny clean car. "I didn't realize how dirty it was," WD said, glancing at the hood.

Uncle Sam reappeared. "Now, if you will follow me. There is a parade waiting."

"Say what?" WD asked.

Chloe shifted upright.

The man smiled. "Yes, sir. There is a parade waiting and you are our honored guests. Now line up. Oh, and lower your top." Looking at Chloe, he said, "And you, young lady, take a seat on the back of the car."

Her smile broadened. "What? Like a homecoming queen?"

Uncle Sam nodded. "Yep, just like a homecoming queen. Now up you go."

They followed his instructions and found themselves behind a line of firetrucks, police cruisers, a marching band and other antique vehicles. Soon they were rolling along through the center of town with scores of people holding signs which read; *Go WD Go*, and *We are 4 U*.

Children tossed confetti in their direction and cheered as they rolled along. It was obvious Toto enjoyed the attention as much as Chloe.

Suddenly, a four-man team of bagpipers fell in line behind them playing an assortment of Celtic tunes.

"I can't believe this," Chloe yelled over the droning of the bagpipes. "Why are they honoring us?"

WD smiled. "I don't know. Just enjoy the moment."

The parade continued through town and ended in the parking lot of a Piggly-Wiggly grocery store. All at once, the old Ford Mustang sputtered and died.

Chapter Sixty-Four

The End of the Line ...

"Uh oh," WD muttered. "I think this is the end of the line."

Eyes rounding, Chloe said, "What? After all we've been through, you're giving up?"

WD's shoulders slumped. "What are we supposed to do? Walk all the way to El Reno, Oklahoma?" His answer was drowned out by the cheering crowd.

Uncle Sam stepped closer. "Is there a problem?" he asked, keeping his distance from Toto's inquisitive nose.

After climbing out, WD placed his hand on the hood of his overheated car, and suddenly pulled back. "Yeah, we've got a problem. We're trying to get to El Reno, on the west side of Oklahoma City and my car just gave up the ghost." Glancing around at the exuberant crowd, he asked, "By the way, how did you know we were coming through this town?"

The man's face brightened. "Awe, laddie that's easy," he said with a slight Scottish accent. "We've been following your progress ever since you left Conway, Arkansas. You're a celebrity of sorts."

WD straightened. "Really?" he asked, eyeing him with suspicion.

"Yep, your story has gone viral. There are Go WD Go supporters all across the nation. There is over one-hundred thousand dollars in your GoFundMe account, and it keeps growing."

Chloe let out a muffled squeal. "Fur rel?" her eyes danced with excitement.

The man nodded. "Fur rel," he echoed, pinching back a grin.

WD squared himself. "Well, I for one don't need their money. I just need to get my car to a service station."

Uncle Sam's face grew somber. "How much money do you have left?"

WD scuffed the ground. "About a hundred dollars." He didn't sound very confident.

"Well, God knows your need before you ask."

Chloe climbed out of the car, came around and stood next to her grandfather. "He's right, G-Diddy."

Arms folded over his chest, he peered down. "Hey, whose side are you on?"

"Both," she grinned. "Remember, I prayed, and you drove."

WD huffed and leveled his gaze at Uncle Sam. "When do you think I can get my car into a shop?"

The man's shoulders hiked up. "That old thing? I doubt you can even find parts for it. Anyway, with it being the Memorial weekend, I'd say it would be around Tuesday."

WD shook his head. "That's not an option. How far is it if we decided to walk?"

Uncle Sam rubbed the patch of white beard jutting from his chin. "I'd say it's about a hundred and forty-four miles, give or take. Could take up to a week to travel on foot. You aren't thinking about—"

WD pushed himself away from the smoking car. "You bet I am. Chloe, get your stuff. We're going on a hike."

Her grin faded. "What? That'll take, like forever."

"The longest journey starts with the first step," he said. "I read that on a bumper sticker." Then he opened the trunk lid and lifted his backpack.

"Grab only what you need," he said, looking at his pouting granddaughter.

"Hey, wait." The man's forehead wrinkled. "Tell you what. I can take you as far as Checotah. Would that be acceptable?"

"What's in Checotah?" Chloe asked.

"A bus station," the man replied.

WD extended his hand. "You've got a deal."

***

After pushing the Mustang off to the side of the road, Chloe, her grandfather and Toto climbed into Uncle Sam's pickup truck.

The man cranked the engine and turned on the air conditioning to full blast.

"Ah, that feels so good," Chloe said, adjusting the vents to blow in her direction.

WD gave his face permission to smile. "Enjoy it now. It'll be hot were we're going."

As they sped along the highway, Sam chattered on about the country's growing interest in their journey.

"Your wife is a real trooper," he said with a smile. "She and your daughter are giving interviews nearly every day. She's like your biggest fanatic, uh, your biggest fan."

WD's ears perked up, but he let the comment pass. Weary from the day's trip, WD settled into silent mode.

Twenty-five miles later, Sam delivered them to the curb of an aging bus station.

"Thanks for the ride," he said, as he reluctantly left the cool interior of the pickup.

"My pleasure, Woodrow. You take care of yourself. You too Miss Chloe."

***

Prince Leo pinched back a grin as WD and his granddaughter exited the pickup truck.

"Not bad," Prince Camael said as he materialized next to his companion. "Except for your two faux pas."

Leo's face went slack. "I thought I did rather well."

Camael lowered his eyelids. "Can I say fanatic?"

"But I corrected myself."

"And Woodrow and 'you too Miss Chloe? He never told you his first name."

Prince Leo's countenance fell. "Oh. Well maybe he didn't catch it."

Prince Camael rocked back on his heels. "He did. Believe me—he did."

***

"Two tickets to O. K. City," WD said, sliding one of his last one-hundred-dollar bills across the counter.

The ticket agent took the money and returned with two tickets and change. "The bus leaves in thirty minutes."

WD thanked him and he took a seat next to Chloe who sat on a hard wooden bench scribbling in her notebook.

"What are you writing?" he asked.

She didn't look up but kept writing. "It's my journal."

"Oh, I wasn't aware that you started one. That's nice."

Keeping her head down, she said, "Well, it's better than just sitting here sweltering. It's really boring. At least this way, I won't feel so, so—"

"Bored?"

"Right, bored. I started it after we left Miss Winnie's." She paused a moment in reflection. "I've added an entry nearly every day since then."

WD leaned over to get a better look, but she slammed the journal shut. "No peeking. Don't you know it's bad luck to read someone else's journal, especially if it belongs to a girl?"

WD shook his head. "No, I hadn't heard that."

"Well, it is."

"All right, but could you at least read a little of it. I'm bored," he grinned.

She flipped to the page dated Friday, May 26th. "It's not much really, just what happened back in Webber Falls. I've never ridden on the back of a convertible."

WD smiled. "Yeah, that was pretty cool."

Twenty-five minutes later, the bus, belching diesel smoke, rolled to a stop. The driver climbed down and opened the storage bay doors. "All aboard!" he yelled.

Once everyone had loaded their gear, the driver retook his seat, closed the door and guided the bus to the highway leading to Henryetta, their first stop. From there, they took another bus to Shawnee, making several stops in small, dusty towns.

Chloe shifted uncomfortably in her seat. "I'm hungry and tired of being cramped in this small seat with that crying baby kicking my seat."

Her grandfather glanced between seats. "I agree. That baby is driving me nuts too. Hopefully this will be the last stop before we get to O. K. City."

By the time the bus rolled to a stop, evening had overtaken them. Exiting the bus, he led Toto and his granddaughter to a bench and set their backpacks down. Toto found a cool spot under the bench and curled up, still panting.

Overhead, a vast display of stars had come out, supported by a slivered moon. Inhaling the fresh night air, WD let it out slowly. "Ah, the familiar smell of the west."

Chloe sniffed the air and wrinkled her nose.

"I'm so tired of hearing Spanish music," WD muttered, eyeing a couple of guys who had serenaded them on an out-of-tune guitar.

Chloe gave them a slight wave, which caused one of them to strum a chord and smile.

Toto released a low growl.

"I thought they were cute," she added, giving them weary sigh.

"I noticed you added it into your journal."

"Nah, I just added it to fill in the rest of the page."

WD nodded knowingly.

"So, what's the plan? Should we push on?" Chloe asked, her shoulders slumping under the day's long journey.

WD checked his watch. "No, it's too late in the day. Let's eat, get a couple of rooms and a good night's sleep. Tomorrow morning, after breakfast we'll resume our trek. It's only about ten miles to my father's ranch."

"That still seems like a long ways; especially for an old man."

Feigning insult, WD bent his arm and formed a muscle. "Old man? Who are you calling old?"

She punched him playfully in the shoulder. "Just kidding. The walk will do me good. It'll give me time to think what I will say when I first meet him."

"Are you nervous about the kind of reception you'll get?"

He pinched his chin between his thumb and forefinger. "Yeah. He could shoot me on sight or sick his dogs on me. But whichever happens, I'm determined to try and get our relationship reconciled. Call it fence mending," he said with a smirk. "By the way, that gives me an idea."

***

The Oklahoma morning started early by most people's standards.

By eight o'clock the cool, crisp morning breeze had been replaced with hot, dry air. After checking out of the motel, WD, Chloe and Toto headed for the nearest diner.

"Follow me. I know of a good restaurant where they serve the best ham and eggs this side of the Mississippi."

"G-Diddy, I'm a vegan, remember?"

He chuckled. "You weren't a vegan at Miss Winnie's cabin."

The days at Miss Winnie's cabin seemed like a million years ago.

"When you sit at Miss Winnie's table, no one, and I mean, no one is a vegan," she smiled.

Nearing a cafe, the door swung open and an elderly man wearing a tight-fitting pair of overalls exited the building.

"By its looks, this must be the best place to eat in town," Chloe quipped, eyeing the parking lot filled with police cars, utility trucks and even the fire chief's vehicle.

Forty-five minutes later, they stepped to the curb under a cobalt sky and waited for their Uber driver to arrive.

"I didn't remember how hot it could get in Oklahoma in the summer," WD said, shielding his eyes from the sun's glare.

Chloe swiped the sweat from her upper lip. "They say it is dry heat, but the way I'm perspiring, it sure doesn't feel dry."

He smiled. "Welcome to Oklahoma, where oil is king, land is cheap, water is scarce, and life is miserable."

After a few minutes, the Uber driver pulled to a stop and waited for them to cram into the back. With Toto sitting in his lap, WD tried to see ahead but the big dog blocked most of his view.

"I've been following your progress all the way from Webber Falls," the driver confessed. "I'm also a Christian and I don't believe what they are saying about you.

"WD forced back a smile. "Thank you for that vote of confidence."

"Mind if I pray," he said expectantly.

A moment later, the driver began. The prayer covered them, their families, the town of Conway, the police, the State Patrol, and anything the driver could think of. By the time he'd finished, they had arrived in Yukon, a city on the eastern side of Canadian County, Oklahoma.

Getting out, Chloe exhaled. "Wow, I feel like a new woman."

Chapter Sixty-Five

Last Stop – the Helpful Hardware Man …

After thanking the Uber driver for his prayers and assistance, WD handed him his last fifty-dollar bill.

"No, Mr. WD this one is on the house," he said with a broad smile.

"Are you sure?" WD asked, still offering him the money.

"Count it my contribution to your GoFundMe account." Revving the engine, the driver sped off for his next fare.

As the car disappeared in traffic, WD shoved the money back into his pocket and led Toto and Chloe to a 7-Eleven store. The cooler air quickly enveloped them. "

"Ah, that's nice," Chloe said, rubbing the chills from her bare arms."

Immediately, Toto headed to a bowl of water the owner provided for the customer's dogs.

"It certainly is, but it won't last. Let's stock up on water. We'll need it," he said, opening a cooler and taking out several store-brand bottles.

Chloe shook her head. "That's boring water. I want the good stuff." Stepping to another door, she swung it open and pulled out several bottles of Perrier. "See? Nothing but the best, thanks to the GoFundMe account."

WD stepped to the snack-food isle and grabbed a few energy bars and placed them on the counter.

"Wait," Chloe said, and added a few other items.

"Will that be all?" asked the young cashier eyeing her with interest.

Chloe glanced at her grandfather. "Oh wait, I need a hat. I lost mine on the bus," Chloe said.

A minute later she returned with a ball cap with the letters, OK emblazoned on the top.

WD handed him the fifty-dollar bill which the Uber driver refused to take. "I think that will do, thank you."

This time, the cashier accepted the proffered money and handed him the change; twenty dollars and a few coins. After stuffing the items in their backpacks, they prepared for the last leg of their journey.

Stepping outside, the arid heat nearly took WD's breath away. "This is going to be harder than I'd thought," he said, glancing at the blistering sun.

Chloe adjusted her new hat and took her place next to him.

"Okay Toto. Let's go. We're off to see the wizard, the wonderful Wizard of Oz," she said in a musical tone.

After walking a few blocks, Chloe moved to the inside, away from the flow of traffic. "I never realized how nerve-racking it is to walk the highway," she admitted. "With everyone honking, and waving, I feel like a marathon runner."

WD remained deep in thought as he put one foot in front of the other. Glancing up, he pointed. "Let's go into that ACE Hardware store. There's something I need."

She gave him a quizzical look. "What G-Diddy?"

As he led Toto and his granddaughter across the road, he said over his shoulder. "You'll see."

A chime sounded as the electric doors receded from view, and they were immediately greeted by a friendly man wearing a red vest. "Can I help you?"

WD nodded, "Yeah, do you carry fence posts. You know, the kind with—"

"You mean a 6' by 1.5" studded T-Post?" He grabbed one from a crate and held it. "'Cause that's the only kind we sell."

It was painted green and nearly dwarfed Chloe.

"That's the one. I'll take it, and I'd also like to purchase a sledgehammer."

The man nodded, handed him the fence post, and then sauntered off.

Chloe watched in silence, her face reflecting confusion.

A few minutes later, the man reappeared carrying a five-pound sledgehammer. "You think this will do?"

WD took the hammer and made like he was hammering. "I think so. That ground out there is mighty hard."

"I can get you a heavier one if you—"

"No, no, this will be fine. Ring me up."

As the man scanned the items, he asked, "Say, aren't you the two people everyone's been talking about?"

WD eyed Chloe. Even with her hat pulled low, she was still unmistakable.

"Yeah, what of it?" WD asked curtly.

The ACE hardware clerk pushed the money back across the counter. "Keep your money. The whole country is pullin' for you. So are we," he said as the other employees gathered and began chanting, "Go WD Go!"

Unable to hide their smiles, WD and Chloe thanked them and headed out the door followed by Toto.

"That was bizarre," Chloe said as they resumed their journey. "I had no idea."

WD glanced ahead. "You might as well get used to it. Look."

Chloe squinted in the bright sunlight and inhaled a sharp breath. "Who are all those people?"

Scores of smiling supporters had lined the street holding banners and homemade posters with the words; Go WD Go hastily painted in bright colors. With each step, more people gathered. Buses began to empty with men and women, boys and girls anxiously trying to catch a glimpse of the elderly man and attractive girl hiking across America.

Cheers rose from the crowd as they trudged along Route 66. And yet more came.

"I can't believe this," Chloe whispered between smiling lips. "You're a celeb."

WD shook off her comment. "I'm no celeb. I'm just one man trying to do the right thing."

Chloe glanced at the cheering crowd. "Not to these people. They see a man finishing the work of his father. Isn't that like Jesus? He came to do His Father's will."

"I'm nothing like Jesus," he said as they plodded along.

Chloe held his gaze. "That's where you're wrong, G-Diddy. You're more like Jesus than you can imagine. And I love you." Then she placed a kiss on his sweaty forehead.

"Ouch!"

***

Trudging along the highway, Chloe asked, "G-Diddy, how did you and G-Ma meet?"

WD waved at a group of supporters and kept going. "It's a long story."

Chloe eyed the road ahead. "I've got time."

Taking a deep breath, he began, "As I told you, after I left the rodeo, I joined the Navy."

"Yes, and you got wounded."

"Right, they sent me to The Naval Hospital in Jacksonville. I was there for several months recuperating. Your grandmother was my physical therapist. She was finishing up her nurses training there and I fell in love with her the first time we met. I told my buddies in the hospital ward, 'I'm going to marry that girl if it's the last thing I do.'

And by golly, she agreed when I asked her. Her family was from Savannah. So, after we got married, we bought a house on the outskirts of town and started a family. We were so in love." He chuckled to himself. "She even got me to go with her to church."

"Fer rel? Like church, church?"

He nodded. "Yep, church church, but just going to church didn't make me a Christian any more than sitting in a garage makes you a car."

She considered his statement for a moment. "That's good, G-Diddy. Real good, G-Ma would be so happy to hear you say that."

Facing the late afternoon sun, his countenance glowed.

Chloe couldn't hide her smile. "Believe me, she's as much in love with you now as she was back then."

"You think so? After all these years?"

She nodded enthusiastically. "Most definitely."

WD stopped to catch his breath. "Have you been talking to your G-Ma?"

"Most definitely."

"What'd she say? I mean, about me? You know, me being on America's Most Wanted list."

She giggled, "Oh G-Diddy, you may not be on America's Most Wanted list, but you for sure are on G-Ma's."

Picking up his pace, he marched on with renewed energy.

All at once, a small private jet buzzed overhead and waggled its wings. The crowd cheered and waved as it disappeared over the horizon.

"I wonder what that was all about," Chloe said as the plane disappeared from sight.

"Probably just more well-wishers."

"Or news media."

"Probably."

Chapter Sixty-Six

Bagpipes and Fence posts ...

They had been walking for nearly two hours and to their relief, the sun grew weary and took a seat on the distant horizon.

As the air cooled, long shadows formed behind the few scattered trees which dotted the landscape. With each step, they grew longer and crossed the highway like black ink. A few brave stars took their places in the darkening night sky and in the distance, a train whistle echoed across the plains.

The weary traveler's steps slowed, and their heads hung low, but they kept moving fearing if they stopped, they might not continue.

"Keep going!" Someone holding a Go WD Go sign hollered.

"How much further, G-Diddy?"

He let out a heavy sigh. "Not much, Honey." His words came in short, and dry syllables.

Chloe reached inside his backpack and drew out two bottles of water. One Perrier and the other store brand. She handed him the store brand.

Twisting off the cap, he took a long pull. "Ah, that hit the spot."

"You sound beat. You want to stop?" she asked.

He didn't answer. Cupping his hand, he poured some water in it and let Toto lap it up. After repeating the action, he straightened and continued, his eyes fixed on a distant object.

From over a crest in the road, an engine sounded, and a golf cart hummed up next to Chloe.

"Want a ride?" the driver asked.

Chloe glanced at her grandfather. "We appreciate it, sir, really we do, but this is something we need to do on foot."

"Suit yourself," he said, and took off in the opposite direction.

As they neared a gravel driveway WD stopped and stared. On either side of the road stood two upright poles. A sign with the words Circle D Ranch were emblazoned on it. Tears welled in his eyes.

"This is it—I'm finally home." His words came out dry and raspy.

Chloe caught him by the arm as his knees buckled.

"This is it? This is where your father lived?"

"Lives. My father is still alive, or at least I hope so."

For several minutes, he stood unmoving. It was as though he couldn't decide if he should take the next step or not. A light wind stirred the air sending the aroma of hickory smoke and beef their direction.

He inhaled. "Ah, that smells good."

Finally, he lifted his leg and stepped across the cattle-gate which separated the ranch from the main highway. In an instant, a cheer rose from the supportive onlookers. In the distance, the drone of bagpipes grew louder.

"What is that sound, G-Diddy?" Chloe asked. Cocking her head around, she squinted and lifted her hand to shield her eyes.

The crowd parted as four men, dressed in forest green kilts marched forward in lockstep.

"It's those bagpipers," he said with a weak smile. "They must have come all the way from Webber Falls."

"And they are playing my favorite song."

WD waited until they were closer. "Mine too. It's the song Sir Isaac Newton, the old slave trader turned Christian wrote, *Amazing Grace*." He began to hum the sweet melody.

As they drew closer, the crowd joined in and lifted their voices.

"I'm so thankful you accompanied me on this journey. I don't think I could have made it without you," his voice broke.

Leaning down, he kissed her cheek.

"Ouch," she giggled. "I wouldn't have missed this for the world, G-Diddy," rubbing the spot where his lips touched her.

Leaning on Chloe for support, WD began the last leg of his journey. Like the prodigal son, he had returned home. Weary, worn, scarred and broken, he had tasted all that the world could offer and found that nothing satisfied. It was not until he surrendered his will to the One who created that longing that he found lasting peace.

No sooner had they entered the ranch, than a pack of dogs raced excitedly up the driveway and met the approaching couple barking and yapping all the way. As they neared, Toto tugged at his leash. Unable to restrain him, Chloe let it go rather than being dragged across the prairie.

"It's all right," WD said. "I think they'll get along."

After the obligatory sniffing, the four furry friends welcomed the newcomer into their pack and ran off across the prairie looking for their own adventure.

"I just hope our welcome is as friendly," WD said as he trudged along the dusty driveway.

"Only without all that sniffing." Chloe said, fanning her blouse.

Chapter Sixty-Seven

Outside the Circle D Ranch ...

"Is everything ready?" a female voice called over a bevy of excited chatter.

Emotions ran high as scores of volunteers lowered their voices. "Yes ma'am," a man hollered. "We're almost finished."

Then the chatter resumed.

Blaine, sitting in his wheelchair, watched the flurry with quiet amusement. It had been years since he'd seen so many people in his home. Most of them he'd met only yesterday, but already they seemed like family.

All at once, someone hollered, "There they are! He's here."

The room grew still as a morgue as anxious guests gathered at the windows, peering out.

"I can't believe it. He really did it," one of the guests cited.

"Shh," a male voice whispered.

"He won't hear us that far away," another person said, their eyes straining to see the two slow-moving figures approaching the house.

"Not over all that cheering," said the first person.

Blaine signaled to his nurse. "Take me to the porch. I want to see his face."

"Don't try to fool me, Blaine. You've been sitting on that porch for years watching for Woodrow to return."

"And now he has." He gave way to the smile which tugged the corners of his mouth. "I suppose you're right. I never thought I'd live to see the day."

"Well, now you have." Taking the two handle grips, his nurse rolled him though the house and onto the porch.

By then, two weary figures, followed by a throng of cheering supporters and accompanied by four bagpipers, had made it half-way down the gravel drive. Above the din, *Amazing Grace* grew louder. One figure carried a six-foot fence post; the other held a sledgehammer.

***

As they neared the porch, WD stopped.

His father remained stoic, not moving. Bending his knees, WD lowered himself to the ground, tears soaking his face. Chloe, not sure what to do, stood as still as a wooden Indian.

"Father, I have sinned against Heaven and in your sight. I am not worthy to be called your son."

Glancing upward, he expected to hear his father's sharp rebuke. Instead, he saw his father's gnarled hands grip the arms of the wheelchair and start to push himself up.

"Here, let me wheel you closer," his nurse said.

"No! I can do this," he snapped.

To everyone's surprise, he gave a grunt and with great effort, pushed himself up on shaky legs. Standing, the older man waited for the blood to reach his head before taking a step. Unsteady at first, the older man hobbled down the steps.

"Dad, I thought—"

"Nonsense, son. Just seeing you here, alive has revived me." He extended his arthritic hands and helped his son up. Then threw his arms around him.

He buried his face in WD's shoulder, and said, "Welcome home, my son. I have prayed every day since you left to see this moment. And today, God has answered my prayers."

Lifting his eyes heavenward, he raised his arms and cried, "Lord, now lettest thou thy servant depart in peace…for mine eyes have seen thy salvation, which Thou hast prepared before the face of all people." Quoting from Luke 2.

***

Looking at Chloe, he asked, "Who is this lovely young lady?"

WD gently brought Chloe out from behind his back. With his chest puffing, he said, "This is Chloe, my granddaughter, your great-granddaughter."

The older Dawson extended his weathered hands, took Chloe by the arms and enfolded her. Holding her at arm's length, he said, "And you came all the way from Georgia just to see me?"

Chloe's knees bent slightly. "Actually no, but now that I'm here—"

"It's a long story Dad," WD interjected saving Chloe the embarrassment of trying to explain everything.

"And who are all these people?" the older Dawson asked, his gray eyes scanning the crowd.

WD straightened and spread his arms out as if trying to encompass the throng. "This is my tribe," he said with a wide grin. "My Fam. They have accompanied Chloe and me for the last mile of our journey."

All at once, a cheer filled the air, and the bagpipers began a new Scottish jig. Soon the entire crowd was swirling and dancing with joy.

As the music and the singing continued, Blaine asked, "What are you doing with that fence post and a sledgehammer?"

WD's face grew sober as a priest. "Father, the last thing I remember before leaving home was you ordering me to put a fence around the family garden."

"I remember it as if it were yesterday," Blaine admitted.

"So do I, Father, so do I. There hasn't been a day go by on this journey that I didn't think of it. Now I am here, I have one more thing to finish." Moving to his right, he led Chloe to the backyard. Not far from the back porch was a single grave.

It was his mother's.

WD paused and looked down. Kneeling, he traced the two dates separated by a small dash. After a moment of reflection, he stood with Chloe's help, and proceeded to the family garden.

"I sure wish mother was here to see this," WD choked out the words.

Blaine patted his son's slumping shoulder. "She is, son. Believe me, she is."

A few yards further down an ancient path lay a large garden. It was overgrown with vines and weeds. Forty years of neglect pressed in hard against WD's heaving chest and tears flooded his eyes.

His father pulled a red handkerchief from his pocket. After wiping his wearing eyes, he handed it to WD. "Here, son. I think you need this more than me."

WD accepted it with a nod and mopped his eyes. When they reached the plot of land, he lifted the iron fence post and stabbed the virgin earth. At first, the stubborn ground resisted, but as he put his back into it, it began to yield.

"Chloe, I need you to hold the post while I pound it in deeper."

She sucked in a halting breath and handed him the sledgehammer.

Gripping the fence post, she said, "Try not to hit me, please."

"I'll do my best," WD answered through tear-stained eyes.

Just before he made the first strike, two more hands gripped the wobbling fence post, then two more.

Blinking back his tears, WD looked up. Madeline and Joyce stood, their hands gripping the iron fence post.

"I thought you might need a hand," Madeline said smiling through her tears.

At last, one more set of hands reached out. They belonged to Blaine Dawson. With one gnarled hand, he gripped the iron post and with the other, he reached for the hammer.

"Let's finish this together, Son."

With tears and sweat dripping down their faces, they began to pound the post into the stubborn soil. Within minutes, they had finished the task and WD dropped the sledgehammer with a heavy thud. Reaching up, he mopped the sweat from his brow and turned. All around the garden, scores of people stood ten feet apart, pounding fence posts into the ground.

Standing in the middle of the garden was Uncle Sam, his arms outstretched like a scarecrow. He had come all the way from Webber Falls to witness this sight. Cupping his hands, he yelled, "The fence will arrive tomorrow, and I know a guy who is pretty good on a tractor who can clear off the foliage."

WD couldn't hide his mirth. "You can count on me," he grinned.

Chapter Sixty-Eight

Inside the Dawson home …

Standing on the back porch, four men watched the festivities unfold with silent amusement.

Princes Camael, Leo, Uriel, and Selaphiel, disguised as ranch hands, tended the large iron smoker. "This sorta reminds me of the day King Solomon dedicated the temple," Prince Leo said, with a Celtic lilt in his voice.

"Aye, laddie," Prince Uriel replied. "And playing those bagpipes added a real nice touch to the whole affair. Don't you think, Prince Camael?"

He tossed another log into the smoker and inhaled. "Ah, that smells so good. Too bad we won't be able to stay and enjoy it. And to your point, yes, those bagpipes were a real nice touch."

They had successfully guided each of their charges to their destination and now, with their task completed, it was time to move on.

Standing in the mystical dimension between the physical and the celestial, they folded their wings, bowed their heads and worshipped their Creator.

"By the way, is that bells I hear?" Prince Leo whispered, his ear pointed heavenward.

Prince Uriel shifted his position. "No, that's not bells. That's the Almighty. He is singing, again.

***

Once Blaine had gotten the crowd to settle down, he said, "Thank you for supporting my son in his quest and thank you for your help in fencing in the garden. As you can see, it is in desperate need of work,"

A round of laughter scattered like windblown hay.

"And in appreciation for all you've done, please stay and enjoy the best barbecue this side of Heaven."

Another cheer rose all around.

"But first, let's all gather around, clasp hands and let me pray over this bounty."

To WD's surprise, his father began.

Hands lifted heavenward, Blaine cried out, "Oh Lord, Maker of Heaven and earth, giver of all good things, who has fed us with bread to strengthen our bones and honey from the comb to sweeten our bitter years; who has brought us rain in due season and sun that our crops would grow thirty, sixty, one hundred fold, and multiplied our cattle, and if that were not enough, You sent Your Son to die in our place, yea, to rise again the third day as the scriptures foretold, and this day sits at Your right hand until You make His enemies His footstool. And now my eyes have seen the completion of my faith in that You have brought my son home who was dead to me, and yet he lives. Thank you Father for Your bounty and blessings. Bless this food and bless Your people, in Jesus' strong name, amen."

WD kept his head bowed for another moment. He'd never known his father to pray, didn't know he was a believer. After thanking his Savior for performing another miracle, he rejoined his family. *I am really looking forward to hearing all about dad's conversion as well as telling him about how God has changed my life,* he told himself.

At Blaine's insistence, the crowd formed a line which stretched nearly to the front of his property. "Eat up, there is plenty for everybody," he said with renewed energy.

Taking WD and Chloe by the hands, he led them into the house. Accompanied by Madeline and Joyce they entered the living room and were immediately engulfed in light.

Holding a microphone, Aimee Waterman waited for her turn to speak. Behind her stood Boomer Pauley; a large camera on his shoulder capturing the events in real time. Next to him stood Tramp Estes; a broad smile stretched across his face. They had arrived a day earlier and informed Blaine of his soon-to-arrive son.

With cameras rolling, Aimee began. "WD, how does it feel to be home again after all these years," she asked rather impertinently.

Blinded by flashes from a dozen lightbulbs and the beam from a halogen spotlight, WD and the others stood like a deer caught in the headlights. He froze, unable to speak.

"I—I don't know," he said absently. "I'm just glad I could finish the job my father asked me to do."

"Do you plan on sticking around, knowing your family's history?"

For a moment, WD remained speechless. Then, with a broad grin, he said, "Dad and I have a lot of catching up to do. So, if it's all right with him, I think I'll stay a while."

Blaine extended his arms and pulled his son into a strong embrace. "Of course, you'll stay. I need someone to plow up the garden. Then we need to decide what to plant, and—"

"All right, all right, Dad. I got the point."

While the two men ribbed each other, Aimee turned to face the camera. Her adoring fans weren't so much interested in seeing WD's rugged face as they were hers. Lifting the microphone to her mouth she began a colorful description of the scene outside.

Chapter Sixty-Nine

Clearing the Air ...

With the attention focused on Aimee, WD took Madeline and Chloe by the hands and led them to a quiet corner.

Lowering his eyes, he began, "I'm so sorry for all the trouble I've caused you and Joyce," he said through trembling lips.

"Hush, WD," Madeline whispered through her tears. "There's enough blame to go around for both of us. Truth is, I was as much at fault as you. My pride, my selfishness, my stubbornness clouded my judgment. By God's grace I'm willing to start all over again."

WD sucked in a halting breath and buried his face in his wife's shoulder. "I think that's a wonderful idea. How about you Chloe?"

She sputtered out a shaky, "Yes! And I think we should do it right here, on the Circle D Ranch," she said, scanning the wide expanse.

Madeline broke from his embrace and pulled Chloe into her arms. "My, my, you have changed so much. I barely recognize you. Just look at you, you're quite a lady."

Chloe glanced down at herself. "Well, I'm not much to look at right now. I have been traveling for about a thousand miles." A crooked smile marked her features.

All at once, Boomer stuck his fat hand out and took Chloe's. "You look bussin," he said appraising her.

She stepped back, "English, please."

His face went slack. "I mean, for a girl who'd traveled halfway across America, you look great."

She shifted uncomfortably. Tucking a strand of hair behind her ear, she said, "Look, Boomer. I'm not the girl you knew two months ago. I have my standards—"

Hands held in surrender, he glanced around. "I—I didn't mean anything by it. It's just, that, well."

WD stepped closer and offered the young man his hand. "Nice to see you again, Boomer. How did your first fishing expedition go?"

Tramp joined them and padded his friend's shoulder. "We loved it, but not at first. It's a long story. Before we go into that, we have an admission."

WD grew serious. "Oh? What is it?"

Tramp scuffed the hart-pine floor with his tennis shoe. "Well, sir, it was me and Boomer who accidentally started the fire in the warehouse. We were fooling around, smoking and stuff and accidentally knocked over a lantern. It spread so fast all we could think of was getting out of there."

WD gave Chloe a knowing smile. Taking the boys by the arm, he said, "I know all about it, Boomer. You may have inadvertently meant it for harm, but God meant it for good. We will speak of this no more."

Boomer smiled through his tears. "Thank you, sir, but there is something else we need to say."

WD stiffened.

Tramp took up the admission. "After we got home, we told our parents that it was us who forced you to drive us to Florida. And that we were responsible for setting the fire, but they didn't listen. So, we went to Mr. Ellis Grayson. He's a real cool guy, if you don't already know it."

WD smiled at the thought.

"Then, with him acting as our attorney, we went to the sheriff. You should have seen the look on old Sheriff Wooten's face when we marched into his office and told him all about the shell company and the plot to swindle your father out of his land. He immediately called off the manhunt and dropped all the charges against you. Then he had his men arrest our Granddad along with my Dad and Boomer's."

"Yeah, and I just got a phone call from the local authorities telling me that they just picked up Ms. Taylor and Uncle Truman. They are being charged with conspiracy to commit fraud and a list of other crimes," Boomer said. "So, I guess they got them all."

"—all except me!" Ellis Grayson's baritone voice sliced through the air.

Joyce turned just as he took her in his arms.

"Oh Ellis, I thought you'd never make it," she said smothering him with kisses.

"My flight was delayed and the road to this ranch was lined with people. I was sure I'd missed the whole thing."

Chloe's forehead wrinkled. "Mom, why are you kissing this—No! Wait! It can't be."

"Your father?" Joyce's eyes glistened with happy tears.

WD stepped closer. "I'm sorry I didn't tell you earlier, but I was sworn to secrecy. Chloe, let me introduce you to your father, Ellis Grayson. Ellis, this is your daughter, Chloe Dawson."

She let out a squeal. "Oh G-Diddy, I'm so happy." Leaning over, she placed a kiss on his cheek.

"Ouch!"

***

As the angelic hosts rose heavenward, *Amazing Grace* vibrated in their chests.

It was a good day for the angels.

It was a good day for the mortals.

A good day, indeed.

Questions to reflect upon.

1. While you read *The Prodigal's Return,* did you sense the call of the Holy Spirit to trust Christ as your Savior?
2. Have you been scripturally baptized by emersion to identify with Christ's death, burial, and resurrection?
3. Are there unresolved issues in your life between you and a family member, a co-worker, a spouse that need to be addressed?
4. Have you, or are you willing to take the seven steps to a restored relationship WD spoke about?
5. How far are you willing to go to make things right with someone who has offended you or someone you have offended?
6. Do you regularly give a witness or a testimony of what Christ has done for you like our friend Arnie?
7. Are there besetting sins like alcohol or over the counter drugs which have taken hold of your life?
8. Are you on the road to recovery?
9. Does selfishness and greed mark your life as it did Ben's, Stephen's and Truman's?
10. Which character did you identify with?
11. What changes in their lives impacted you the most?
12. Is there a prodigal you are praying for?

Books by Bryan M. Powell

<u>Christian Fantasy Series</u>
The Witch and the Wise Men*
The Lost Medallion
The Last Magi
Journey to Edenstrae
<u>The Jared Russell Series</u>
Sisters of the Veil
Power Play
The Final Countdown
<u>The Chase Newton Series</u>
The Order
The Oath
The Outsider
<u>Mystery Series</u>
Million Dollar Murder
Snapshot of a Killer
In the Line of Fire
Uncaged
Undetected
<u>Historical Fiction</u>
Sins of the Fathers*
Sins of the Mothers
<u>Southern Humor</u>
Loving Miss Bessie*
<u>Non-Fiction/Devotional</u>
Seeing Jesus – A Three Dimensional Look at Worship
Show Us the Father – A 30-Day Devotional
Faith, Family, and a Lot of hard Work –
The Grady Gillis Story
*** = Available on Audible**